Metanoia

THE EUNOIA SERIES
BOOK TWO

HANNAH BREE CAMPBELL

Paperback ISBN: 978-1-63337-788-2
E-Book ISBN: 978-1-63337-789-9

Printed in the United States of America
1 3 5 7 9 10 8 6 4 2

Artist: Alexandra Russell
Editor: Kyla Jones
Photography: Donna Jung

Metanoia

Dear Azalea, you are me and I am you.

Chapter 1

LIFE THROUGH YOUR PERSPECTIVE

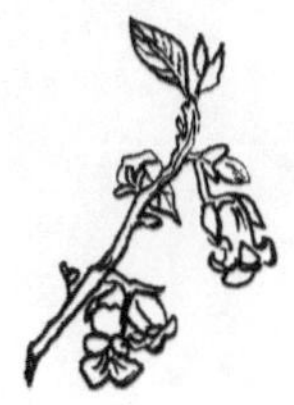

MY EYES FLUTTER OPEN to the orange light that streams in from the window and across the wooden floorboards to my tear-stained cheeks. The rhythm of Azalea's breathing is all I hold on to in this moment.

Memories of my life play in my mind, overtaking my vision: crying on the terrace at the Brockschmidt ball, Christmas morning when my fingers gingerly unwrapped an embroidered apron from my sister, secretly watching her climb up the roof each morning even after she sprained her ankle that one time, blowing out the candles on each of my birthdays, traveling from Colorado to Wyoming, Azalea convincing me to run alongside the wagon with our arms outstretched because there was a chance we might take off in flight just like the hawks that soared above, playing in mounds of snow until the coldness stung my face, frolicking outside with a rag doll when I was a child. What a beautiful life I have been so fortunate to live!

"Thank you for the memories, the moments, the laughter, the smiles, the tears, the heartbreak, and the adventure. Thank you for it all," I whisper as one last tear travels down my face before landing on my shoulder. For a second the sunlight blinks as if God is saying, "You are most welcome, my daughter."

"Aren't the views just ravishing?" My chest rises and falls as my eyes slowly flutter closed, and the light in my vision overcomes my worldly existence.

Chapter 2

LETUM NON OMNIA FINIT

LIFE HAS PROGRESSED; it is not the same…but it has moved on. The only difference is that I have been left behind. The world has continued—clouds race one another gayly, flowers blossom and smile, and the sun gazes down warmly. With all this light, why does it feel so dark? Today's weather seems to mirror my troubled soul.

The meadow sways as the wind rolls over it. My fingertips reach up delicately from the nest of wild grass that engulfs me. Each morning the sunrises are seamless and instantaneous, while the sunsets are exquisitely unhurried. The crisp air fills my lungs as I rise from my makeshift cradle and face the fading light of a summer's day that is overtaken by darkness.

Sometimes I awaken with the impression that this is all a dream, a simple figment of my immense imagination, but I always come to remember that the rattle of the covered wagon, the call of hawks flying overhead looking for a snack, and the lonesome howl of a gray wolf at twilight are the symphony of my new reality. Calamitous clouds cover the sun, threatening to spill over with water droplets as I run with my arms outstretched. This is it, everything I have ever dreamt of and held in my heart! "Perfect" doesn't do the scenery any justice…the word "idyllic" is only fitting for this countryside!

The only thing it lacks is her presence. The most heart-wrenching moment in my lifetime was bidding that final goodbye to the person I could have spent the rest of my life with. It has been almost four weeks since her passing, and each night I wake with a scream that sends my family into a panic. Mother does her best to soothe me by smoothing my hair and saying they are just nightmares, but it is no use. The uncontrollable trembling of my hands cannot be quieted with words.

I shake the thought away from my mind, trying to find happiness in watching a herd of mule deer prancing past, frightened by the passing thunder. Pa unhitches the team of horses from the wagon and ties the duo to picket lines so they can graze nearby whilst we prepare dinner. After we come to the conclusion that the storm will pass us by, leaving us untouched, I help Mother unpack the few dishes we decided to bring along, unravel the blanket to lie on the grass as the sun disappears, and gather dry twigs for the fire.

Pa brought his gun despite Mother's detestation of weapons. Its permanent place is at the jockey box in the event he would need to fire it at any bandits or wild animals, but each day when we stop to eat, he uses it to hunt. We anxiously await the familiar sound of a gunshot ringing through the air, announcing that meat will soon be sizzling in the pan over the fire.

Anxious and inpatient, I walk around our temporary campsite barefoot, feeling the dirt between my toes. Mother constantly scoffs at the sight because of how unrefined it is—not that I take this too much to heart. After many failed attempts, along with bruises dotting my torso, I have finally mastered the skill of climbing into the wagon bed, where Mother and I spend most of the day as we travel. Besides that, the vast majority of my days are spent passing the time by reading the small dictionary that sits atop the trunk that belonged to my sister.

A couple of years ago, I would commit words to memory in the hopes that one could be used in a conversation so I would appear smarter than Florence. Looking back on the memory, it really was foolish of me to do so considering I had no clue as to what "keen," "auspicious," "perfidious," or "verdant" meant. Now, it means something else to sit for hours reading the definitions; I never comprehended how important my education as a young woman was until I met the woman standing in the park in Brockschmidt waving pamphlets filled with things I had no knowledge of. I can almost hear her booming voice now, yelling for justice and attention from anyone who cared for the matter of women's voting rights.

It seems like months have passed since we were in Brockschmidt—a city near our small town of Lorretta, Wyoming, to which we had made the strenuous journey so my sister could find a proper husband. But we were hoodwinked. No proposal was made, and our reputations were disgraced by dirty rumors. *Has it truly only been nearly seven weeks since then?*

After supper, it is time to hitch up the team, clear away the dishes—which will be washed once we locate a stream—and fold up the blanket. I place it where I sit at the back of the wagon bed, the wagon's cover shading me from the sun's rays that have emerged from the passing storm clouds.

"Pa?" My voice later rings out above the endless rattle of the wagon, which drives me to insanity, especially when the iron tires go over a rock, jolting me awake from much-needed slumber. "How ever do you know where we are located? You have told me before, but I must admit it slipped my mind from the instant you last explained it. Please, do remind me of it." I cling to the wooden boards of the wagon bed as we hit yet another rock.

A hearty chuckle sounds at my words, and he turns to shout over his shoulder whilst driving the team. "Well, Bluebird, we have been following the tracks of the other wagons that've come before us on the journey westward. You also have to use the sun to your personal advantage; it rises in the east and sets west." My eyes travel to the tracks made from wagon tires and where the fiery orb of the sun is already lowering in the sky. Out here, there are so many things that boggle my mind that I have not had the opportunity to learn before!

The remainder of the afternoon is whisked away in the breeze as we all find things to occupy our minds. I spend a good deal of time sitting at the rear of the wagon with my legs stretched out the width of the wagon bed, peeking my head out of the canvas cover and simply taking in the scenery. The mountains are already thinning away into the background, trees are becoming a rare sight, and there is no sign of civilization as far as the eye can see!

Another caravan of darkening clouds looms above, threatening to spill over. Drizzle has such a pleasant sound as it rushes from the atmosphere to the earthly soil below. Oh, how I long for the pitter-patter of a summer's rainstorm on the roof of our house! Florence would have loved to be here traveling along with us. What fun we had journeying from Colorado. It is as if that was a lifetime away!

"Pa, why ever is this called a prairie schooner?" My eyes scan the interior of our wagon, which Pa bought before we left Lorretta. In order to afford the supplies, wagon, and two Percheron horses, we sold everything, including my two beloved cows, Sense and Sensibility. Pa has forbade me from going anywhere near the towering horses, but I at least dubbed them Cobalt and Tempest. They are both a sophisticated raven black, and even though Pa said it would be too dangerous for a little girl to ride them, it still gives me such a thrill to imagine it!

Cobalt releases a high-pitched whinny, as if he has suddenly obtained the ability to read my thoughts, and continues beating his hooves at a steady trot. A chuckle and a twitch of the reins are Pa's only response to Cobalt's attitude. With the wave of Pa's hand, I am ushered to sit on the jockey box. In order to do so, I have to scramble over Mother, who has succumbed to sleep's convincing grasp. The sun is shielded from our eyes as thunder sends the earth quaking. A temporary darkness blankets the meadows of mixed grasses, making the landscape appear as eerie as fog settling over creeping waves.

"Well, it's said to have come from the appearance of a schooner ship with white sails that might resemble the wagon's canvas cover. As long as we do not have any run-ins with Indians, we should make good time. Do not worry, Bluebird—you'll learn a great heap of knowledge in school this winter," he comments with a twinkle in his eyes.

A fire ignites in my heart, fueling an interest that otherwise would have never happened had he not mentioned it. "Oh, Pa, will I really be going to school? Why, this is better than I ever could have imagined! It has been a secret desire of mine even though Mother's Sunday schooling has been a blessing in itself! Do you suppose we might see an Indian? How fascinating it would be to really see one, for I have only ever read about them in books. To be captivated by their painted skin, feathers from exotic birds, animal skins sewn into clothes, and predator's claws worn as jewelry would be a true honor!"

"Indians aren't as common here anymore, what with them being driven off their lands. Horrible thing that is, but people have a habit of fearing for the worst. I don't know how many tribes there are nowadays, but there are quite a few in Oklahoma, Missouri, Washington, Montana. Some would shoot you down before asking if you were friend or foe."

My eyes acutely scan the horizon as the sun lowers in the sky, as if an Indian will be standing there watching us rattle past in the wagon. "Goodness! How horrible to be treated like that when they inhabited America long before it existed! What fun it must have been before the Brits came and all of this was wilderness." I gesture to the rolling hills, painted orange and absent of any sign of civilization. Birds caw above us as they swoop back to their nests, stray mule deer wander around looking for their herds, and the grasses sway in the small zephyr sweeping by. The heaven-touching apex of a mountain holds glittering snow reflecting rays back at me. "How wonderful it is to be older and traveling since I cannot remember much of our journey to Wyoming. Do you think I will be terribly behind in school? I shall have a horrid trepidation of that now. There is much that Mother never taught us, not that I am blaming her for lack of resources or knowledge!"

A glimmer of a fatherly smile flashes as he responds, "Our current travels are definitely different than before." His gaze seems lost in the distance, and he tries to hide a chuckle. The moment disappears as quickly as it had materialized, and the conversation is kept afloat amongst a sea of concealed emotions. "As for school, you'll do great, Bluebird. You might even *soar* above the rest of them." Managing the reins, he shoots a playful look at me, causing a giggle to emerge at his attempted humor. The worries settle at the mercy of humor, and Pa says with a satisfied air, "This is a good camping spot for the night." The wagon eases to a halt as he pulls back on the leather reins and then hops down from the box.

Tempest paws anxiously at the ground, awaiting the moment he will be released. I help unload the blankets, making a makeshift bed for Mother and Pa under the wagon just as Mother awakens to find us stationary and immediately locates work to be done. My conversation with Pa trails off as we each prepare different things. Mother has already begun clearing a spot for the fire by ripping out the grass, Pa ties the horses to their picket lines, and I shuffle the cargo around in the wagon to create more room.

Before long, the three-legged iron spider skillet—containing some of the grouse Pa was able to shoot before the stars arose—sits over a crackling fire. The three of us perch around the petite fire, eating the grouse along with the handful of crackers left in the tin and the trickle of water left in the canister.

Prior to her passing, Florence told me to take care of our parents, sensing that her death would be a life-altering event. Often enough, I contemplate every sentence uttered from her lips, attempting to find what role I can play in their care. *I am trying, Florence, but the three of us are lost without you.*

The sun bows below the horizon, its last light stretching over the mountaintops in the distance as the stars reveal a whole galaxy to me. I anxiously wait for the glorious sight of Earth's rotation. Each heavenly body twinkles and winks as if they each know this fourteen-year-old girl gazing up at them, thinking only of her sister. The fire's embers glow orange with hope but eventually die with the breeze. I stifle a yawn while climbing into the wagon, not bothering to change into my nightgown, for I will wear this same brown dress tomorrow. I whisper a brief prayer just as my eyelids close, whisking me away to dreamland before the tears can streak down my face.

⌐

I awake with a fright, bursts of breaths coming out in puffs as my palm presses against my pulsing heart. Why won't my consciousness relent? Cursed am I, who must endure the torment of my own memories that haunt me and loom in my head each night!

Give it time, a soothing voice says in my ear. When my screams awake Mother, she always rushes to me, repeating, "Only time can cure the cursed memories.". Time cannot pass quickly enough, no matter how much I distract myself with hopes of school or even our future house that awaits us, wherever our destination is! Tears pool at my eyes and blur my vision as my head tilts backwards. I pull at my blanket and wrap it around my shoulders to mimic an embrace. *God, please free me from this endless torment!* my mind screams.

"I cannot bear it anymore," I mumble under my breath as another droplet trickles down my cheeks, searing my skin. "I cannot bear seeing it every night…thinking of the moment when I awoke to find every sense of familiarity gone from my life! It is as though life punishes me for wanting her here with us. Please, make it depart from my mind! Take it all away, for it cannot compare to feeling nothing at all…a different type of grief in itself, but at least it did not cause this persistent throbbing agony! She did not mean everything to the world, but she meant the world to me." It is no use. Saying the words aloud only verifies the truth: I am broken without Florence and may never be repaired.

Rays burn through the canvas cover, causing immense pain to my eyes. I rub them, squinting at the light as I poke my head through the hole at the rear of the cover, finding Mother crouched down jabbing at the coals of a fire. My bare feet hit the ground with a thud, my eyes missing no small detail as I look for a distraction. Cobalt grazes on the other side of the wagon, lifting his head to stare as I step closer.

I verify the absence of Mother and Pa with a single scan. My fingertips brush Cobalt's muzzle delicately before running down his scraggly mane. His brown eyes look imploringly at me as he chews a mouthful of grass. Tempest cautiously takes a few steps toward me, reaching his head out to be stroked. The morning light gleams off their bare backs, and they gawk at me as I admire their dazzling physiques. Ears twitching at all the sounds of nature, Cobalt snaps his head upright at the sight of Pa rushing to me.

"Azalea Bree Stanton, get away from those animals!" His voice booms and echoes over the hills. He snatches me by the arm, yanking me out of their midst. Every bird in our vicinity is alarmed by the sudden outburst and squawks a call of warning, taking off from their vulnerable spots on the ground.

"Pa, stop it! They are not the least bit aggressive. You are overreacting! I am no feeble little girl who cannot manage herself around horses," I scoff, crossing my arms defensively over my chest. Pa has rarely ever been cross with me before, except when I was a child and disobeyed his orders or sassed Mother. It is usually Mother who finds faults in my actions and punishes me severely for it.

His face turns to stone as he lifts a finger and points at Tempest and Cobalt. "You blatantly disobeyed my orders; I warned you not to step one foot near those horses! Your Mother and I have a good mind to forbid you from going to school this winter." With his words still booming at me, Pa whips around, storming off towards the wagon, the sight of his red face seared into my mind.

I am fully aware of my temper and stubbornness, but after that last sentence Pa spoke, my previously stony expression is paved into a look of pure remorse. "Pa, no! Please, you are aware that since yesterday it is my utmost desire to attend school this autumn!" The pleading scream is said to his back as he stomps further away from me. I take off after him. A pause ensues as I dash to his side. He begins swinging a hammer at the wagon's iron tires where the band has separated from the wooden wheel. "How can you be this villainous toward me? Ever since we bought those horses, I have been keen on riding them. I will admit I contravened your orders, but please do not prohibit me from going to school! What about my education? Are you willing to throw away my whole future over this one indiscretion?"

His green eyes remain focused as he swings the hammer, bending the band back around the wheel. Tears flood my eyes with every word that departs my lips; nonetheless, they are met with utter silence. The wind tosses my hair into my face as I await an answer. The pound of his hammer against the tire, pop of the firewood on the other side of the schooner, and whoosh of the wind clouds my eardrums. Anxious, I pick at the dirt under my fingernails and chew on my chapped lips.

When he finally turns around, his face turns fear-stricken, his wrinkles deepening as the tension builds. Knitting my brow, I follow his line of sight over my shoulder to a wide hill in the distance. An eerie feeling prickles down my spine as I squint. What appeared to be trees at first glance is actually a handful of people staring at us.

"Indians," I croak like a frog that has lost its voice. I look down for confirmation, and sure enough, my hands are shaking uncontrollably. The words spoken to me yesterday waft into my brain. *Some would shoot you before asking friend or foe.*

"Indians." Pa has always been able to filter his fear—better than I can because my face is an open book—nevertheless, he repeats the word, sounding equally as terrified as I did. "Margaret!" He calls her name in a low voice that strikes my heart as the shock begins to set in. The world begins to sway; I press my palm to my forehead in an unsuccessful attempt to make it stop. Oh gosh, the nausea is becoming unbearable!

"Albert?" she calls from the other side of the schooner, confusion leaking into her tone. Footsteps thump behind us whilst our eyes remain fixated on the people in the distance.

Even though it is just barely visible, I can see them waving and pointing at us. One of them mounts a horse, riding quickly toward us as the others remain stationary. The beating of my heart overtakes my hearing as my eyes fasten upon the rider gradually getting closer to us.

Brushing the wisps of hair from my face, I plead with urgency and gape at the stranger. "Pa, what do we do? Pa!" The answer, however, is undeniable: we are stuck here waiting as this Indian rides up to us and determines whether we deserve to live another day.

My eyelids are squeezed shut, nails dug into my palms, and ears focused on the thudding of hooves getting louder until it stops. Someone lets out a sigh of relief as a horse whinnies close by. In a moment of absolute dread, my eyelids flutter open to find a stubby, bearded man holding no resemblance to an Indian standing before us with his horse's reins in one hand and hat in the other. Mother lets out an, "Oh, goodness me," as I let out a monosyllabic laugh at our misconception.

The stranger, who is quite short compared to his towering steed and no older than the fair age of forty, gazes questioningly between our awe-struck faces as he speaks in a low grumble. "Sorry, folks, didn't mean to give you a fright!"

A hearty chuckle escapes Pa's lips as he saunters up to the stranger, cordially shaking his hand wordlessly.

The stranger continues. "We noticed your wagon and thought it good to offer the invitation to join us. You heading to Idaho? Perfect! I'm Samuel. Most call me Uncle Sam, but you're welcome to whichever." Every sentence the stranger—or Uncle Sam—yells out is followed by a chuckle, and his unbothered horse chews grass around the bit in its mouth.

He displays a wide grin along with another friendly handshake. Pa jumps at the invitation—for what I am not quite sure of at the moment, although his happiness brings a smile to my face despite our argument lingering in the air. Uncle Sam watches with an animated twinkle as we pack the wagon in great haste, simultaneously calling out instructions to follow him to the rest of the "wagon train."

I crane my neck over Mother's and Pa's shoulders, which block my view of the supposed wagon train, which I imagine is a train whose cars look like wagons. My query is answered as we arrive a few minutes later to the wide hill. The wagon train is a line of what must be more than twenty wagons like ours, all with numerous families aboard them directing welcoming smiles at us.

"Azalea! Sit down before you injure yourself!"

"Oh, Mother, how can I sit while we are approaching such an unexpecting group of people? Why is it called a wagon train, and why do these people travel in it? Surely, they are not all related to one another," my feathery voice asks above the rattle of the wheels. Pa pipes in, explaining that it is called a wagon train because the wagons' close proximity and formation are similar to a train's cars, travelers are often invited to join but have no relation to each other, and most travel this way for safety.

Uncle Sam directs us to join at the back of the train. He then proceeds to ride ahead to the front to speak with the lead wagon, whose occupant seems to be named Mr. Etton. Upon our inclusion, the train progresses. Leaning against the driver's seat where Mother and Pa are sitting, I can just make out the sight of children walking alongside their families' wagons.

A notion hops into my mind, provoking me to jump out the back of our slow-moving wagon and prance alongside the children, who seem to range in age from about five to eighteen. The breeze whistles beautifully against my face as I take my place next to a red-headed girl who looks around twelve years old. On account of her whoops and hollers that are echoed by the others, along with the expression on her face, I can infer that she too is deeply enjoying the wonderful weather. I join in the hollering while holding my skirts out of reach from the briars that try to scratch them to pieces.

Oh, what a joyous time it is until an hour passes. My feet begin to ache, and gopher burrows do their best to hide in plain sight. My bonnet fails to keep the sun off my neck, resulting in a scorched patch, the wagons kick up so much dust that I develop a dry cough, and my lips become cracked and bleed. Even souvenir hunting does not occupy my mind long—even though I find a genuine arrowhead shortly into my search.

"Colleen O'Reilly," says the red-headed girl, suddenly offering her hand to me as we continue walking. A touch of an accent alters the two words.

Astonished by the sudden sound of her voice after nearly an hour of silence, I grin wildly, shaking her hand just as Pa did with Uncle Sam. "Azalea Stanton. Pleasure to make your acquaintance! I have attempted to conjure up a number of conversational pieces in the hopes of making a friend out of you but failed to articulate them into words. 'O'Reilly' is Irish, is it not? My Pa says Stanton is originated from England; therefore, we are practically neighbors!" I bite my lip, abashed by the sudden confession and rambling, but Colleen pays no mind and conveys the same enthusiasm in her response.

"Why, yes! I'm not one for greetings—it took me twice the time it should've to work up the courage to introduce myself. My family's wagon is in front of yours! That means we will be together every day! Being at the back is horrible because of the dust, but tomorrow the second wagon will be in the back and so on up the line. The only one that stays put is the lead wagon because the Etton family started this train. Do you like the eagle feather in my hair?"

Stuck firmly at the top of her left braid is a glorious brown and white plume. I noticed it previously but show the highest praise in response to her question, calling it "a wonderful work of natural décor."

"Thanks!" Colleen replies. "Y'all joined after dinner, but I think we will stop to collect some more meat soon. Look at all that." Colleen gestures to the animal carcasses that lie out in the field, and the revolting smell makes me pinch my nose until we pass. We halt our conversation for a few moments as the child in charge of dispersing water to each member of the train offers each of us a cup. We both quench our thirst and Colleen goes right back to talking.

"The plains are full of carcasses because most hunters only take the skins. Lucky for us, the meat makes for a decent stew. Oh goodness, my brother has been bitten by a snakelet. Excuse me!"

My head spins, trying to snatch up all the new information as Colleen speaks at such a rate before calmly rushing off to tend to her wailing brother, who had stepped on a tiny snake. Heart swelling with pride after making a new friend, I watch as a prairie dog sits on its haunches, peering at us as the wagons rattle by, sending up a cloud of dust in their wake.

Not long after the riders are sent ahead to scout out a camping spot, Mr. Etton calls, "Wagons ho!" Every wagon soon halts to form a large circle. All the horses and oxen are unhitched and turned loose to roam around in the enclosed area.

Chatting while we wait in line for supper, Colleen graciously explains that the trains often form a circle for safety from Indian attacks. In my hand is a tin cup held out for a ration of burgoo. Uncle Sam generously fills our cups while offering a friendly beam.

The fire crackles and pops, sending ashes up into the air. The smell of smoke sticks to my skin. I am a firm believer that one aroma can characterize a memory; maybe one day I will look back on this eventful day and recall the campfire smell latching onto me. A fiddle and banjo are struck up as hollers echo around the circle.

"Come now, Azalea!" Colleen yanks my arm playfully to the side, nearly dumping the remainder of my supper. With great haste, I place my cup—holding my half-finished meal—on the ground next to hers and rush to the roaring flames.

The sun offers a slow wave as it starts to dip below the horizon. Spontaneously creating moves to match the tempo, we parade around the fire, shouting out the lyrics from "Happy Land" as the instruments play even louder. Several others join in our efforts as we jump and holler. The euphoria refuses to diminish even after the song ends, for soon another song is on the fiddle's strings! Before I can settle back down or even catch my breath after the first round of gallivanting, Colleen begs me to go along again!

"What a capital time this is!" I shout between lyrics as the entirety of the travelers join hands and skip around the diminishing flames. The last chord strikes, and a round of thundering applause rises as people retreat to their supper, which is surely cold. In one great laugh, I collapse to the ground, lying on the dry grass with my hands tucked under my head and my cheeks aching.

How long has it been since I have truly found myself in this mood? All my internal battles slipped away when we were dancing, and suddenly I was the same Azalea I was before Florence died. Could I finally be recovering, healing, and moving on? But…how could I be healed this quickly? I have not faced any greater feat nor come to terms with my grief. Perhaps the only way to fix what is broken internally is to bury the past and leave it behind. But am I ready to forget my darling sister and everything she had to offer?

Colleen prances over and collapses next to me in a flurry of gasps. "Wasn't that exciting!" Her eyes fall upon my furrowed brow and distant eyes. "Penny for your thoughts?"

I offer my hand out jokingly as she digs through the pocket of her calico dress for a coin. She places it in my hand with a friendly grin, waiting for the contents of my mind to be unfolded.

Twirling the coin in my fingers, I begin reluctantly, "If someone says, 'You are full of life,' shouldn't that be a good thing?" She purses her lips, clearly taken aback by my rhetorical question. "When I hear that someone is 'full of life,' I imagine somebody with millions of questions waiting to be answered, eyes aglow with possibilities, and a grin on their lips because they find the good in everything." Words concerning Florence's death follow without registering in my mind. Mother and Pa never asked me how I felt after her death; I have kept these feelings bottled inside just waiting to be released. "After all this time, I still do not know how to live without her! Every moment that went by while she was alive was wasted as if it never mattered. How do I…how can I keep living without her?" Maybe dumping this trauma on someone a little more than a stranger is not the wisest way to make a friend, yet that is the only way these thoughts can escape.

My emerald eyes plead for an answer as I turn my attention away from the hypnotizing stars to watch as the expressions play across Colleen's face. The wrinkles from her furrowed brow lessened when I spoke of Florence as if she too understands the grief of losing someone. "Don't dwell too much on the past because you might miss the future. Azalea, you cannot be angry at the world for what has happened to you! You must move on, forgive what has happened but don't forget her. And try not to feel guilty for living."

My heart beats faster as I realize how much truth the words hold; nonetheless, my conscience is weighed down from the guilt. Without saying anything else, Colleen stands and strolls away in the direction of her family's wagon. The embers of the fire glow orange, refusing to die as I stumble to our wagon and settle on the blanket next to Mother, who has already fallen asleep.

⌒

Just as the sky begins to lighten, everyone pitches in to collect chips, build the fire, prepare breakfast, and hitch the horses and oxen. One of the families offers their milking cow, and a line forms with people waiting their turn for a cup before she runs out. After a breakfast of cornbread, bacon, and coffee, the train resumes pace once the sun reaches above the horizon.

Colleen skips next to me, her hair tangled in knots from the wind. "Whatever are you wearing?" I exclaim upon noticing the absence of her calico dress. My eyes widen as I scan the area for any sign of a man who might see.

Overcome by a forceful laugh, she bends over, slapping her knee. Once tranquility returns, she explains, "They are just bloomers! My mother said women often abandon their hoopskirts and dresses on the trail. You should try it! The heat makes it almost unbearable with all the skirts on anyways." She shrugs while gesturing to three of the women standing a few yards before us also equipped in their bloomers. With an awestruck expression painted on my face, I pull my horrendous brown dress over my head and toss it over my arm. A rebellious laugh bursts out of my mouth.

My wild moment of impropriety does not go unnoticed by Mother, who screams loudly from the wagon. "Azalea Bree Stanton, why do you not have your dress on?!"

In an effort to prevent this personal conversation from being overheard by the children and women walking, I dash over to our wagon. "Colleen told me most women just wear their bloomers on account of those pesky weeds that catch hold of your dress!"

Pa attempts to conceal a chuckle behind a cough as he focuses on driving the horses. Has he finally forgiven my indiscretion? Why hasn't he said anything to me about my attendance in school this forthcoming autumn? I too stifle a giggle at Mother's exasperated face. Staring at me with astonished eyes and perilous brows, she holds a hand underneath her bonnet to massage the growing wrinkles on her forehead.

"Dear child, you are putting that dress back on this very minute! I shall not hear of this notion of bloomers anymore. It is highly improper!" I offer a single nod and yank the dress, which is caked in dirt, back over my head.

Mother's shouts echo in my mind. I try to shake away the feeling of her disappointment, but it seems to have hit a nerve and seeped into me. It's almost as if I can feel her eyes on my hair, which I attempted to brush and braid this morning but now sticks out messily, tangled in the buttons of my dress. Due to Mother's outburst, I decide against walking barefoot like some of the others do to save their shoes.

"Your mother won't permit you wearing bloomers?" Colleen questions as I rejoin her. With a shrug, I turn my attention to one of her younger brothers, who is walking up to us with a toad in his hands. After he exclaims that he is going to care for it as a pet, Colleen shoos him away and he traipses off willingly to show the other children. My eyes follow him as he bolts between the wagons, holding the creature for all to see.

A sullen-faced little boy near the age of seven sits on the back of a wagon, staring at me with teary eyes. My friend takes notice of our shared eyesight and comments, "His family won't let him near us. They say he's possessed by the devil, so they hide him out of shame. I tried to comfort him our first day with the train, but his mother exclaimed that his mind is ruined and muddled. It's a shame. He seems like a sweet child." A crop of blonde curls frames his small face.

"How horrible it must be to live like that!" Sympathy leaks into my voice as I lift a hand to wave to him. Upon first glance, a smile brims his lips, and he even lifts a pale white hand to wave back at me.

The weather takes a turn for the worse a few hours later, ominous gray clouds unleashing perpetual raindrops that send us running for the cover of the canvas. Pa remains outside the wagon to drive the horses whilst Mother and I take shelter inside. Battling relentless winds, Mother does her best to tighten the canvas at the back of the wagon, but the shower still makes its way through the same hole.

The wagon behind us blocks my view of the summer rainstorm that bores down upon us. I can only make out the droplets sliding down the wagon cover. Howls come as the horses struggle to regain their footing on the muddy ground. A scruffy voice yells above the fray, telling the men to continue driving. A rock tosses Mother and me against the planks as our speed suddenly increases. Goosebumps prickle my skin as coldness nips at my toes, and my head snaps around as screams echo from the family behind us. Mother immediately wraps her arms around me and shuffles the pair of us between the wooden trunk and boxes. The sight of the wind pulling the canvas off the wagon behind us, the women and children inside screaming at the direct downpour, sends shivers down my spine.

"We are okay," Mother repeats as droplets blow into our safe haven and soak us to the bone. Her voice quivers like a bow across fiddle strings, striking fear into my resilient heart. My eyes are constantly blinded from the lightning flashes, my eardrums throbbing from the booming thunder and the relentless chattering of my teeth driving me to insanity. Seeking comfort and warmth, I nestle into Mother's shoulder, wrapping my arms around her neck like a helpless infant.

Despite the raging storm, only one thing occupies my mind. I have no control over my circumstances; humans are at the mercy of the obstacles that present themselves. Like a boat in the raging waves of a perilous ocean, I am knocked down time and time again, desperately clawing for something to lift me back up. I am drowning in a sea of worries, forever surrendering to the greater power.

Considering the trials and tribulations we have encountered on our travels, I feel as though stability is an element missing from my life. Here I am, forced to wait for the day when I shall be deemed old enough to make my own decisions; no wonder I feel so helpless in the attempts at a solution for whatever problem shall occur! This fact does nothing except distract me from the nipping cold that makes my nose and hands ache. For now, I must close my eyes to all my grievances and wait for the end of judgment day.

Chapter 3

LEST WE FORGET

WHEN THE STORM CEASES, all the wagons are ordered to halt in circle formation, and the damage becomes clear. Canvases have been ripped to pieces or blown away completely, a horse injured and unable to travel for the next few days, belongings littered on the dirt path behind us, the food stored on the chuckwagon soiled and ruined, and everything drenched.

We lay all our clothing out to dry in the warm grass as we wash the dishes. My hair remains untidy as I lift the heavy water tub, which is filled to the brim with dirty, soapy water. It splashes against me, and with a sigh I turn it over, waiting until every drop has spilled out. Feet caked in mud, sweat running down my brow, and hands wrinkled and dry from the sun's rays that bore down upon me, I wave a quick hello to Colleen and her family where they stand at the edge of the creek.

Afterward, I return the tub to the wagon and fetch one of the few books that went untouched by the downpour. Shade offered by the occasional tree is taken advantage of by all, especially the younger children. Despite my horrid appearance, I cannot help but feel at peace about the fact that we survived that horrid storm!

A red-tailed chipmunk chitters a hello before disappearing into its burrow. With the mountains as my background, I gaze upward at the pleasantly white pillows that float just above my reach along the azure sea. My book lies open, pages flipping involuntarily in the wind. Life is like a book; the chapters are people, paragraphs are memories, and sentences are unspoken words. Another day goes by where I am yet again astounded by the Earth in all its heavenly beauty.

"Azalea, please pack the last of your things!"

"Yes, Mother!" I call as I climb into the wagon bed, stuffing a dress, a broken compass I found yesterday afternoon, and a bird feather Colleen gifted me this morning into Florence's wooden trunk.

Cobalt lets out a high-pitched whinny as Pa tries to hitch him next to the wagon shaft. Without much of a struggle, I jump out of the back and scurry to Pa and Cobalt. Cobalt is grappling with the rope tied to his halter, beating his hoof on the ground defiantly.

"Get back, Azalea." Pa cranes his neck slightly so that I might see the fierceness in his eyes. With an agitated sigh, I relinquish my stubbornness, stepping back to watch him spar with the task. After the fifth attempt of trying to corral Cobalt in between the jockey yoke and singletree, he finally relents and accepts my aid. With Cobalt being obstinate and our water barrel stilled needing to be filled at the stream, time is slipping through our fingers. Most of the train already filled their barrels at the last creek, but after the hot day yesterday and the washing, a few families, ours included, are without water.

Colleen skips up to us, twirling a lock of brilliant red hair around her finger. "Azalea, Mr. Etton just came down to the creek and told my Pa that the train is about to leave—" Distracted by the task at hand, I'm caught off guard by her unanticipated pause. Tossing a glance over my shoulder, I catch the moment she clutches her stomach before continuing. "You must hurry if you wish to get water."

"Dear friend, are you unwell?" I ask, abandoning Pa and Cobalt, the latter finally standing still long enough to be hitched. "What ails you?" My eyes scan her for any infected cut or snake bite, but there is not even a scratch on her skin. I flash a look of worry to Pa, and he raises a brow and nods at Colleen.

After a long pause, she sucks in air through her teeth. "I don't know. I have felt this way since yesterday morning. A few of my brothers and sisters are sick too. I must get back to the wagon." With that, she slouches and trudges back to her family's wagon, leaving our stupefied faces creased with worry.

"We have to hurry if we are going to continue with the wagon train. Margaret, we are going down to the creek!"

Pa rolls the barrel, and I snatch a wooden bucket as Mother echoes that she will join us momentarily. Thankfully, the creek is only a few minutes' walk from the train. Weeds pull at the hem of my dress as I perch on the bank, gleaming blue water rushing by whilst being sliced by sharp rocks that dare to poke out.

Pa has thankfully brought his cup along. He goes a few yards upstream from me and sets the barrel down on the ground. The warm water laps at my fingertips as I skim them along the surface. While I lower the bucket into the water, my eyes shift to a nearby boulder with something carved into it. The oddly scrawled letters arrange themselves in my mind just as Pa scoops a cupful of water, then raises it to his lips.

"Water poisonous."

A wheezy breath eases out of my lungs as time slows for a moment.

"Pa!" The scream echoes and sweeps over the meadow, but the volume is degraded by the rush of the creek. The bucket falls from my grasp and clatters to the ground by gravity's forceful pull until every last droplet leaks out. Shoes pounding on the ground, my hand flies to the cup just before he can take a sip. Pa's stunned expression disappears as he reads the words on the boulder in utter silence.

But my relief soon vanishes like sunlight covered by an ominous cloud; the rest of the train remains unaware of the danger. My vision focuses to see Mother walking toward us; reaching up a hand to adjust a pin in her hair, eyes glancing up at us with a momentary smile that fades upon the sight of our ghostly white frames.

Heart beating like a war drum in my chest, my family races to the camp with such urgency only permitted for Jesus's second return. A crowd of people is gathered near the side of a wagon muttering questions. My legs sting from the scratches made by thorny vines, arms shaking as I push through the men and women. In the middle of the crowd is Colleen in her mother's arms, the latter's pale face searching people for answers as someone mutters to Pa that Colleen has collapsed.

I can feel the color trickling out of my face as a cold wave sweeps over my rigid frame. My hands quiver violently as I cover my mouth and sink to the ground, whispering, "This cannot be happening again! She's young. Younger than…"

Her younger brothers and sisters, not looking well themselves, stand behind Mrs. O'Reilly, gazing curiously at the display. Colleen's chest rises and falls rapidly as her mother strokes her face. I faintly hear Pa's voice telling everyone that the creek's water is poison. They remain confused or even hesitant for a second before a widespread panic sets in.

Colleen does not wake up, her condition worsening by the hour. I remain by her side for a time, placing a cool rag on her forehead. Sometime around midnight, her eyes begin to roll back in her head and her body shakes uncontrollably, sending her mother into hysteria. She calls out for help even though none can be provided.

Less than one day after Colleen suffers a seizure, her pulse stops. She is buried along with her younger brother, who succumbed to the same illness. Their graves lie under a young willow tree and are each marked with rocks.

The rest of her siblings did not drink enough water for it to be fatal, although they remain indisposed. Only two other families drank from the creek, and they too were buried or remain hopelessly clinging to life.

For the second time this year I am forced by fate to wear a black dress. It is as if I carry the kiss of death; no matter which corner of the Earth we travel to escape it, it shall always prevail and claim yet another. An end to yet another friendship that would have blossomed beautifully.

It seems like I have been befallen by a horrid curse that deprives me of ever having a lifelong friend: Nora, Evelyn, Mrs. Jones, Florence, and now Colleen! How woeful it is that such a glimmering soul has been taken so soon; I struggle to grasp the concept that the fiery red-headed girl who was like a kindred spirit has been stolen away. Why does this keep happening? I cannot handle it. How can I carry Florence's *and* Colleen's deaths upon my shoulders? If only I stopped her from going to the creek, then none of this would have happened and she would still be here next to me!

A lump rises in my throat, choking me until the tears are released with excruciating pain. Nail-shaped indents mark my palms, but the pain feels like less than a sting when compared to the internal gnawing.

It is now, as I sob alone next to Colleen's grave, that an epiphany settles upon me: Florence is gone. Of course, I previously realized she is no longer here when I awoke that fateful morning and had to witness her funeral, but it feels final now, as if I have forgiven myself, the world, and God for letting her die. *My dear friend Colleen…why couldn't I save you either?*

The train moves on two days after the funerals. Pa glances at me worriedly as I stare blankly out of the back of the wagon. I no longer feel the need to walk outside with the other children because unlike them, I am old enough to realize the severity of what has happened. A once-blank journal sits open in my lap with words written in my handwriting, "*I still search for you; when someone laughs, when a moment aches of your presence, in the sunrise and wide-open fields. It's been forever since your name has been spoken aloud.*"

Chapter 4

MY HEART ACHES FOR YOU

FAMILIES JOIN AND LEAVE the train each day. As we travel, I have started to notice the mounds of dirt with rocks marking them. My eyes have been opened to just how many graves there are on the trails, and each morning I consider myself in God's grace to have lived this long. although I am not quite sure how merciful it can be to bear witness to these tragedies each daybreak.

My supper—salted pork and beans that were cooked in the embers of the campfire—sits untouched on my plate. Coffee fills my cup to the brim; I have always found the smell rather addicting, but the taste is anything but pleasurable. Wispy clouds shield the stars; without the light from them or the moon, the night feels like an endless pit of darkness gradually closing in.

A booming chorus of laughter comes from a nearby campfire, a group of women sharing in a jocular mood. How can others do that—go on with life as if unaffected? Every thought, breath, and moment are inundated with Colleen, to the point where happiness feels blameworthy. Abandoning the sustenance, I stumble gloomily to bed, my mind whisking me off to dreamland as soon as my head touches the lumpy pillow.

A deep voice calls out for help as a woman screams. The voices feel far away, as if whispered down a tunnel. My eyelids flicker open, and my vision adjusts to the darkness of the night. The sight of Mother and Pa missing from the wagon invokes a jab of terror, like the blade of a knife piercing my skin. A faint glimmer of the moon peeks out wickedly from behind the clouds as if withholding an ominous secret. Panic pulses through my veins, a shiver takes over, and my skin is prickled with goosebumps. The humidity sticks to my skin, forcefully weighing me down.

My bare feet hit the ground as I jump out of the wagon, searching the circle for where the voices are coming from. Grasshoppers play sweetly while the scene unfolds from across the circle; the canvas of someone's wagon is ablaze. Orange light grows quickly as the whole wagon goes up in flames within minutes.

Pa's gruff holler diverts my attention. I catch sight of him in the group of men as they race around the camp, alerting everybody of the danger and locating buckets to fill with water. The heat warms my skin as I mindlessly walk closer, eyes wide as if I am a lost child. The family who owns this wagon stands nearby, watching in horror as all of their belongings burn during this summer night.

Mother holds the woman, shushing her sobs and rubbing her arms. Her child clings to her leg with tears dripping off his cheeks and a hand-sewn doll in his clutches. My head spins wildly as a bucket is thrust into my arms and I am dragged to the creek whilst my vision remains fastened on the blaze that has fully engulfed the wagon. It takes me a moment to realize it is Pa who is pulling me.

"Azalea!"

My name seems foreign in my groggy mind. I lower the bucket into the water and allow it to fill halfway before I run toward the line of bodies waiting for me. The bucket leaves my grasp in an instant and is passed up the line of men and women until the water is tossed on the flames.

Water splashes against me repeatedly as I race alongside others to retrieve and deliver water. The wagons and livestock in close proximity are moved away for fear of an outbreak. A dark cloud of smoke drifts above until the wind sends it over to us. Ashes hit my eyes, slowing my efforts down tremendously. *Heavenly Father, please help us!*

Lungs screaming for pure air and muscles throbbing from lifting buckets, I could just collapse from exhaustion in this spot, and nobody would ever notice my disappearance. My life is filled with "what if's" that are never answered, so I must ask myself once again, what if the past few months had never occurred in history? Would my fate be considerably changed? Is it God's plan to have me struggle through so much grief and misery for some deeper unknown reason or is all of this my own doing? Nonetheless, I must continue waiting for someone or something to drive my journey forward.

The crowd of wanderers' stare in agony as the last bucket is passed down the line and thrown onto the glowing embers that threaten to spark again. Chest rapidly releasing sighs of relief, I wipe the sweat from my brow, streaking soot across my face in the process.

The family is boarded for the night in a tent that escaped the blaze. Their only worldly possessions are some mementos that were moderately unharmed. Everyone returns to sleep as if it is as easy as breathing whilst I toss and turn under my thinly knit blanket. Swollen mosquito bites dot my skin and itch profusely, which only contributes to my negative mood. The moon peers down unfeelingly and a coyote yip echoes somewhere far away.

It is nights like these when random glimpses of the past seep into my mind. For instance, there is this particular memory that has resurfaced of me dashing around the house with a blanket draped over my shoulders and pinned at the throat with one of Mother's brooches. The ends of the blanket flap as I run down the hallway, looking over my shoulder at my sister, who mirrors my strange appearance. Laughter echoes as we skip into her room and find the object in our imaginations. A bonnet is mistaken for a crown and placed on her head as she sinks into a low bow, then rises to greet the crowd of faithful admirers who chant, "God save the Queen," upon seeing her smile.

What a mirthful memory it is! Nearly every childhood memory appears that way as you get older. A grin brims my cupid's bow, which is swollen from constant lip-biting.

"I desperately wish to speak with you. But you are no longer here. Perhaps it is selfish of me to wish you were, considering this is God's plan. Nevertheless, I have nobody else!" My voice whispers into the dead of night. A shaky breath invokes a heart-wrenching sob. When Florence died, I never thought I would ache for those days when shock overshadowed grief, for now it seems like the pain has made a home in my heart.

"It pains me deeply every time I remember you are not with us on this journey. The one thing I want, I can never truly have…Perhaps I am making too much of a fuss over your death. People die every day, yet the world keeps rotating without them. It still feels as though my life is centered around you and I am clueless as to how to fix my brokenness. Goodnight, my dear sister." A star winks as my eyelids flutter to a close and a huff forces the agony back into the confines of my soul.

∿

"What shall become of them?" My eyes waver to the family whose wagon burned last night. Their faces convey misery to anyone who sees them. Pitying condolences have been uttered all morning. What sorrow they must feel to be without nearly every belonging they hold dear!

Pa looks over his shoulder as he collects the reins. "A family will carry them to the nearest town, and they will have to find their way from there." Mother climbs up to sit next to him and adjusts her bonnet to shield her alabaster skin from the brutal summer rays.

"All their belongings gone in an instant. Is there not something we can do?"

They smile, yet I am answered with an order from Mother. "Azalea, do not fret about them. Please, sit down so your Pa can start the team! Albert, how much longer are we traveling with the wagon train?"

My only response is a disappointed sigh as I release my grip on the back of the box they sit on and sandwich myself uncomfortably between the boxes and trunks. Mother has always shown a certain distrust for being around strangers, but for the life of me I have never comprehended why.

"We can stray from the rest of them today, if it pleases you. We need to stop at some point to fill the water barrel." After Colleen's death, everyone has taken extra precautions to boil their water, mix it with charcoal, and filter it through a handkerchief to make it potable.

It takes several hours to reach water after we branch off from the train. The liquid reaches my knees as I stand on the bank of a large river. A cloudless sky stretches above while the smell of pancakes wafts over to me. Mother's shrill voice calls for me to join them for dinner, and my stomach forces me to hasten my pace and trot the short way to camp. A tiny fire crackles next to our wagon along with an iron spider holding a pan of fresh batter poured on it. I fetch the ceramic syrup jug and pour a generous amount over my pancakes. Pa settles next to me, forking a cut of the fluffy cakes into his mouth.

A sudden breeze sends my loose hair whipping in front of my face rather vexatiously. Mother takes the pan off the spider, flipping the flat cake with great ease onto her plate. Cobalt looks up at me with watchful eyes and twitching ears before returning to grazing alongside Tempest. My heart yearns to ride Cobalt. How wonderful it would be if I could acquire my own horse when we settle!

A glance at our box of provisions shows me that it is vacant. My fork lifts the syrup-covered cake to my mouth as I'm overwhelmed with guilt for not realizing the absence sooner. The feeble attempt to play it off is clear as I say, "Pa, when shall we reach our destination? How odd it is to not know where one is traveling to."

"Albert, we are scarce on supplies and rations," says my mother in a soft voice.

Placing his empty plate on the ground, Pa finishes the task of chewing before speaking. "Today is the day we arrive in Winfield."

My head snaps up to meet his eyes, which express a certain glow of a metaphorical grin. Could it be true? Winfield…What an exquisite name for a place, one I am quite sure could not have been imagined on my own merit! The name is like something out of the deepest dream of one's consciousness, similar to a slow summer breeze sweeping over rolling hills and sending wildflowers and tulips waving.

Pa continues, "The ferry upstream will take us across the river. It should be another eight miles south 'til we reach town." The horizon gleams brighter as if the star of Bethlehem glows over it on this serene afternoon, guiding us to our destination.

"A ferry?" My smile quickly fades at Mother's words and intense stare directed at Pa, who appears perplexed at the question.

Silence hangs between the three of us for several moments before it is cut like a knife. "Yes, Margaret. How else would we cross the river? Mr. Etton advised me that it will be too deep to float or plow through." Even though his tone is placid, Mother's brown eyes tell the story of how perilous a ferry is.

There are many things about which I lack knowledge, a ferry being one of them, so I quickly adopt a carefree outlook on the method transportation. If Pa is not worried, then why should I be? After all, Mother overreacts to everything! Nothing more is said as we hasten to pack the dishes, spider, and blankets, then follow along a short trail upstream with a wooden sign pointing us in the right direction.

It takes us about twenty minutes to follow the thin dirt path along the riverbank until we reach a small log cabin with two log rafts securely floating in the water. A stout man waves us over to where he stands near the house.

"My goodness!" Mother mumbles under her breath once the rafts come into view. A palm is pressed to her stomach as if to settle her nerves. Deeply confused, I observe the rafts as they sway with the fast-moving water.

"Howdy, sir! One dollar for a ferry ride," the scruffy man bellows as he swaggers up to where Pa sits on the box. Mother pulls out her small purse, unclasps it, and counts out a dollar in coins, placing them in the palm of Pa's hand. The money is transferred and counted again before we start moving closer to the landing.

One raft is larger than the other, but both are a bit wider and longer than the wagon. My shoulders fall upon the realization that we are to cross the raging river on one of these objects.

Held by pegs and ropes, the raft remains steady as the man directs our horses to it. Their eyes flash wildly at the object in which they are asked to step upon, and in doing so they yank the wagon suddenly before smoothly moving forward onto the raft. Water kicks and splashes against the raft as the man grabs a large wooden paddle and steps on board.

Mother glances over her shoulder to where I sit in the wagon bed, her eyes conveying a thousand words as she holds the palm of her hand to her chest whilst the other remains tightly fastened on the seat. Her knuckles begin to turn a ghostly white. Pa firms his grip on the leather reins as the man unties the ropes that hold the raft.

In a lurch, the ferry sweeps downstream, and we are left clutching for stability. The man stands at the back of our wagon. I can just barely see him out of the untightened canvas, paddle half in the water he peers around the wagon and directs the raft. Another lurch comes, sending a small box crashing onto my foot. I cry out, releasing my grip on the sides of the wagon bed to shove the box away and comfort my throbbing ankle.

"Azalea?" Pa pauses his shouts to calm the horses to look over his shoulder at me. I wince at the pain but smooth my face into a normal expression. My lips part to respond, but too much time has already passed. Mother does her best to look at me to make sure I am alright.

"Albert, it's her ankle. I think she is injured. I must check on her!" Mother yells over the horse's whinnies and the rushing water. Just as she attempts to throw her leg over the box and climb into the wagon bed, Pa shuffles both reins into his other hand and holds her in place.

"It is too dangerous! Stay put until we get to the riverbank. Azalea, hang on for now!"

Defeated but sensible enough to absorb the warning, Mother remains in her place next to him on the box while briefly peeking at me every few moments. If a lurch were to come or a current were to sweep us further downstream while she tries to climb back here, then she could be thrust into the raging water and gone in an instant. Pa always thinks two steps ahead; I have noticed that about him as I've gotten older. I sometimes wonder when he became so equipped to speculate at the unknown.

Oxygen fills my lungs before being swiftly expelled back out through my mouth, and my eyelids shield me from witnessing any more of this so-called "adventure". Let it be over already!

A few minutes later, we float close to the riverbank, where another small cabin is located with a stranger standing outside. The young man on the bank catches the ropes thrown by our ferry guide and wraps them around pegs fixed to the riverbank. In an instant, our horses are directed and our wagon safely pulled onto the bank.

Almost in unison, our shoulders ease, minds relax, and lungs heave out sighs of relief at our survival. Embedded into the palms of each of my hands are four crescent moons from where my nails dug into the skin.

I take notice of the darkening scar on my right palm, inflicted by a piece of wood that cut me when Mother, Florence, and I camped after our stagecoach got robbed a few months ago. That was the day we met Russell;

I often wonder how he is doing on account of his last letter; he practically proclaimed that he wanted to marry me!

The ring necklace he gifted me is tucked safely in a trunk, awaiting the moment I take it out, along with every memory and feeling that is captured with it. My responding letter told him about Florence's death and about my family's travels elsewhere with the promise of writing to him once our new address is established. A voice in my head questions if he will ever write me back, even after I send a letter from our new home. I am not quite sure if I could bear losing him too. My feelings toward Russell have never been clear—even to me—but cutting him out of my life completely would be utter torture. His face is still so familiar to my eyes…

"Are you well?" Mother's voice questions. My mystified eyes focus on her presence next to me in the wagon. My heart skips a beat; I must have fallen out of attention and not noticed her climbing into the wagon bed! She tenderly pokes at my puffy ankle and convinces me to extend the leg. "It appears swollen! We are going to have to prepare a poultice. I will collect some chickweed. Azalea, stay put!" To some it may appear as though these words are spoken with the tenderness of a mother, but from the mouth of mine, it comes as the sternest of enforcements.

Pa directs the horses to a grassy area and holds them steadfast while Mother searches around, eyeing the ground. The sunlight gleams off her pale blonde hair. Ever since I was a child, she has styled it the same way: wrapped up in a bun with five pins poked strategically in it to keep it in place in any conditions. It is a rare sight to see her hair down, a sight that I can only recall a handful of times. Even at nighttime, she brushes it until smooth, then braids it only to wrap it up again in the morning.

She hastens back to the shade of the wagon, holding up a leafy plant with small white flowers. I stare, riveted in place as she locates the petite stone bowl and mortar, sprinkles the plant in, adds a few drops of water from the barrel, then grinds it into a liquid serum. Mother directs me to sit on the edge of the wagon bed as she smears the poultice on my ankle, and afterward she wraps it in fabric torn from the hem of her dress.

With my mind greatly enticed by the display of medical practice, questions fly quizzingly from my lips without a moment's thought. "Where ever did you learn such a thing? Is that plant chickweed? What an odd name to be dubbed to such an interesting specimen! Shall it heal my ankle?" My gaze flickers between her face and the bandaged ankle, and a smile lifts my cheeks and brings my mood up to par.

A sigh escapes her mouth as if annoyed, cutting into my endless curiosity like a knife does butter. "In my younger days, a few years before you were born, I was a nurse. There were many battles, one in particular called the Red River War. Some doctors used medicinal plants and herbs. I adapted to the practice quickly and applied it to some of the injured men." Heart skipping a beat, my reaction is delayed for a moment as the words swirl in my mind. The sun peeks out from behind a cloud, temporarily blinding me as Mother pins the fabric together and examines her work carefully.

"Why is this the first I have heard about this? Did you treat many wounded soldiers? What a noble profession that must be, and how romantic to cure such ailments! Medicinal herbs…how interesting. Could you—"

"Azalea, enough! I do not wish to recall such events! Leave well enough alone." She stomps off, face reddening as she takes her place on the box. Pa climbs up next to her, peering at me with a solemn shrug of his shoulders, and clucks for the horses to giddy up.

Did Florence know Mother was a nurse in the war? She would not have been born yet, but perhaps the story was told to her. I cannot imagine the ensuing horrors in one's mind after witnessing such death and destruction. Could that be the reasoning behind her discontentment with the subject? Thoughts cloud my mind as the grasses sway under my feet, which swing above the moving ground. We continue for several miles on a sandy dirt road until turning into Winfield.

The name "Winfield" has been chiseled into a birch wood sign; the surrounding wood stained a dark brown to make the name catch any eye. The sign stands at the base of a young willow tree tilted north, its limbs stretching green leaves to visitors who pass by it. As our wagon rolls down the dirt road, which is wide enough for two wagons, I reach out and gently pluck a single leaf, holding it in my grasp to later press between the pages of my journal. In a flurry of excitement, I smooth my hair and hobble on my knees to the front of the wagon to peer over Mother's and Pa's shoulders. Tightly-packed buildings painted an array of colors adorn each side of the road for about twenty yards before ending in more prairie.

My smile quickly falters as I ask, "Pa, this cannot truly be all of Winfield! Where are the school, church, and houses? A town cannot be comprised of only a mercantile, dress shop, blacksmith, and a handful of homes!" My mouth reads the words off the signs that hang over each building.

"Bluebird, do calm down. I'm sure there is more to the town than this! Margaret, hold the team for a moment, and I will run into the mercantile." Mother bobs her head once and grabs hold of the horses' reins determinedly as Pa takes a few bills out of the purse, walks up the three dusty wooden steps, and disappears behind the two glass doors. Just barely visible under the beige shade is a counter with a line of glass jars filled what I speculate is candy in several different colors, from red to blue to purple.

The words "The Mercantile" are painted on the wide window to the left of the doors in bright red with gold around each letter. A large porch wraps around the front of the shop, similar to the rest of the buildings. Whether it be red brick, wood panels, or stone, every building has a common theme: long porch, chimney on the left corner of the black shingled roof, windows facing the road giving travelers an insight into the lives of Winfield's residents, and a congenial ambience.

Similar to a place that could only be experienced in one's dreams, Winfield appears to be something out of my own imagination, not by the look of it but by the eerie feel of déjà vu. Maybe I have seen this in a dream before, for it appears to be the town which I briefly described to Florence when the news of her diagnosis was delivered from my lips. The dress shop I spoke about then is located a few yards away from where I peer over Mother and the horses. The two wide, sparkling windows on either side of the faded-blue door reveal two dresses sitting on mannequins made in a suitable and plain fashion, spools of a few different kinds of fabric on the wall behind the counter, and a sewing machine on a marble-topped desk.

"It is an interesting town," Mother comments while gazing cautiously at the handful of structures. She picks at her fingernails every couple of moments as if anxiously awaiting Pa's return. To be perfectly honest, I too am agitated that Pa has not returned sooner; at least ten minutes have passed us by as we sit in quietude on this empty road.

Please let there be a school! My heart beats in rhythm to the words.

"I must say, I expected something a little more populated and civilized! Lorretta was a city in comparison to this." This seems to be Mother's way of not getting her hopes up. For all we know, Pa could be mistaken and there could be no occupations available. And without a steady income, we cannot survive here. I choose not to respond. On the contrary, I offer a wordless nod.

A bell rings as the store's front door swings open. Pa's chuckle fills the summer afternoon as it is carried to us through the breeze. Leaves rustle as he walks toward us with a toothy grin and a piece of paper in his hand. Perplexed, Mother and I exchange a look of great curiosity before our questions shoot at him like cannonballs during a battle.

"Albert, where are the supplies?"

"Pa, do tell us there is more to Winfield than this!" Our voices overlap as he climbs up to sit on the box, folds the paper, tucks it away for safekeeping, and then turns to face us. The shadow from his worn slouch hat covers his tan skin from the brutal rays.

He lifts his hands in defense as his playful grin widens, revealing dimpled cheeks. "All in good time. I will ride into town later today to fetch supplies, but for now we have a house to get to! Giddy up!" The reins crack and up the horses go, trotting up a dust cloud that lingers for a few moments, reminding the town of our presence.

"House?" Mother shrieks and clutches the side of the box. The sudden speed caught her off-guard and she almost tumbled out of the wagon from shock!

In unison, my ears perk up, my eyes widen, and my mouth opens. It takes less than a second for my mood to change, and when it does it is the best feeling! Euphoria sparks in my mind and heart instantly, and soon I am hanging on to Pa's every word as we dash along the road, past the houses, and over an old bridge.

The sight of a trickling river under the bridge and evergreen fir trees surrounding us temporarily distract me from my intention of asking Pa about every detail of the house, to which we will surely arrive at any moment.

"Albert, how can we afford a house? We barely have twenty dollars to our name!" Mother covers her mouth with the tips of her fingers and snaps her head around to gaze at me. In an instant, my face changes to a distracted expression as I resume staring at the forest on either side of the path.

Pa clears his throat, then clucks at the horses, twitching the reins and pulling back when their heads get too high. "Margaret, do calm down. We'll do just fine here!" His honey voice is a great contrast to Mother's shrill pitch, but they go hand-in-hand nicely. "Robert Huxley and his family own the mercantile. He promised me a good deal on the place on account of it being uninhabited for the past few years. I used half of our money as a down payment, and the rest of the mortgage will be paid in an installment plan between Robert and me. There are a few jobs in town for carpenters and joiners with new houses and such being built. I'll start work in town and begin putting the house in order in the spare hours. The horses and wagon ought to be sold once we move in! Azalea, I made sure to ask about the school on your behalf—"

"Does this mean you will allow me to go to school?" My question is met with the slight inclination of his head, confirming that the answer is yes. "Do tell what he said! There must be more branches of Winfield if our house is not located on the main road. What do you suppose this house looks like? Shall it be in great disrepair or need work done before we get situated?"

Wildlife seems to be in great abundance here, for I have already spotted several species of birds and a small herd of deer standing in a grove. I also hear the croak of frogs and chirp of insects. A European starling gleams past, barely missing the horses' pounding hooves. My imagination swirls with the prospect of what our home looks like. How odd it is to say that after a long time of feeling displaced: "our home!" I enjoy the stability in the sense that it does not include the reoccurring chores, rations of beans and watered stew, and sleeping on the hard wagon bed.

Pa laughs at my eagerness, not minding my rudeness in cutting his sentence short. "As I was saying, Bluebird…School starts the first of November. Winter term, they call it. Don't expect too many kids there. This is farming country and most everyone will be busy preparing a crop for spring. Robert said the town stretches several miles in all directions, the main street being for the businesses and smaller homes. Paths lead to properties and neighboring towns. As for the house, I'm not sure what it looks like. My knowledge only goes to the fact that it was a low price, located two miles along the right side of the fork in the road, and not a soul has lived there since '89."

Heart content with this newfound knowledge, I settle down in the back of the wagon while counting my blessings and thanking God for this altered course. We trot along the path until we pass through the gate of an old split-rail fence that had once been painted some color related to white. On we go, bouncing at every rock that the wheel hits and fearfully anticipating the state of our new home. The wagon slowly halts where the dirt path ends at the base of an idyllic countryside farmhouse. A glance at the surrounding land beholds the occasional tree that stands like a main character when compared to the blank landscape.

I jump out of the wagon and hobble around the side to achieve a better perspective, and what a wonderful view it is! Two stories, a lengthy front porch, white exterior matched with a gray-shingled roof, and quantities of windows with light indigo blue shutters spaced along every available area. A first-floor mansard roof with the second floor owning a gable style, and large square footage. On the house's left is a blooming Black Tartarian cherry tree, identifiable upon first glance, no more than nine feet tall. What a wonderful spot to read!

A walk around the other side of the home reveals a red brick chimney, which I suppose opens to a fireplace in the parlor. A small cluster of dandelions are grouped around my ankles, carefully awaiting movement. I must oblige them, so I give a few twirls—heedful of my injured ankle— matched with a giggle and stop to watch the seeds disperse in the air before being carried away by the breeze.

The first-floor windows are covered by screens and speckled with dirt beyond belief, making it impossible to see inside! What color is the wallpaper in the parlor or my bedroom? I can spot a bay window on the second floor from where I stand. Please let that be the perfect nook for reading a hearty novel like *Jane Eyre*! A circular window is located on each side of the house near the gable roof— perhaps the house contains a garret! A garret would be a splendid location for a collection: leaves of all natures, pinned-up butterflies, Colleen's feather, my arrowhead, and the occasional rock or pinecone that seems captivating in natural architecture. Some of Florence's beloved mementos shall be tucked safely away in that garret; I could never truly forgive myself if some possession of hers were to be damaged beyond repair.

Occasionally, when nobody is around, I lift the lid of the heavy wooden trunk that once belonged to her and observe the objects that have been packaged away since our return from Brockschmidt: dresses, blouses, skirts, and hair ribbons all exactly as she left them. It's as if the entities anticipate her return. Often enough I question whether she will ever leave my mind or if that is something I even desire. The memories of our past life in Wyoming—and inquires of how she would react to the natural occurrences that have happened in my life since she died—pain me deeply, but would it be even more unbearable to erase the suffering entirely?

I must constantly remind myself of the words she wrote to me in her final goodbye: *"God makes everything happen for a reason, even if we may not know what that is yet."* They rarely provide me enough comfort to persevere through the days. Nothing could ever come between my relationship with my religion and partnership with God as one of His children. Nonetheless, that does not dissipate the doubt in this all being for my own good. The last of the daylight shines upon me in blissful rays as I sit here on the ground experiencing my first sunset in Winfield, Idaho.

Later, Pa proclaims after his inspection of the structure that "the house is unsuitable and will need fixing up." When I ask by the glow of the firelight in what way it is unsuitable, he responds with the orders not to set foot in the home because some the floors need replacing and the staircase is rickety. In the coming weeks, I shall have to remain content in exploring our small parcel of land…

"Bluebird, I suppose you will have some catching up to do to with the rest of your class," Pa comments as he puts another spoonful of oatmeal in his mouth, chewing thoughtfully.

I quickly steal a glance in the direction of the wagon. Mother retired to bed just as the moon rose overhead, so I respond in a whisper. "I am, of course, grateful for our Sunday schooling. Nonetheless, Mother could not teach us in-depth things that were beyond her knowledge. For example, the Revolutionary War or harder aspects of arithmetic. Hopefully, the rest of the children are not incredibly studious or else I shall feel like a black sheep in a flock of purity!" His eyes reflect my smirk right back at me.

"Well, why don't you help me with some simple arithmetic?" He pulls a short and thin branch out from the wood pile, handing it to me. He clears a small area of grass so that I can copy the numbers down, just like a slate and pencil. "Now then, the house cost five hundred dollars. Add twenty acres of land at five dollars an acre, a homestead filing fee of ten dollars, and a pound of oats at seven cents. How much does that add to?"

My quiet contemplation is disrupted by the sound of chirping crickets performing their nighttime opera. Still, I scratch the numbers into the dirt, carry the one over, and write the answer at the bottom. "Six hundred ten dollars and seven cents."

"Very good. Now we can subtract the profits we'll make; the wagon is worth sixty dollars and the horses about a hundred each."

Another few tranquil moments. "Three hundred fifty dollars and seven cents. Pa, are you truly going to sell Cobalt *and* Tempest? I figured you would let me keep at least one to ride. You could teach me to ride, of course."

He inclines his head at the number with a grin, conveying a job well done. "Sorry, Bluebird, we have to sell them to the livery as soon as possible. Only way to pay off the house. And you will need a good bit of things for school. How does a new dress sound?"

A moment of hesitation passes by, carrying great tension. "I was actually hoping to wear one of Florence's dresses when the day comes. If that is all right with you?" His reaction, a wince of pain at the sound of her name and the concealment by looking over his shoulder, was expected but still gut-wrenching to watch. "Pa?"

He snaps back into the moment as if lightning has struck. "Of course, you may wear her clothes." The absence of her name has not gone unnoticed by me; neither one of my parents have spoken her name aloud since her untimely demise. I suppose child loss inflicts unimaginable grief onto the overseers. "Maybe you can have a horse of your own by wintertime. We'll have to see what money the jobs in town bring in, so do not get your hopes up! You should get to bed now." I stand, looking back at him once to evaluate the expressions playing across his face, then walk to the wagon bed where I settle down and wait for my subconscious to locate dreamland.

Chapter 5

SELFLESS NATURE OF HOPE

FOR THE LAST TWO WEEKS of June, Mother and I rarely leave the property, doing any task that will occupy our time whilst Pa works in town. Even on Saturday and after church on the Sabbath—despite Mother's constant scolding that "we do not work on the Lord's Day"—Pa works dawn to dusk.

One day, Pa marches outside with a saw in hand, the light reflecting off the blade and alerting me instantly. Curious at first, my eyes follow him to the side of the house, where the cherry tree branches sway in the wind. Oh, what a heavenly sound it is when the breeze shakes the canopies, almost like a chorus of humming vocal cords rather than words. It is only when he clutches the trunk that the realization hits me furiously. Before my mind can formulate a thought, my feet are hitting the ground.

Screeching to a sudden halt, fighting to regain my footing, I hold a hand over his on the handle of the saw.

"Please do not cut it down!" His startled eyes look into mine as my chest heaves. "What a wonderful spot it is to read! How ever can you look at this little sapling that has only existed a short while and think to cut it down?" In an attempt to stage my protest and declare the severity of my intentions, I try to hoist myself up into its branches. Comprehending that the thin young branches above my head will not hold my weight, I instead spread my arm across the front with my chest against the wooden trunk stemming higher than me, wrapping it in a one-armed bear hug. It isn't until now that I fully understand how absurd a tree hugger looks.

Whether it is the brimming of tears in my pleading green eyes or the fact that I will not unhand the saw whose blade points at me dangerously, Pa relents and promises no harm to the sapling. My gaze wavers to it now as the shadow casts on me while I sit in the naturally carved nook of its base.

I have been tasked with naming our new property, something unique yet simple to pronounce so that travelers may marvel at the brilliance of it. So far, a short list comprised of four possibilities is written in my journal. None of them produce a euphonious enough sound for this place. "Further contemplation is required," I say when asked of my progress.

In a twist of events, I have gone stir-crazy in the confines of the fence whilst Mother appears content in our confinement! The first couple days were sublime. I had a capital time chasing my shadow, resulting in many victories, sitting under the elderly willow tree at the corner of the two fences (what a brilliant place for a swing that would be), reading numerous books I have in my collection, and starting my collection of natural artifacts.

Repetition certainly is not absent from my life, for I seem to be stuck in an alternate universe where each day plays out the same as the one before it! The sound of the hammer is an infinite echo around us that dares to drive our minds to insanity. It starts to feel like my existence is bound by the fences that surround our property, heart yearning for the adventure promised to me once we completed the journey here. I grow bored of the constant cycle and move on to helping Mother mend holes in clothes, wash dishes, and weed the flowerbeds on either side of the stairs to the front door. In order to prepare proper flowerbeds, we pull the deteriorating rose bushes out of the ground, bring them to the edge of the property, and toss them into the forest, then work on our hands and knees to uproot the buckhorn plantain, a weed Mother pointed out to me. The sunshine scorched my neck yesterday, turning it a blistering red on account of the absence of my bonnet, so Mother has forced a blue bonnet upon my head today. To fill the silent void, I take to whistling no tune in particular as I yank the leafy plants from the earth.

"Stop that infernal racket, child! I cannot hear myself think," Mother exclaims so suddenly that the sound is sucked back into my vocal cords before it has the chance to be heard. She leans back, pulling off her glove to wipe the sweat from her brow. Lips pursed, I too steal a break from the work at hand. "Sorry, dear. How about you go frolicking? Promise to stay within view of the fence, and you can go a few steps into the forest and find more of those leaves you like to collect."

Something between a gasp and a sputter comes from my lungs. "Thank you, Mother!" I yell while tossing my dirt-covered gloves on the ground next to her.

My heart pulses with a yearning to find new items, balance on fallen logs, examine the grubs on the underside of rocks, and befriend the birds so that one day I may observe them from a lesser distance. The fence is nearly five feet tall, but I easily climb my way up the first two rails, then toss my leg over, pushing off from the fence line. Gravity quickly pulls me to the forest floor as I jump down. I pick myself up and continue walking with one arm gilding along the fence as I follow it south.

Our home stands in the middle of the twenty acres with the fence creating a rectangle around the property line and curving up and down with every hill that it meets. The front of the house faces north, toward the road, and on the east side where the sun rises are uninhabited rolling green hills and the occasional tree. The west—where I am located—is the forest that is home to a great deal of wildlife and the river that must go all the way to that bridge I saw our first day. And finally, the land to the south goes down in elevation only to shoot back up again and has a lovely Queen Anne-style house sitting on it. A white picket fence surrounds the majestic home, whose detail is too far away to properly see. The wraparound porch and turrets contribute to its asymmetrical beauty; I wonder at the intrinsic beauty that one could observe if they were in its proximity.

A few days ago, I asked Pa how far away that house is from ours, and he estimated half a mile. I wish I could encounter the people who live there! Interaction has been limited to the three of us, besides Pa when he goes to town to work, and conversation consists of worn subjects such as supper, the weather, and the itinerary of our day. A friend would be a great help to my imagination. Oh, what adventures we could dream up!

Exhaustion takes hold, forcing my legs to the ground after a long time of walking through the forest along our fence. The grass tickles my face as I lie back and take in the warmth of the afternoon. A breeze whispers through the canopies, and silence follows in its wake. The river is too far away to be heard, but rest assured it is there. Birds flutter from branch to branch effortlessly. Moss and lush brush cradle me like a baby, creating a soft bed for me to rest on. Time seems to disappear altogether.

My slim fingers twist a lock of my gleaming hair as my mind races with thoughts and ideas. The fragrance of summer flowers fuels my creativity, and before long I have crafted an entire story in my mind to entertain myself. Books—worlds and kingdoms built on pages—are my weakness. For I have been known to fall in love with characters with whom I can never truly become acquainted, worlds which I long to experience, and adventures that are unimaginable in this universe. It is strange; I can hear their voices, and sometimes a particular character may materialize beside me if I envisage them. Their touch, however, is ghostly, their face only a jumble of words, for I have never seen it—it is similar to awaking from the most realistic dream. For a time, the characters in my novels were my only friends. I could not bear to be around Florence and witness her perfection be praised, so I was whirled away to fairytale lands where people understood the envy of being the second-born child. My imagination is both a gift and a curse—it whisks me away only to later torment me with these desires.

Oh, how beautiful those rays of sunshine look as they light the forest after a momentary darkness from the shade of a cloud! For a moment the question becomes engraved in my heart: How could I ever wish to exchange this awe-inspiring natural world for a different one?

The snapping of a twig yanks me out of my previous state of internal contemplation. My eyes scan between the trees, over mossy logs, and behind me looking for the cause of such disturbance. Another branch snaps as the large berry bush to my left rustles, and my heart pounds in fearful suspense as a girl near in age to me emerges with an expression of equal shock.

A sigh blows out of my mouth as I press the palm of my hand to my rapid heart. "My goodness, you gave me quite the fright!" A single laugh escapes her lips as she stands over me, offering her hand. I gladly take it and stand, a couple inches shorter than her.

"Sorry! I spotted you sitting there and had to formally introduce myself. Nannie Fraser." Her modulated voice sounds trustworthy. Glowing amber eyes accompany her long, chocolate-brown hair.

"Pleasure to meet you, Nannie. My name is Azalea Stanton." We partake in shaking hands, but unlike adults, we hold steadfast to a jokingly dignified manner fit for children. How odd it is that my request for a friend has been fulfilled so quickly! Here we stand at the edge of the forest carrying on a conversation. I could think of no other way to meet a chum.

"What a nice name! I have been walking along this fence nearly every day since I heard that house was sold, hoping that whoever moved into the home had children my age. How old are you?" Once I respond, Nannie exclaims joyously, "I too am fourteen! My birthday was April seventh. I do believe God has fated us to meet, Azalea!" We begin to stroll alongside the fence as she talks, relying heavily on hand gestures to convey her emotions. "I have not seen you in church or town. Do you not leave your house often? My mother allows me a maximum of two hours to 'adventure.' It's ridiculous to limit fun. Don't you agree?"

There is a certain sporadic aspect to conversing with a friend, for the topic often wavers before coming full circle. This is evident in our gibbering. "Thank you! Certain people find my name too unconventional to be labeled a respectable girl because how could you be perfectly studious and obedient with a name like Azalea over Jane or Mary?"

"No, I do not find it…*unconventional?* It is a breath of fresh air when compared to the other overused, plain names."

"I am elated you think so! My parents and I have not ventured much outside of our property, although I am not quite sure why. I assume we are to attend sermons and any town functions on a regular basis once the house is fixed up, which shall not require more than a fortnight. Also, I do believe our mothers are cut from the same cloth." We exchange a moment of giggles as I attempt to imagine someone in close physical resemblance to Nannie and similar in nature to Mother. Everything about Nannie's manner, speech, and visual appearance paints her as kind-hearted, benevolent, and a patient soul. "Do tell me, is Winfield terribly exciting? We lived in a small town in Wyoming, and although I loved it dearly, I feel the need to experience more of what the world and life have to offer!" Holding my thumb and forefinger close together, I emphasize the petiteness of Lorretta.

"Winfield is filled with kind, God-fearing people. It is a very dignified town when it wants to be; even so, it does have certain faults. Summer is incredibly boring because school is not until the first of November and there is nothing else to do except chores. Most families choose to travel during the warm months, so the population is low for the time being. The mothers have their own society and activities: quilting bees, teas, and the like. I will warn you that the teas are a lengthy experience, for I had to attend one last September and it lasted nearly three hours! There are only so many miniature sandwiches and cups of tea I can hold without developing a hankering for entertainment or mischief!

"In the spring we have church sermons outside sometimes, along with picnics, socials, hoedowns or dances, et cetera. Oh, you shall come to love the town debates! The topics typically remain the same, but there is a new twist each conversation! My family has lived here for almost my whole life, so I would be honored to be your friend and give you the 'bird's eye view' of Winfield, if you would have me?"

A smile erupts on my face upon the question, and Nannie graciously grins in return. "That would be sublime! We shall be sworn friends and soul sisters until the end of time. I will eagerly await the events you mentioned, but for now we must go our separate ways before our mothers come hunting us down."

"Dear me, it is almost sundown! Until next time, my friend." Exchanging a hug, we part ways. I wave a final goodbye as she steps around a mossy stump and I climb over the fence. Mark my words, this will be the chapter of new beginnings!

Nannie shall be my confidant who will guide me through life in Winfield, no matter how pleasant or vexatious it may turn out to be. How wonderful it is to acquire a friend! Tomorrow I must write to Evelyn and Russell to inform them of the events that have transpired.

In all honesty, even though I now have an address to give him, I have been avoiding writing to Russell out of fear of his reaction. I cannot help but speculate that his feelings for me have not vanished as easily as I asked they would. Although there might be some part of my heart that wishes to entertain the thought of Russell and me, the truth remains that I am too young for an engagement or betrothal, and I am not sure if there is anything but fondness between me and him.

The sun dips just below the horizon as I stumble up the hill and arrive at the crackling fire by the wagon. Cobalt and Tempest were sold almost a week ago. It was a hushed goodbye considering I was forbidden to go up to either one of them, but our eyes conveyed a thousand words. Pa said it was for the best because the money from the sale goes toward the house, the interior of which I have yet to see besides small glimpses through dust-covered window panes. I believe that one day Pa will let me choose my own horse and teach me to ride. After all, I have waited this long to own a horse, so what are a few more months compared to that?

"There you are, Bluebird! We were about to send a search party out for you," Pa jokes as I take my place on the ground next to him, grinning at the attempted humor. He yanks his boots off his feet, letting them fall to the ground with exhausted thumps. Both soles are worn beyond belief and have been repaired countless times. Picking up a stick from the nearby woodpile, he pokes at the embers of the fire. Mother settles across from us, distractedly staring into the flames as she sips on watered-down coffee every few moments.

"I met a friend out by the woods. Nannie Fraser. Her family lives in that lovely Queen Anne house over yonder. She shared Winfield's upcoming events with me. Apparently there are all sorts of wonderful things to look forward to in this town! Mother, I think you shall enjoy the local society of mothers. They engage in quilting bees and teas. Mother, did you hear me?"

Caught in a daze, she abruptly raises her eyes to meet Pa's and my perplexed stares. "That sounds wonderful." Half-hearted is the response that comes from a distracted mind. What burdens her on this day? I have done nothing to agitate her except to grant her wish of being left alone to pull the weeds in the flowerbeds. It seems as though I am always the one at fault, even if no indicator is conveyed verbally. Whatever action I take is the cause of her vexed nature! Even when I have attempted to make a real connection, it goes unheard! Why do I even try? Though this internal argument may tear at me inside, I cannot express these feelings for fear of offending her.

"That reminds me! While I was working at the Jenkins' house, I heard about something you both might be interested in. It would give us a chance to meet our neighbors and get a view of life in Winfield." The Jenkinses hired Pa and a few other men to fix their barn after it caught fire a week ago. "Mr. Jenkins explained that when a barn is built or fixed up around here, the whole community comes together for a barn dance. A good old-fashioned hoedown is exactly what we need!"

"A dance?" My voice sounds outlandish.

"A *barn* dance." He jokingly mocks my excitement.

"Oh, that would be wonderful! I could even wear the pearl necklace that Mrs. Jones gave me and one of…the dresses." When Florence's name comes to my lips, I cannot bring myself to say it in the presence of my parents. I sense their hurt, anger, and fear even if it is only expressed through the lonely twinkle in their eyes or in a distracted moment.

My attention snaps to Mother upon this observation. Is that why she seems different this evening? Every time that I think we—or I—have gotten past her death, it seems as though a thought, moment, or event takes us right back to the mindset we were in before we left Lorretta. Time does not seem to heal anything when we are continuously hurting.

"Mother, we could try and prepare something to bring to the dance. Maybe your wild berry pie? Pa, when shall the dance take place?" Stars glimmer overhead as my eyes come alive at the possibility of attending my very first barn dance. Every dream or thought from now until then will be occupied with the prospect of the dance.

"I think that's a great idea, Bluebird! You'll have to make the pie next Wednesday because the dance is on Thursday evening."

To think that in less than five nights' sleep I will be at the dance! Mother leaves us by the fireside to discuss the details along with the basics of some dances they might play. She later returns with three portions of bean porridge that was prepared earlier today, but by that time Pa is cheering me on as I reenact the dance moves he explained are part of the polka. My smile stays permanently fixed on my face until the arrival of the dance on Thursday evening.

Chapter 6

THE NIGHT WE MET

MY FINGERTIPS STROKE the soft blue dress with the white wrists, hem, and collar. It is not as extravagant or as complimentary on me as it was on Florence, but it is the only outfit of hers that does not bring back painful memories. Upon opening the trunk, my hands hovered over the daisy dress, questioning whether or not to wear it and ultimately deciding against it.

I inhale a breath of the warm summer's air before stepping out from behind the wagon. Mother adjusts a handheld mirror to examine every side of her hair before catching sight of me. She presses her hand against her heart as she hesitantly walks over to me. A breeze sends the grass swaying as she lifts her other hand to touch my hair, which has been brushed to perfection. My green eyes stare into her brown ones as they gaze at me with a certain fondness I thought was reserved for my sister.

"You look just like…" her voice whispers to nobody in particular as her hand moves a lock of my hair behind my shoulder. Eyes glistening with the prospect of tears, she turns away, appearing ashamed of missing her daughter. Over these past two months my skin has become tanned, and my hair has lightened greatly from the sunshine. It is almost the same shade as Florence's golden blonde that dazzled in the sunlight and gleamed in angelic beauty. I hadn't taken notice of that until now.

"Are my girls ready?" Pa asks as he positions his hat on the top of his head and tugs on a thin jacket. Mother forces a smile and brushes away a wisp of hair from her eyes as Pa looks at us with profound pride. "You look perfect, Bluebird," he whispers in my ear as he places a kiss on my brow. With a grin I reach up to touch the string of pearls around my throat, making sure their presence is accounted for.

"You ought to be careful wearing such an expensive gift. It would be a shame for something like that to break because you were not careful, Azalea," Mother says in all-knowing manner as if the necklace is bound to fall into ruin at my hands.

"If Mrs. Jones did not wish for me to value this necklace—that she bestowed upon me—then I would not wear it proudly around my throat and the delicate object would be confined to a life in a dark jewelry tin." With a simple sentence Mother's warning is put to rest, and a smile brims Pa's lips as she huffs defeatedly.

Mother and I each take one of Pa's arms and stroll down the lane toward the Jenkins property. The sun dips below the trees, proclaiming nightfall just as we walk into the spacious red barn. Fiddles run at a fast tempo, and footsteps thud in rhythm on the wood-planked floor. Numerous candles dot the room, giving it a well-lit glow as we stroll through the doors. The one-room barn holds nearly sixty strangers who talk and laugh joyously as they stand along the walls, prance in the middle of the floor in pairs, or aid in serving the sustenance that is spread out on a lengthy table covered in a perfectly white tablecloth. Mother promptly marches over to the table, declaring her identity to the women standing there and offering the wild berry pie that has my initials edged into the crust, a little detail I added before Mother baked it. I smirk at my slyness before scanning the room for a certain dark-haired girl.

"Azalea! You came!" Nannie exclaims above the music as we engulf each other in a quick embrace. "Oh, I am so glad you heard about the dance. I forgot to mention it to you when we met! I wanted to run right over to your house when I realized my mistake, but my mother refused to let me spend any more time outside. 'It is too hot, you'll run yourself ragged!' she said, then added that I am 'going to adventure myself into a grave one of these days.' Do come and meet the girls. I have informed them of you!"

Pa merrily waves a goodbye to me before I turn and dash into the crowd of people, Nannie leading the way. A moment later, I hear his voice yell out a hearty hello to one of the men who helped fix this structure. What a fine job they did, for it looks nothing like the ramshackle place Pa described when they first started work.

Hands clap in a thunderous rhythm as a young couple twirls onto the dance floor and captures everyone's attention with their lovestruck gaze. A smile emerges on my lips as I catch sight of them between the towering shoulders that surround me and block my view. Nannie risks a collision with some innocent bystander as she tosses her chin over her shoulder to catch a glimpse at my awestruck expression. A shared laugh bursts from our mouths as if she shares my surprise at what a wonderful event this is! We travel to the back right corner of the spacious building, where a ladder to the hayloft above is located. Six girls around my age talk quietly in the corner, all of them dressed in different colors.

They all turn in unison as Nannie and I screech to a halt in a bundle of laughter due to a joke I just told about the owl-eyed old man who dropped his glass at my feet because I startled him while running. A few of the girls join in with a giggle, although they are oblivious to our debacle.

"My goodness, have you ever seen such a face as his? I thought I had spooked him so dearly that he would fall right over from a heart attack!" I huff while distractedly scanning the room to make sure the man is not coming after us.

"I would like to introduce you to the girls. Everyone, this is Azalea Stanton. Her family has just bought that lovely property adjacent to my house. She is to attend school with us this autumn!" I whip my head back around. My breath catches and my heart flutters. I offer a silent nod to the group of girls who examine me with an array of expressions. Some of them stare at me like I am an unmannerly girl who has just offended them in some way, while the others tilt their heads and grin at me like I am a lost dog that has wandered into their midst. "This is Wilhelmina Koller, Henrietta and Catalina Dawson, Phoebe Peterson, Matilda Jenkins, and Ophelia Cassidy." Each name flies into the air as Nannie points them out. Embarrassed, I nod upon each title as they curtsy in greeting.

The colors of their dresses are all different, as are the designs of their hair; the sight of my unstyled locks stands out amongst their Dutch braids, simple buns, and extravagant curls. Most of the older women here are embellished with loose lace blouses and walking skirts matched with their hair swooped up in an array of buns. I feel overdressed in comparison, a prickling feeling of awkwardness traveling up my arms at the realization. The men all look quite similar in terms of fashion; the majority are clothed in white cotton shirts and brown or black trousers with striped suspenders and the occasional jacket. The fiddles have transitioned from a melancholy waltz to a gradually growing tempo.

"Pleasure to make your acquaintance!" I exclaim with a crack in my voice, glancing to each person, waiting for a conversation to emerge. Embarrassment is the most excruciating form of torture! My skin tingles as warmth floods my cheeks.

Phoebe Peterson—a girl clothed in a bright blue calico dress—steps forward, turning her nose up at me while the girls behind her await verbal approval. A moment of confusion passes as I steal a glance at Nannie out of the corner of my eye. Nannie's smile has faltered slightly as if she awaits Phoebe's confirmation of whether I am suitable to join their inner circle.

"My, how skinny you are." It comes out as less than complimentary, almost like an insult. This predicament feels all too similar to the soiree in Brockschmidt—snooty girls who stare at you to make you feel small. I remember Evelyn telling me that.

"Well, I suppose you could join us. We are an exclusive group, so don't get any ideas about bringing anyone else in. Yes, I will make an exception this one time." Phoebe saunters off, followed by the other girls.

"I love your hair!" Ophelia whispers as she passes by. Her rosy cheeks tell me her character is not as monotonous as I previously speculated. Perhaps when I get to know the girls better, they may open up to me! I can only hope that in the future they do not show the same coldness.

Nannie exhales a breath and a laugh in one fell swoop as my head turns to follow the girls snake between people in the crowd. "Do not take Phoebe's words to heart. She is easily intimidated. Her family has lived in Winfield the longest and they practically run the town. Nearly every mother hangs on to Mrs. Peterson's every word, and Mr. Peterson owns the bank, so he makes more than enough money. The girls are not normally that reserved, but Phoebe is the self-proclaimed leader of the group, so they tend to follow her; like mother, like daughter. In time, they will come to accept you just as I have done!" She gives a glimmering smile that I joyfully reciprocate as the music strikes one last chord in the song.

I whip my head around to the dance floor to confirm my speculation. "They are about to start another song; we must join in at least one dance for the evening or else we shall be labeled as uppity girls!" I snatch Nannie's hand and we both run to the middle of the floor, awaiting instructions.

Couples join in, creating a circle as the striking chords are played in a hypnotizing manner. Nannie and I join hands, tapping the heels of our shoes into the circle before prancing into the middle along with the other pairs. The circle shrinks before expanding to its original size. The deafening clapping of hands is met with the stomping of heels as the crowd around the floor encourages us. My cheeks ache from the undisguisable grin on my face due to the buoyant ambience around me.

Nannie and I join our right elbows and skip around once clockwise before switching partners. I turn my eyes away from my friend as we share one last laugh before halting at the sight of a boy's gray eyes staring deeply into mine, as if reading my character with one look. A small percent of the population possesses this skill; when they stare into your eyes they can read every intricate thought, prodigious memory, and arduous challenge you have experienced. This stranger has somehow mastered this skill to perfection.

Heart skipping a beat, I feel his fingers brush along the palm of my hand as we maintain eye contact. For a moment, it seems as though we have been whisked away to a metaphorical place existing only in our imaginations; nobody else seems to exist as of now. This selcouth feeling overwhelms my heart as his face stays mere inches away from mine and we mindlessly follow the steps of the dance. My cheeks fill with warmth as a smile brims this stranger's lips upon seeing the infatuated expression that has immersed me.

It is as if I have forgotten myself; nonetheless, I have willfully chosen to stay in this moment with the awareness of what is happening and how many stares are following the pair of us. His short golden-brown hair is untamed and swooped to the left. The quiver of the fiddles, clap of palms, and stomp of heels do not divert my attention away from him even though they should. Who is this boy who has bewitched me? Why is his gaze an unwavering force that controls me so? His name is not to my knowledge and his presence has not previously been documented in my mind. It is as if he has appeared out of my imagination to promenade beside me.

My eyes glance over his shoulder, immediately locating a jealous glare from Phoebe Peterson as she crosses her arms defensively. The rest of the girls stand alongside her, their faces painted with wide-eyed expressions of awe. I blush deeply as we join elbows, skipping around once, but instead of switching partners, he clutches my hand at the last second and we stumble past a lady who clearly looked forward to having him as her partner. She instead has to settle for a white-haired man who tries his best to keep up with the tempo. The two of us take notice of her grimace as he messily steps on her foot. Our eyes focus back on one another as we prance to the center with the rest of the couples.

"Hi," I whisper in a tremulous voice as our fingertips brush against each other.

"Hi," he says in a quiet voice as if the greeting is in secret. An embarrassed laugh brims my lips just as he speaks. A few small freckles dot his nose and upper right cheekbone. "Francis," the stranger whispers into my ear. The single word is a somewhat unusual introduction that I return in the same fashion. I bite the corner of my bottom lip nervously as the name sinks into my brain. Francis—meaning "free."

We are no longer two people fastened to this Earth by gravity, for it does not exist in this moment. Instead, we are in limbo, lost in a field of wildflowers, dancing to the orchestra of nature. This is one of those rare events when your heart grows so fond of a moment that it becomes devoured by and ingrained in that feeling. Verbal communication is cut short by the sudden applause, which pulls us apart instantly. Lost in thought, neither of us cared to realize that the dance finished and the crowd around the floor is clapping for the musicians.

In a parting gesture, Francis takes my hand in his, staring deeply into my eyes one last time, and places a soft kiss on my knuckles before turning around and being engulfed by the crowd. This beautiful stranger—who may not be a stranger now that a name has been put to his face—has disappeared from my view. I reach up and touch the pearl necklace around my throat. It seems as if this old thing still has some luck in it after all! Without a second thought, I rush in the direction he went, unaware of what I shall say or do when I locate him, but Nannie interrupts my quest.

I shake away the thoughts and put a smile on my face as she exclaims a huff of words. "Wasn't that exhilarating?! I am so glad the Jenkins decided to have this dance; she almost decided against it. You look flushed. Should we get some cider?" For a moment I was about to reveal my questions about Francis to her—surely Nannie must know something of him—but my lips purse and I decide to keep the moment to myself. Arm in arm and echoing laughter, we prance over to the refreshment table, where the ladies of Winfield are immersed in conversation.

Nannie requests two cups of cider, and a woman pours the liquid into two fine glasses using a ladle, then hands us the ice-cold beverages. The cider quenches my thirst after such an extemporaneous dance, giving me a few unhurried moments to contemplate tonight's events. I must admit I was quite nervous to meet Nannie's friends along with the rest of the townsfolk, but it has gone exemplary! In the fall, I shall attend school and perhaps become familiarized with the girls. How wonderful it would be to have a group of friends; I hope they share the same imagination I have!

Florence would have loved this town. I can see her now, dancing to song after song to her heart's content. Every pair of eyes would be on the golden-haired beauty as her smile gleamed like sunlight; it is only now, when I have lost her, that my mind has come to revere the aurorean person she was. Florence seemed to radiate sunlight and a certain charisma. It is nights like these, ones that make up lifelong memories, that I become rather sentimental. I have spent all my life alone while my mind held on to the concept that nobody truly understood me, but that foolishness and jealously cost me years of memories that could've been shared with my sister. Now I rely on words to describe my feelings that seem to pour out of me in an endless manner; nonetheless, life's deepest feelings can never fully be put into words.

⸺

"'Dost thou weep to see my anguish? Mark me and escape my woe. When men flatter, sigh, and languish, think them false—I found them so!'" Pa and I sing out as we skip along the dirt road while the moon lights our path. Mother's spirits have soared greatly on account of interacting with the other ladies at the dance, so she even joined in yelling out the lyrics of "Crazy Jane." Every now and then at the dance, I would peek over my shoulder and see her conversing with one of the ladies, face painted with a carefree gleam. I am unaware of the contents of the conversations in which she partook, but they have clearly had a positive effect because for the first time in weeks there is a genuine smile on her face.

I promised myself and Florence that I would be there for our parents. She always had the all-seeing eye when it came to their feelings. *Tell me, God, are we moving on or are we in a state of suspension? Has progress truly been made, or are we simply stuck in a temporary lull that distracts us from pain?* There is no doubt in my mind that we are still grieving such a loss, but there is a point when the heartache will start to heal. I just have to locate which point we are at. At times I am not sure if Mother has come to terms with it or if just the memory sends her into a sulking state. Yesterday night, her mind was in the past, but right now the three of us are living in the moment.

Tomorrow shall be our first church service in Winfield. Earlier, Mother informed us that the pastor has just returned from his missionary trip south and that "we must be in the house of the Lord this Sunday morning." There is no doubt in my mind that she obtained this information about the pastor through one of the ladies she met tonight. I know her eagerness to attend church goes beyond hearing a sermon; she wishes to socialize with the other ladies. I am not the only one starved for friends and tired of the endless emptiness of our property.

As we return to the wagon just outside our house, I do not bother brushing my hair or even changing into my nightgown. Stars twinkle above me as I lie down on the blankets in the wagon bed, and a midsummer night's breeze sweeps by, softly kissing me goodnight. The sight of Francis is still fresh in my mind as I wonder when we shall meet again.

THE OCCUPANT OF MY MIND

NOT EVEN A STRAY HAIR can escape Mother's watchful eye as we walk toward the heavenly structure. It is but a short distance away. The road that goes by our house continues until it curves to the right, then splits in two. Both paths wrap around a small grove of trees with a short trail connecting the two. The left path has unmarked trails leading to dispersed houses whose chimneys are vacant of smoke of this clear blue morning, and the right path borders a large cornfield that anxiously awaits its October harvest.

Families stroll in front of and behind us, eyeing the newest inhabitants of Winfield with a certain curiosity. This stare, however, does not distract Mother, who walks smugly and grows increasingly confident with every whisper and finger directed at us. As we round the corner, the grove abruptly ends and the two paths forge into one leading up to the white building that gleams in the morning sunlight. When I briefly mentioned our attendance to church to Nannie yesterday evening, she quickly informed me that, come November, the building acts as our schoolhouse every weekday and a church on the Sabbath.

A crimson wooden door stands in the middle of the front wall with two stone-carved steps leading up to it. Three medium-sized tracery windows are on either side of the door, a dark shingled gable roof holds up a small belltower with a tiny cross at its cone-shaped peak, and a thin arched stone bridge reaches a few feet over the petite brook. Trees shelter the building from anything other than a delicate breeze, and water from the brook trickles by silently as the soles of our shoes clop on the small bridge.

Murmurs echo in the cloakroom as each family hangs their shawls and hats on the row of coat hooks that wraps around the wall. A pot-belly stove stands at the back left corner of the one-room schoolhouse, the teacher's desk situated to the front left with a blank blackboard stretched out along the middle of the wall. On either side of the aisle are long benches with desks on the backs.

Morning sunlight streams in on the left side of the room as seats fill up quickly. We rush to grab the last available bench at the back of the room. The late attendees are forced to stand and lean against the wall once they arrive. The bench is just big enough for the three of us, with Pa on the aisle seat, Mother in the middle, and me on the right.

My eyes scan the room for Francis, but alas, he is either absent or lost in the sea of townsfolk. I notice Nannie and her family sitting a few rows ahead of us, so I attempt to hiss her name quietly but receive only a handful of odd stares from the people in front of us in response. Mother thwacks at my arm, forcing me to sit down as she nervously laughs at my display to anyone that noticed. In a huff, I cross my arms and stare out the nearest window until the pastor trudges to the front of the room.

His black clothes and clerical collar stand out among the bright colors and patterns of everyone's Sunday best. A leather bible is situated in his right hand, and his white hair is slicked back on his half-bald head. Everyone quiets as a hoarse, monotone voice emerges from his mouth to lead the church in prayer. Each crack in his voice is met by the flinch of my closed eyes as I try my very best to stay focused on his words and not the giggle I'm forcibly holding back. Upon the "amen," I open my eyelids and gaze at the cavetto crown molding on the ceiling as the words fly right over my head. Mother and Pa, on the other hand, are focused on the pastor as he speaks, standing rigid at the front of the room.

I would much rather be out in nature, surrounded solely by God's presence, to witness an internal sermon. Even if there were a downpour of rain, it would only make the moment more romantic, and I would remain out there! Perhaps the sermon could be witnessed in a field of wildflowers or among a forest of trees. I run each scenario in my mind, trying to choose which option would ameliorate this day. Nonetheless, I shall be forced to return every Sunday to this manmade structure and sit still for nearly two hours whilst listening to a monotoned sermon. I have no doubt in my faith, but there is something about a lesson being delivered in such a scratchy voice that makes everything dull!

Several times throughout the service, I catch myself growing drowsy as I prop my elbow on the desk and hold my fist to my cheek. My growing energy for the first town church service in quite a time has died down tremendously. I am not the only soul to have noticed this, for even Mother seems disgruntled by the fourth "thou art" the pastor speaks during the closing prayer.

Pa appears to take on a more relaxed position as the service lags on; the other attendees mimic this as their sharp shoulders and stiff postures gradually slump. The pastor suddenly stops talking, lazily looking around and obviously awaiting the accolade of applause that is pitifully given when it finally arrives. How long have the residents of the town endured his tedious sermons and given deceitful compliments like, "What a lovely message it was today," as one lady comments to her husband, who unethically agrees?

Birds hide in the boughs of nearby trees, tweeting hellos as the townsfolk step outside onto the front lawn to converse. Mother hastily locates a group of ladies, most of whom I recognize from the dance, and tugs me along with her to greet them. Pa shakes the pastor's hand as he introduces himself; the latter, however, seems only mildly interested in the former and the topic of our relocation to Winfield.

"Hello, Mrs. Stanton, I was just speaking to the ladies about you moments ago!" a tall woman says smoothly as she gestures to Mother with her gloved hand. Her hazel eyes glance at me with fake sweetness as if she is only playing the role of a cordial neighbor. "Who do we have here?"

Mother's grin is like that of the Cheshire Cat, expanding with every second that passes by. With any luck, a rabbit hole might just open up, swallowing me whole so I do not have to bear witness to Mother's social agenda and boring conversations!

"Ladies," she responds in greeting with the inclination of her head, "this is my daughter, Azalea. She is to attend school this coming November. I am so glad we have run into you all, as I wanted to introduce her yesterday evening but did not get the chance!" A series of coos compliment my appearance as Mother speaks. I purse my lips tightly as I try to smile a hello at the several pairs of glassy eyes staring at me like a specimen.

"She is just darling! How old are you, dear?" One woman pipes up as she leans in to ask the question.

"Fourteen." Mother throws a prickling stare at me as if to enforce my best behavior. I add a "ma'am" to make up for my lack of manners. "What a…lovely message it was today. The pastor did a wonderful job with his… um…pronunciation." Out of the corner of my eye I can see my mother discreetly press her fingertips to her temple as if to shield her eyes from the reactions. My cheeks flush with warmth as my callow words sink into the women's brains.

"Yes, well…Mrs. Stanton, we would like to invite you to tea sometime soon. Our society, The Maidens, is for the married ladies of Winfield. We work on improvements to the community, organize social activities, and observe the children's education. Now, I must warn you, we are a rather prestigious group. Therefore, invite only!" she whispers with a wink.

Mother's face explodes with happiness, as she has just been handed an invitation to join Winfield's ladies' society. In order to not let her efforts go to waste, she deviously meets each pair of eyes, as if she is an empress looking at her subjects, and responds in a courteous manner.

"What a wonderful idea! If I may, perhaps you ladies would enjoy an afternoon tea at our home? Shall we say two o'clock Wednesday? We are located at the white ranch house: down Main Street two miles and right at the fork in the road. It was a pleasure meeting you all!" Her hand lies on my shoulder as we turn around in unison and march away, the ladies' eyes hot on our backs. Mother and I share a peek over our shoulders at their awed faces as they whisper to each other. Rather smug smirks are on our lips as we join Pa, who is still talking to the pastor.

My heart stops completely as I realize who is standing between Pa and the pastor. Francis's gray eyes smile as I take my place and stand across from him. The pastor's hebetude suddenly no longer bothers me in this moment as a flutter stirs in my stomach. Since my eyelids opened to the morning sunlight on this very day, I have questioned the world if I would see Francis, but failed to think of what action I would take once in his presence. His Sunday best consists of a seamless white cotton shirt with a small folded-down collar, formal black trousers, perfectly polished shoes, and a light gray wool cap in his hand. I cannot help but notice his symmetrical face, which shows every emotion that crosses his heart. A prickling sensation travels up my arms as his glorifying stare never ceases. With much effort, I turn to Pa, who is conversing about something.

"Pastor Jonathan, thank you again for the service," Pa says while nodding his head in farewell. Pastor Jonathan solemnly dips his head, then returns to the church, somewhat ignoring the remarks from other people congratulating him on "yet another splendid preaching."

My eyes follow the pastor as he walks to the door of the church, which shuts with a squeak. I do pity the poor old man, for he has no excitement or entertaining hue when reading from the Bible. Perhaps it is a skill one must be born with.

A woman passes by our small group, reaching up to pin an eccentric hat atop her head. I have noticed that the fashion of the people of Winfield, both last night and this morning, is subtly fancy; gigot sleeves seem to be on every woman's shoulder today. As much as I enjoy the ecstasy of puff sleeves, these seem overdramatic and so huge to the point where you cannot tell where the fabric ends and the human flesh begins! I can only hope that the fashion of puff sleeves changes to a much subtler and frill-bearing nature when I am old enough to have them adorn me.

A sudden voice jolts me out of my daydream and makes me look around for the source.

"Mr. Stanton, pleasure meeting you," Francis's deep voice says as he firmly shakes Pa's hand. Pa voices his gratitude for Francis taking time to speak with him, to which Francis replies, "I'll send word to Mr. Huxley about the mercantile job."

I anxiously skip over his words in my mind, anticipating a final glance into my eyes, but I am left standing like a child awaiting vocal permission to join the conversation. My heart falters seeing him saunter away without so much as one last glimpse in my direction.

"Well, girls, we should start heading back home!" Pa says with a chuckle as our shoes begin to carry us away from the picturesque scene of people talking in groups on the church lawn. It stills boggles my mind that I shall be attending school for the first time in my life in that building come autumn!

Halfway down the dirt road, Mother beats me to the question that has been at the tip of my tongue. "What did that young man mean about the mercantile job? Albert, you must not strain yourself with finishing the house and working two jobs!"

"Do not worry, I am not taking on another job." My brow furrows at the grin that accompanies his response, as if there is some important detail that has been left from Mother's and my knowledge. We exchange a curious glance before turning our eyes back to Pa, who is just about exploding with excitement! "Francis Southerland mentioned that he met Azalea at the barn dance." My eyes widen and blood runs cold as Mother's head snaps to me, her face perplexed at the relation between me, Francis, and the job at the mercantile. My skin grows hot as embarrassment creeps down my spine.

"Yes…well, I recall seeing him, but we never spoke more than a hello." Pa, however, seems to be unsurprised at me meeting the boy. Perhaps Francis is just another person in town to him. Mother opens her mouth, raising up her hand to gesture at whatever comment is about to emerge.

Before she can get a word in edgewise, Pa continues, "Anyway, Mr. Huxley's wife has her hands full with their children, and they need someone to help with the upkeep of the mercantile at least a day or two each week. Francis mentioned Azalea might be the right fit for the job." Pa speaks these simple words as if he's reading a storybook that is building to a climax. At the mention of a job, my eyebrows raise and lips purse; this is certainly not the direction in which I expected this conversation to be heading! Francis recommended me for a job at the mercantile? Why on earth would he do that when he is no more than a stranger whom I have come across twice?

Mother's scoff averts my gaze from the path ahead of us. Her eyes roll as she begins her sentence with the know-it-all voice of a scholar. The invitation to join The Maidens has certainly made her confidence soar to great heights! "A girl should not be working unless she is directly related to the proprietor or her family has no money. It is anything but proper! I must strictly forbid it. Young girls cannot be trusted with money, anyway."

My pout promptly sways Pa to defend my case. "Now, Margaret, times are changing and there is no harm in Azalea making money. She could even it put in an account at the bank if you're concerned about wasteful spending! The Huxleys are good folks, and she won't be in any harm while sweeping or dusting." A giggle escapes my mouth at Pa's mild joke, but it only seems to further infuriate Mother. I see an internal battle cross her face as she wrestles between putting her foot down and releasing her hold on her only child.

A bird swoops across the path right in front of us as Mother's shrill voice pipes up after several moments. "If you insist, then we will put it to a trial run. Azalea, if you can go one week without making trouble or causing stress to the Huxleys, then you may keep the job. But one mistake and you must give an apology to those folks and revoke the offer." The tension that has been slowly building upon my shoulders begins to melt away as Mother gives her permission. Then she turns to Pa. "I have invited some of the women over to the house Wednesday afternoon for tea. Will that be enough time for the house to be completed?"

Her raised eyebrow is like a bottle of poison that could be released if the answer is not acceptable. I suppose the stakes are high for this tea. If the ladies enjoy the afternoon, then my mother shall join The Maidens and that shall fill up her time. Mother possesses the ability to be quite malleable and conform to any mold when it comes to something she desires; it would not astonish me if she convinced her way into The Maidens. A simple nod from me satisfies her intense stare. The countryside captures my attention and lures me away from Mother's ramblings, which expand on the upcoming tea party.

"A job at the mercantile..." My whisper trails off as I contemplate the idea of making my own money and finally going beyond the everyday bounds of the fence. What an adventure this could be!

Chapter 8

WHERE THERE IS LOVE, THERE IS PAIN

I TWIDDLE MY HANDS, peering through the crack of the door and trying to get a glimpse inside our long-awaited home. Not a day has passed since we have moved to Winfield that I have not set my imagination loose to dream up the interior of this beautiful haven. Pa promised us at breakfast that it would be completed today, and my stomach has been a bundle of nerves every second since then! Mother sent me away from her after proclaiming she could not "stand the infernal racket" of my unceasing blabbering whose purpose was to occupy the minutes that ticked by as we waited. Without the outlet of speaking, I must continue to try and peer between the door and its frame to catch a snippet of our forever home!

The thudding of incoming footsteps does not register in my mind until the door I am leaning against swings open and I am flying across the threshold. A chuckle sounds above me as I pick up my embarrassed frame, concealing the mishap with a giggle as I catch the glimmer in Pa's eyes. A nonverbal message is conveyed in the single look, giving me permission to become acquaintances with our new sanctuary. I pick myself up and begin to dash through the rooms with Florence's old straw boater hat in hand. I forgot it was on my head until I tripped through the doorway!

Upon entering the house, I see a lovely white archway to my left that leads to a simple parlor where a stone hearth sits on the opposite wall. I imagine the hefty rocks were collected one at a time and carefully placed whilst the house was being built. A short mantle holds an intriguing photo of who I assume are the previous inhabitants.

My fingertip strokes the oval frame and the glass where a man stands solemnly behind a woman sitting in a calico chair, both of them near in age to thirty. I almost don't notice the snippet of a young girl cut off by the frame. What possessed them to abandon the home which they strived to build?

Slivers of light leak in through the screen in front of the window next to the hearth. Few pieces of furniture remain in the room and are covered with sheets that have yellowed with age. Peeking under each sheet, I see a black rocking chair quite similar to the one we left in Lorretta and a petite round oak table sitting before an exquisite camelback sofa that has been upholstered in a lovely mauve velvet fabric.

Unable to resist the temptation that has been gnawing at me for the past minute, my hands grip the sheet and toss it away to where it flutters onto the wide-plank pine floors. A cloud of dust settles as I delicately sit on the edge of the cushion whilst taking in the beauty of this handcrafted piece. A piece of dark wood with ivy vines carved into it stretches across the back of the sofa, dipping down softly on either side and adjoining on the arch that is but a few inches taller. When I lie with my head on the scroll arm, my bare feet reach the other arm perfectly. I do not consider myself rather tall—Pa recently estimated that I can be no more than five feet and three inches—so this sofa seems to be made for me.

It is upon this quiet contemplation that I finally lift my green eyes to the painting above the mantle. Due to my buzzing excitement, I hadn't given my brain the time to soak in my surroundings. I begin to study the landscape that sits in a giltwood frame, tacked to the wall. The artist, whomever they may be, has set their sights on a brook (similar in size to the one in the church yard) with trees placed sporadically on either side of the reflecting water. Ferns and small shrubs sit on the water's edge, golden and white clouds obscuring the sun and giving the viewer a sense of what phase in the day it is. There are serene rolling hills in the background and gleaming green grass throughout the picture. It is not invaded by human subjects nor civilization; perhaps that is what makes it so alluring to me.

The densely packed burgundy flower crests stand out on the cream wallpaper that surrounds this room, making it feel smaller than it is. When the ambience of the nearly empty room is soaked into my memory, I rise from the sofa and skip through the other archway about six feet of undecorated wall from the other entryway.

A small hallway leads from the front door to the back of the home where the kitchen is located. From what I gather as I walk to the kitchen, the dining room is on the right side of the house, parlor to the left, and hallway in the middle. The two arches lead to the parlor, one door near the front leads to the dining room, and the open frame at the end of the hall goes to the kitchen.

The pine floors, with a few sparkly new boards that Pa put in, go through the hallway and parlor before stopping at the kitchen doorway where I stand. On the left of the room is a baluster staircase leading to the second floor, dark wood slabs contrasting with the white risers. In small basic frames, hung up the side of the stairs, are mirrors, paintings, and photographs of places hung on the daisy wallpaper. Why did the previous owners leave all their belongings? I have come to notice that this daisy wallpaper is everywhere but the parlor, just a snippet of it is visible upstairs and the dining room that I only caught a glimpse of while rushing through the front door. *Daisies.* My fingertips gently brush over one of the flowers, recalling a certain dress and a memory.

Beyond a wide window in the middle of the wall, a clear meadow goes for miles on the hilly earth. A table covered with a sheet sits alone in the middle of the kitchen, with a latched door likely leading to an underground cellar hidden under it. A stove similar to ours back in Wyoming sits in a nook in the middle of the staircase wall, another wide window above the water pump and sink at the right wall. Even Mother will have to appreciate this picturesque view whilst doing the dishes on a glorious morning soon! Next to the sink is a compact pantry with four bare shelves. The pantry creates a wall between the open kitchen and the dining room, the only entryway being the door near the front.

The black ribbon tied on Florence's hat swishes as I stroll back through the hallway and into the dining space. Six armless chairs surround a solid wood table. There are no paintings nor photographs on the walls of this space. I wonder why? Three connected windows line the opposing wall, letting in an enormous amount of the setting sunlight as I pull the screens up. What a joyous feeling it will be to eat supper each evening bathed in the setting sun!

I walk through this place in awe, a slow gait satisfactory as I try to etch every detail into my mind. Exactly eleven stairs lead up to the second floor, where the banister continues into the hallway for a short distance before stopping at a door down the hall. Despite my great interest to see what lies behind said door, I peek into the first door.

A bed is in the middle of the wall covered by a sheet with a cedar trunk at the foot of it, two barren side tables are located on either side of the bed, and one lonely window is opposite of me from where I stand in the doorway. Between the blank walls and the simple furniture, it is quite dreary in comparison to the rest of the house.

A grin brims my lips as I hasten to the last room, which I fully anticipate shall be mine; the bay window must be located here. As I amble in, a gasp escapes my mouth at the drastic change!

The walls were perhaps once a dark pine color but have been seasoned over time and faded into a lovely light green. Realistic, hand-painted greenery of all natures sprouts from the floor to the ceiling. Primroses, honeysuckles, ferns, carnations, tulips, berry plants, and more are visible everywhere!

I let out a squeal of delight as I jump a few steps forward to the bay window, then spin in a circle with my arms lengthened out, hat swaying in my hand and hair flying around me. With a laugh, I am overcome with dizziness that forces the twirling to cease. In time I shall find objects and mementoes to personalize my room, but for now it is undeniably befitting to someone of my nature.

Upon a small desk is a single object covered in a layer of dust. My soft fingertips stroke the ancient book, carefully opening it and flipping through the contents as my mind ponders its previous owners. How many people have pored over its contents, contemplating the words written in the text? How many more keepers shall this novel meet in its lifetime? I have grown fond of old things; they tell a story I have never read. There is something so special about objects that have lived other lives in the hands of strangers.

A simple bed lies to the left of the doorway, pushed into the corner. On the opposite side of the room is a ladder leading upward to the dreamt-of attic. Making a rash, youthful decision, I crawl up the ladder and toss back the small trapdoor, revealing the secret room.

Two circular windows are on either wall near the tip of the gable roof. There is but one other source of light. Dust thickly covers the glass panes of the rectangular window; the world appears morphed through them as if seen by old, weathered eyes. This room is quaint and barren, as if the past owner came up here to be alone with his or her thoughts.

This garret shall be my secluded hideaway where memories shall be recalled, thoughts scrawled upon blank papers, and my own lonesome presence enjoyed. Florence would have dearly appreciated this house; if only she were here to see it.

Later that day, Pa puts the small sign up at the front gate along the road, carved with the name "Aspenmoore." What an exquisite word to describe this heavenly place we shall forevermore claim as our home.

⌒

My dress is ironed to perfection, but my face remains wrinkled with worry as Mother swats my fidgeting hands. The table has been set with the few dishes we brought along from Lorretta, along with a decent amount of sustenance.

Upon our descent into the newly finished house, every window was flung open and every available bucket filled with soapy water and a scrub brush. Mother took one look at the cobwebs and shuddered in dismay, ordering me to thwart them with the duster in hand. The scratch of the broom was followed by a cloud of dirt that remained for nearly an hour before we went down on our hands and knees to scrub the floor to perfection. The linens were washed, starched, and set out for today's tea. By noon, not a speck of filth dare stick to a windowpane or floorboard or tile, for they all flew away with the breeze to escape Mother's vigilant stare. Cleaning bores me to disarray, so I spent every second imagining upcoming events and what they shall behold.

Luckily, there was a little change left over in the budget to spend on the refreshments for today's tea. Pa went to town and bought all the ingredients that Mother ordered, and so the morning was spent in careful preparation. As a result, white bread with strawberry jam, slices of sponge cake, and a kettle of herbal tea sit on the table in the dining room.

This morning, to my great surprise, Mother waltzed into my room as I brushed my hair; Florence's daisy dress had been extracted from the trunk and was draped over her arm. I strongly believe that there is some deeper reason for Mother's touchy feelings at the mention of Florence, although I am clueless as to finding it out. Now that I think about it, ever since that fateful morning, Mother has avoided the subject and tried to hide any emotion related to grief, although sometimes it seeps through the cracks.

The zest goes out of me as soon as my mother declares I cannot decorate the parlor or dining room with acorns, wildflowers, or any natural objects. With a huff, I clutch the empty glass vase in my hands and carry it back into the kitchen. How splendid it would look if filled with a few grass-widows or pink pyrolas! Since the night of the Brockschmidt ball, when the mysterious old woman offered direction on which flowers for me to pluck, I have developed an interest in botany. Most flora and fauna have been dubbed with amusing names that bewitch my heart.

"My goodness!" Mother mumbles under her breath while she stares out the north-facing window. A hand gingerly touches her chest in a delicate manner whilst her feet remain fastened to the floor. Before I have a chance to question the declaration, I am whisked out of the kitchen and forced to stand beside her behind our closed front door.

Several lingering moments tick by in utter silence as I glance around, wondering why our presence is requested in this spot. My internal inquiry is soon answered by the dainty knock on the other side of the door. After pausing for a few more seconds, Mother reaches over and swings the door inward with a grin plastered on her face. It is quite an applaudable skill to master: answering a door to four intimidating women, all possessing effortless classy appearances.

"Welcome, ladies! Let us take your parasols and bonnets." My mother's voice turns sweet as honey at the sight of the women we met at church three days ago. There is no doubt in my mind that Mother's performance this afternoon will be driven by the intent of earning a formal invitation into The Maidens. Unseen by anyone, a shudder crosses me as I prepare for the worst. "Azalea, take these to the kitchen and put them on the bench by the door," she says in a quick whisper.

While the guests are led into the spotless parlor, I do as Mother instructed, then join the party. Nearly an hour of stiff conversation that lacks any sort of genuine enthusiasm passes by in a grueling manner. My back begins to ache from the stiff posture I have to maintain.

Despite Florence's dress being too large in some areas as it hangs across my frame, a compliment is thrown my way by one of the women. A simple thank you suffices, and I once again mentally retreat from the conversation. Bobbing my head, quietly exclaiming an 'oh' at every dramatic pause in conversation, and being seen more often than heard fulfills the unspoken request in my mother's eyes. A few of the women collectively begin speaking of their daughters—who I assume are the ones I met at the barn dance—as refined young ladies with such poise and elegance. It is in Mother's nature to ensure the flawless and untarnished perception of Winfield's newest family: the Stantons.

With a delicate "ahem," five pairs of eyes, myself included, are snatched then surrendered to Mother's mercy. Her plain white blouse and navy walking skirt clash with the extravagant wallpaper behind her shoulders. Brushing an invisible wisp of hair behind her ear, she begins, "Have I informed you of Azalea's latest hobby? She has a new interest in learning French. It's a lovely language, wouldn't you agree?"

A series of murmurs filled with awe follow the question. My brow furrows at the falsehood; not once in my life have I expressed an interest in learning another language! While it is invigorating to think of speaking some romantic foreign tongue, I am a dunce at the pronunciation and recollection required for learning a new language. My perplexed look does not bother her, as she meets every gaze except mine, continuing to coo false factoids. "Her needlework has become better than mine! Just last winter, she knit *three* pairs of mittens."

My blood turns cold at the realization. While these words spoken to a room full of complete strangers may seem to describe me, they point out someone else entirely. Someone to whom I have been compared for most of my life, whose lacking presence has inflicted a void in my heart and whose name has purposefully been left out of every sentence my parents have spoken since May tenth.

Heart burning with fury, I try to politely excuse the two of us as I grab Mother's hand and pull her out onto the front porch. The front door slams, followed by a tremulous quake of the nearby windows. My lethal gaze is directed solely at my mother. An agitated squint, raised eyebrows, and crossed arms proclaim her innocence in the matter.

"Azalea, we have guests!" Although not spoken, the words "behave yourself" fly in the wind.

A scoff escapes my mouth as I mimic her stance. "Why are you doing this? Has this been your plan from the crack of dawn?" Before any words can escape her mouth, I explode, releasing the wrath that has gradually been building for these past couple months. "Painting me as the exact replica of Florence! The dress, along with saying I enjoy sewing and knitting, both of which I despise to an indescribable extent!" There is no doubt in my mind that every soul in that parlor can hear my booming voice through the walls of our house; nonetheless, how can I care about appearances at a time like this?

Her eye begins to twitch as she takes a defensive position, as if I am in the wrong! "What is wrong with that?" A gulp travels down her throat.

Heart pulsing wickedly, my cheeks heat to an unbearable degree. "I am not her! She is *dead*. Florence is gone." A flinch of hurt crosses her face as if the truth is a knife plunged between her ribs. A pang of remorse stings me as the words settle between us. Nonetheless, the anger is not so easily extinguished from a personality as stubborn as mine. "And you punish me for it. From the day Florence died, you have been trying to change me into her! When is the last time you've spoken her name aloud?"

Why do all my arguments normally end with me pouring out things I have tried to keep within the confines of my soul? As if trying to hold it back, Mother turns her eyes away from me as words continue to whiz into the air, echoing down the lane and into the world. The birds, properly shocked by the dramatic display, clamp their beaks shut for a moment to watch from afar.

Maybe humans are inherently sinful creatures; after all, we continue the awful habits that are a disgrace with our permission. Like a wave crashing onto the shoreline, the words and their meaning chase you until there is nowhere left to run.

"I bet you wish it were me who got typhus instead of her. Then you would have your perfect daughter." This is the truth that has burdened me for months, and here it has been let out in one fell swoop.

Mother has always been a pacifist. Whether it is from the things she has witnessed or that the general idea of brawls disturbs her refined manner, not once in my life have I witnessed any outward aggression from her. That is, until now.

Her palm whips across my cheek at such a speed it makes me question if it even happened. Every sound dies, words drop off our lips as my face sizzles from the sudden contact. As if instantaneous, tears stream down my face, exposing my vulnerability. My cold fingertips gingerly touch my jaw, providing a momentary relief to the burning.

Is my head spinning or am I walking? Before I can fully comprehend what is happening, the knob turns in my hand. I solemnly march through our house, ignoring the perplexed stares from the ladies as I pass the parlor, storming up the staircase whilst steadying myself with the handrail before settling on my bed for the rest of the evening.

Nothing could remove me from this seclusion—not the echo of Pa's questions when he arrives home after working in town, nor the grumble of my stomach as I lay my tear-stained cheeks on the pillow. Sleep cannot come soon enough, and daylight breaks through before enough hours have passed.

Starvation compels me to finally put the feud to rest, join breakfast, and look forward to the excitement of today, but my obstinate personality plunges the meal into a dismal affair of state. Conversation is nonexistent as I pick at the fragrant food that my stomach aches for. Mother and I possess two different characters, so arguments are inevitable. This one, however, is different, as if its impact struck a nerve too deep to recover from. It is, after all, the first real fight we have had since Florence's death.

"Honestly." Pa scoffs under his breath as he crumbles the napkin in his hand and tosses it onto the table. "This is ridiculous! Margaret and Azalea, you ought to—"

"I must leave for work before it gets too late in the morning." My voice holds a certain demanding tone that cannot be put out. If this tone were used in any other circumstance, I would be whacked over the head! "We should start the trek to town." How dull it sounds! My chair screeches on the floor as I stand, carrying my plate to the kitchen at a strenuous pace.

Just as I set the dish in the sink, Mother's vexed voice echoes to my ears. "That is a wonderful idea." The responding scuff of chair legs against the floor announces her departure from the table. In an effort to avoid another awkward encounter, I snatch my dinner pail and glass bottle of water, then walk out the door with my nose in the air.

Once I arrive at the mercantile, Mrs. Huxley gives me a quick tour of the place while pointing out tasks to complete at a head-spinning rate.

My neck constantly whips around as she directs me to a broom behind the counter, examines the dust on the shelf with a swipe of her finger, and calls for her husband.

"Robert!" the towering red-headed woman yells in a shrill voice. He races down the staircase at an impossible speed, taking his place next to his wife. Her frown is undeniable and clearly directed at her husband. "Do take over. The baby is crying in the other room." She marches behind the counter and through a doorway to the earth-shattering wails of an infant.

"Hello, Azalea!" His jubilant personality erupts as his hand grasps mine and shakes it. "I *suppose* the shelves need a dust. Might you take care of that? Or rather sweep the floor, if I can find that broom. Ah, here you are!" I suppress a grin and take the broom from his hand before starting the task. Mr. Huxley is in every way dissimilar to his wife; his laugh lines show a sense of humor whilst hers possess the ghost of a grimace. A smile is a greeting to him, and he looks to others for direction. I have heard the expression, "Some men are born to be ruled over," but I have only ever witnessed it in this case.

Although the mercantile is rather small, the work Mrs. Huxley can dream up seems to be endless. While I was in the middle of sweeping, she reentered the room and instructed me to reorganize the shelves and give them a "thorough" cleaning. When I parted my lips to ask what that included, her exact words were, "You seem to be a capable girl. Figure it out yourself." Then she went on to complain about today's youth being "unenlightened." Only when every shelf was dusted and their contents repositioned did I receive a positive remark.

The clock above the doorway chimes twelve o'clock as I finish my dinner behind the counter. A select few roam the streets at the time of midday, and not a single customer has entered the store since I arrived at nine. What a horrible morning this has turned out to be, and the day is only halfway over!

The bristles flick along the hardwood floors as I resume my duties, making this task take much longer than necessary in order to delay any more that may come. In the next hour, three people enter the store without pausing to glance at the girl sweeping an already spotless floor. Mr. Huxley helps every customer after engaging a lengthy conversation with them. Each time the bell at the door rings, alerting us that a customer has entered the store, I hardly glance up.

"Francis! Good to see you, son. How's the Tammy house coming along?" Mr. Huxley's voice yells out as I turn my head to the dashing young man walking across my path.

Francis's bewitching eyes capture my attention once more; we maintain eye contact as he journeys to the counter. While his back is turned to me, I madly tuck the stray hairs sticking out behind my ears. Thank goodness I did not braid my hair today or else the top of my head would be nothing more than a frizz of untamed strands! If Mother and I were not engaged in a lasting argument, then she would have ordered me to put the locks in two unflattering braids.

Try as I might to focus on sweeping, Francis's and Mr. Huxley's conversation is within earshot.

"Very good, sir." Francis's voice smooths out the line as if it is poetry, leaving his audience to guess at some deeper meaning that may or may not exist. "Mr. Stanton estimates it to be finished by next weekend. I see you have found a helper." Both pairs of eyes glance at me in unison, causing a blush to rise to my cheeks. I try to look down and hide it but fail miserably.

"Yes, indeed! Thank you for the recommendation." Mr. Huxley chuckles as our bodies tense up. Francis recommended me for the job? I thought he only mentioned it to Pa! Why ever would he do that? His anxious glance over his shoulder reveals the fact that the recommendation was classified information. As a result, the room suffers a few moments of gruesome silence.

A clearing of his throat cuts it like a knife. "Are the deliveries ready? I should hurry if I am to get back to the Tammy house before it gets too late." Tension prickles along my shoulders as I finally sweep the nonexistent dirt into a corner. As if beckoned by my moment of rest, Mrs. Huxley appears out of thin air and joins the conversation.

She sets four brown paper bags with food staples peeking out on the counter. "Will you be able to carry them all, dear? I wouldn't want you to make another trip in this heat!" Mrs. Huxley coos at Francis as if he is her next-of-kin. It is more kindness than I have ever seen her express!

With a perkish grin, Francis turns to me while resting one arm on the counter. "Well…I would not mind the help—or company."

All emotion drains from me as I witness Mrs. Huxley nodding as if proclaiming it a brilliant idea for me to tag along. "Azalea, you may help Francis with the deliveries, then return home. I'll see you tomorrow! Goodbye, dear." With a relived huff, I locate my bottle and empty dinner pail before grasping a bag in my left arm, clutching it with all my might to ward off any forthcoming embarrassment of dropping it. Francis, ever the gentleman, carries the other three bags and opens the door for me as we walk out onto the dusty road.

Birds swoop across the path and into the canopies as we stroll along the main road silently. Conversation seems to be brimming on both of our lips but has yet to emerge. Francis's gray eyes merely waver to me for a moment before his attention is directed elsewhere. The fact that two strangers have greeted him since we started our journey gives me the impression of just how valuable Francis is to this community. Even the Huxleys' conversation with him went well beyond a neighborly greeting.

In some ways, I envy him for having so many people who take the time out of their lives to stop and converse. He displays a naturally amiable manner to everyone. I have tried to duplicate, or rather adopt, the manner of being convivial to all whose paths intertwine with mine, but strangers seem to have a belittling effect on me—not in their intentions from what I can tell—that causes every prospective topic to be unattainable. In some circumstances it is the opposite, like if I have a friend like Nannie or Evelyn there to guide me.

"You can go down this path to the Dawsons' place. It is the beige house on the left. I will take these to the Frasers' house, then we can meet back at the bridge."

With a sheepish nod, I saunter down the wooded path until arriving at the described house. Henrietta Dawson, a girl I briefly became acquainted with at the dance, answers the door just as my pathetic knock sounds. Her hazel eyes examine me before coming to the conclusion that I am a stranger.

"Who might you be?" her sharp voice catechizes, accompanied by a raised brow.

Henrietta does not strike me as a rather welcoming girl, but I doubt that our quick encounter at the dance has left her mind completely.

"Azalea Stanton." My response is met with a slow blink. "We met at the barn dance last week." Another blink. Nothing seems to register in her mind, and if it does then she intentionally chooses to blankly stare. "Here are your groceries," I huff while placing the bag in her arms.

She does not say anything as I turn and walk back along the stone trail and through the front gate. Thinking it safe due to the minute that has passed, I turn to glance over my shoulder. Henrietta is still standing in the doorway with the deadpan expression and bag in hand. Honestly, why must the girls around here look at me as if I am some exotic bird?

The bridge lingers a mere five feet above the water that rushes past. It has an almost imperceptible curve to it that can only be seen and not felt when on a wagon going to or from town. Following the road from town to the bridge, then taking a right at the fork leads to Aspenmoore. Winfield is quite the spread-out town, just as Pa said when we road into it.

Setting my bottle and pail down, I lean over the bridge railing to gaze at my reflection, which waves hello. The river stretches onward with a few trees along the banks before snaking around a corner. Although the depth of the river cannot be more than seven feet, the darkness of the water gives it an eerie feeling. A cardinal swoops by in all its crimson glory before settling on a tree bough as a woodpecker's knock travels to my ears. The wildlife accepts my observation of them as if I am an old friend. It is quite a special thrill to see these wild animals up close and feel as though I too belong in the wilderness with them. A certain zephyr contributes to the wonderful orchestra of nature.

I drink in the sunlight that kisses my freckle-sprinkled cheeks and let the sweet breeze be complemented by a growing smile and closed eyes. This is it; this is the feeling that I have been searching for! Everything, here and in the world, is absolutely faultless in its current state. My mind has finally reverted to the way it was, when innocence dwelled in me before I ever realized the extent of Earth and when living in the moment was the key to happiness. I wish to retrogress to those days; the agonizing thing about the past is that it has already abandoned you, then the future grabs hold, yanking you into the present.

A creaking sound disrupts the moment, causing my eyelids to flutter open in annoyance. At first the sound is as low as a mouse squeak then becomes deafening in an instant; with my head in the clouds, I mistake the noise for a wagon rolling past behind me.

I have always had the gift of rapid thinking and perceptiveness in my grasp, but a gasp barely escapes my throat as the wooden railing breaks away, sending me plunging into the turbulent water. Falling is a graceful thing—whether intentional or accidental, literally or metaphorically—surrendering every will and power that you hold inside of you, only to leap into the unknown is splendiferous! Putting it into perspective: human-kind exists within the boundaries of Earth, a sphere hurtling through time and space at an unimaginable pace; bringing us to the realization that we possess no control over the events that take place.

Time halts as I claw the air for some object to grab on to. The slow progression of plummeting to the water gives just enough time for fear to take hold. Fear is a peculiar thing; after all, it is something that we come to learn over time.

The insistent current sends me below the surface as I slash my way through the water. The force of it lifts me and carries me downstream, tossing and turning me around jagged rocks. I desperately flail my arms, forcing my face to break through the surface for a mere second. In that moment, I gargle a cry for help, unaware if someone is here to hear it.

Below the water is a place of terrifying peace. Sun rays glimmer through the cracks of the surface, and silence is a virtue that engulfs my mind. The moment my mouth resurfaces for a second, I take short sips of air before being whisked back under. My racing thoughts, which demand that I try to grab hold of a rock along the riverbank or attempt to fight the menacing current, are soothed and quieted by the silence below. Muddled ideas disappear as the line between the depths of the water and the rest of the world feel miles apart, like trying to reach through the mirror to touch your reflection. It is the river's wicked trick to lure people to their death—their willfulness falters at the lullaby, sending them into a trance that eventually delivers their soul to the grim reaper. My lungs scream and plead for air as I clutch my chest in agony.

Oh, please, let it be quick! my mind screams to God. I have often wondered what death is like, not in a morbid sense but merely out of curiosity. Does everyone feel its cold grasp as I do now? Is the terrifying end met with peaceful surroundings that deliver you to the pearly gates leading to eternity?

My strength gradually diminishes as I close my eyes one last time, and a growing tiredness takes place of any resentment I hold against the water. I shall never see my parents again, nor will I have the chance to tell Mother how sorry I am for the useless fight. I'll never witness the dawn breaking through the morning mist or any other simplistic moment of God's divine creation.

This is the abandonment of every hope, wish, and desire I have ever held for the future, for my future. Is this how my sister felt when her diagnosis proclaimed the end of everything? How did she come to terms with it? How did she become content with the fact that her existence was concluding and her presence would soon be missed? How did she reach the conclusion of her story with peace of mind and soul?

A murmur comes from somewhere nearby, barely audible, calling to me from every direction. The fey voice is familiar to me, for it is deeply rooted in my soul. It is the voice that has comprised my childhood.

It is Florence's voice.

RETROUVAILLES

A GOLDEN WALKWAY stretches across lush fields of green as light comes from the clouds above. But the sky is not of Earth. Every inch is white, something like sunlight gleaming behind it in a restful manner. I have been fortunate to witness auspicious views of God's creation, such as natural human beauty and resplendent sunrises that awaken the day from the dark cover of night; nonetheless, nothing has ever amounted to this place. This creation, wherever it may be, appears so vast that there is neither end nor beginning to it. I feel as though I am attempting to describe a fantasy place that has shattered all possible odds of pertaining to Earth. The appropriate elucidation is nonexistent, for such words in the English language have yet to exist.

There is no throbbing pain nor gnawing grief inside of me. Instead, something mirthful and pure engulfs me as I leisurely gaze around. I am nothing more than a form of consciousness in this place where everything feels like home.

An angel with flowing locks of golden hair quite similar to mine peacefully emerges before me. Her blue eyes send a thrill to my heart. Every scar and mark upon her skin has been replaced with a glowing pale complexion as if erased.

A smile brims my lush lips as my voice speaks calmly. "Florence? Is it really you or a figment of my imagination?" Our hands wrap around each other for a moment, verifying that this is not a dream, before we share a hug. We only break the embrace to stare at one another in childish amazement. Everything about her is so different, yet familiar, as if Earth could never flatter her heavenly appearance.

Her voice is filled with adoration as she speaks to me. "Yes, dear Azalea, I am truly here with you. God has granted us time together." Such delicate sentences she speaks! I half expect them to be followed by sentimental violins or harps!

"I have longed every moment to hear your voice, to witness your alluring smile, and to hold your hand one last time!" A pause creates a gap in our reunion as I realize what this place must be. It is, after all, too enchanting to be terrestrial. "Florence, if this is heaven…am I—"

As if by her nature, Florence reads every thought and emotion inside of me with one gaze. "No, Azalea, you have not died. You, Pa, and Mother still have much more life left on Earth. There are still lives for you to change, journeys to aid, and people for you to meet! As for heaven, we are at the gates of what lies beyond life. God has pieced together such an eternal paradise for us here. But our time is coming to a close, and you must return."

Every emotion is easily expressed here, as if second-guessing is of human nature alone. "No, I shall not abandon you! I do not wish to be alone anymore! Everyday has been utter torture without you, sister. Can't I come with you?"

Florence smiles with motherly affection as the palm of her hand touches my cheek. "God has shown me what your life will look like, and it is far from over! As we part, my beloved sister, I gift you this final advice so that you may carry on. I cannot tell you how to survive without me; I can only say that I want you to. Live every day to the fullest, and laugh until tears start in your eyes and you feel that lovely ache from smiling. Find love and affection in the people around you. Face hardships with resilience. Do not view a challenge as a reason to surrender but as a mountain to climb, and whilst you witness the sunrise on top, think of why the journey was worth the struggle.

"I wish for you to fall in love with being alive instead of feeling guilty for it. Pick flowers in a field and contemplate the book you are reading because there is so much more to your existence than grieving my death. And if you see something that needs to be changed, then invoke the change. Do not think this is the last time we will be together; I will be waiting to spend an eternity with you! I love you, Azalea, and shall watch over our family until we are all home together."

Tears stream down my cheeks but are wiped away by my sister, who stands before me in all her ethereal excellence. This is the goodbye I have desired. It isn't until after someone passes that you can formulate proper departing words.

"I will, Florence. I give you my word. I shall love you even after the last breath escapes my lungs. Even in the afterlife, we will be together. We shall meet again in heaven someday soon." I wrap my arms around her one last time as my heart returns to its normal thump. We exchange a final nod before Florence turns around and steadily walks away into the light that grows brighter with every moment that passes. In the blink of an eye, her charming smile fades and I am left to myself. My chin is lifted by some unseen hand as I look hopefully into the blinding light. "Thank you, God, for letting me say a final farewell." My eyelids slide shut as the light carries me back to Earth in an instant.

‽

The burning feeling in my lungs devours me until it becomes utterly unbearable. A gag sends me heaving out a mouthful of water into the grass nearby. I hear a sigh of relief breathed at my ear, and I turn to see Francis huffing and lying on the ground. His short, dark hair sticks out in all directions and his clothes are soaked through. I sit up on the riverbank, taking in my surroundings with a new perspective on life. Every gasp of air pulled through my lungs stings, the once soft afternoon light is now blinding, and it feels as though a piece has been torn from within me. A breeze kisses my face with such tenderness that tears brim my eyes, I brush them away so Francis does not see. The silence between us is deafening; an orchestra of sounds echoes through the forest, but it fades away into the background.

"Who is Florence?"

A prickle runs down my spine as I snap my posture up. Our eyes meet as his brow purses in confusion. "I—" With a simple question, every word ever created has left my vocabulary. How does he know her name? I ransack my mind for any previous mention of her but come up shorthanded. The heartbeat in my chest quakes in time with my shivering frame as we stand up in unison. "She was my sister. Florence…died a few months ago." His gaze is unceasing. I stare at the ground in an attempt to convey my feelings in the matter of discussing her. Francis, however, ignores every hint thrown his way or simply does not realize them.

"You were yelling her name. If I had not heard it, then I wouldn't have known you fell in. Were you two close?" I whip my head up to meet his eyes, as if asking if the question is genuine. His gray eyes shine with pity as if reading my pain. But the last thing I want is for Francis Southerland to feel sorry for me! My muscles tense and a burning desire to scream ignites inside of me as my feet carry me past him and toward the road. *What an ignorant boy, asking such personal questions when my feelings on the topic are transparent! Is home left or right? Why must Winfield have so many forks in the roads! How infuriating!* His footsteps stomp on the ground behind me as he yells out my name. "Azalea, wait!" Heat builds in my cheeks as I flinch at the touch of his hand against my arm.

"What do you wish to know?" My voice booms, echoing down the lane and throughout the trees. He tenses as if prepared for a fight, and yet his lips remained fastened. Why is he insistent on this inquiry? Upon our first meeting I took Francis for a rather canny, albeit bewitching boy. Now my mind has been swayed to label him as dim-witted and inconsiderate! "No, we were not close, at least not until the end. Is that what you wanted to know? That I was jealous of her all my childhood and that the events in Brockschmidt finally opened my eyes to my own self-worth? If I could take it all back, I would in a heartbeat. If I could take her place…*I would.* It is really none of your business, sir! Thank you for saving me, but I am quite content walking back home. I won't be treated as an imbecile just because I fell into a river."

The final words come out as a poisonous mumble, but no doubt he heard them considering the twitch of pain on his face. A pang of regret strikes my heart and extinguishes the preceding indignation. Piled on everything else is my sincere remorse for my savior. Embarrassed to let another minute linger between us, as our faces are inches away, I depart from his presence and trudge down the dirt road.

Even the sight of the house does not lift my melancholy disposition. In the events that transpired today, the lingering feud between Mother and me vanished from my mind. I am reminded as soon as I walk through the door, as if our shouts are ingrained in the floors. A voice hums a church hymn as footsteps click on the kitchen tile. With a huff I pick my heavy feet up, shuffle down the hall, and take a leap off the metaphorical cliffside.

"Dear child!" Whilst Mother has always had a flair for the dramatic when it comes to my adventures, nothing amounts to her shrill declaration that sends my ears ringing in dismay. The iron skillet in her hand slips through her grasp and clatters to the floor, a pathetic crack assuring me that the tile on which it has fallen is now broken. A hand flies to her chest, desperately searching for evidence that this is reality and she is not dreaming. It's not every day that your daughter returns from her first day of work, soaked from head to toe and hair wound in knots, standing dismally in the kitchen.

My eyes widen at the unanticipated grasping of my shoulders as she pulls me into an embrace. I flinch when she touches a tender place on my skull that a rock must have hit. "What has happened to you? Are you hurt?" Mother questions as she holds me at arm's length and scans my frame for any sign of injury. Her eyes finally travel to mine, and my lip quivers at the sight of her worry. How could I ever have accused her of not loving me when this display proves just how much the thought of losing another daughter terrifies her?

⌒

The never-ending sound of chirping crickets and croaking frogs is enough to drive anyone to insanity. A huff of defeat escapes my lips as I sit up in bed, running my hands through my loose hair. Catching a knot, I pull through the tangle defiantly. Darkness engulfs my room as stars twinkle from outside my window.

After my impromptu arrival, Mother ordered me out of my sopping, grass-stained dress and sent me to bed despite it being near supper time. An untouched meal of bread slathered with butter and a bowl of bean soup taunts me in a relentless manner until quieted with the haughty snatching of a slice. The bite of sustenance fails at dismissing the lump that is permanently fixed in my throat. Throwing it back on the plate with disappointment radiating off my skin, I pull my knees to my chest. I bite my lip, my eyelids fluttering to a close as I face the shadows in the nearest corner. A flash of blue eyes and golden hair appears as I try to bring forth the memory from earlier today. A quiver of my heart sends tears to my eyes as I feebly grasp at the gnawing pain inside of me.

"You have to let me go," a disembodied voice whispers in my ear. As if by magic, every noise belonging to the night, every self-deprecating thought, and every labored breath from my lips are shushed by the words.

"What if I can't?" my cracked voice asks in a hushed tone. "I know you are at peace. I just wish I was too." *You are a part of me. You are my childhood companion, my lifelong friend, and my only sister. I am afraid a goodbye translates to the abandonment of that side of myself. Who am I without you?*

A hot tear streaks down my cheek and lands on the shoulder of my nightgown as I await an answer that may never come. Maybe this is God's way of saying the answer is for me to determine. I have grown up listening to His word through the Bible and hearing stories of disciples who faithfully walked with Him. Although I am no Daniel and this is no lion's den, can I do the same thing he did and put the metaphorical blindfold over my eyes while being guided by His hand?

The echo of a conversation travels under the crack of my bedroom door, then to my ear. My discontent with my unspoken inquiries vanishes in a moment. Curiosity overcomes me as I toss my blanket away, run across the grainy floor, and slowly rotate the doorknob in the palm of my hand.

A small glimmer of firelight travels from the kitchen, and I tiptoe toward an almost inaudible murmur coming from the downstairs hallway. My eyes peek around the archway entrance and find Mother sitting solemnly by the crackling fire. The needle in her hand jabs through the fabric with growing vexation as Pa stands across the room, watching.

Mother huffs and throws the embroidery down in her lap, rubbing at her weary eyes. I shrink down and press my back to the wall, my ears twitching as she speaks. "I can't shake the feeling that—" Her eyes travel to Pa's pursed lips. "I am at fault for everything."

Despite the several moments of silence that tick by on the mantle clock, it looks as though thousands of words are exchanged between the two of them. Mother bites down on her lip as she turns to gaze into the fire. A cricket chirps on as Pa saunters over and settles on the sofa near to her, his back to me.

"Margaret, you are not at fault for Florence's death. How could you be? Our Lord always has a plan, and even if we do not know its contents, we must continue to follow Him. This could be a test of faith. If so, we must stay with the flock." The moment Florence's name is spoken aloud, it feels like an invisible barrier has been shattered. *Mother blames herself for Florence's death?*

Her responding whisper is filled with melancholy. "It is my fault, Albert. I *insisted* that we go to Brockschmidt. If I had not, then nothing would have happened to her. Nothing would have changed. Ever since that morning, I carry this weight in my chest from her missing presence. Is God punishing me by letting this pain stay? Then today Azalea could have…and where would we be then? Those last words would have been spoken in anger. I cannot do it. I cannot live with myself because of that one mistake!"

Only in two circumstances have I witnessed my mother crying: when the news of Grandma Flora's death reached us and when Florence died. Is this similar? It is conceivable that this breakdown and relinquishment of this guilt may be the death of her hope related to Florence, hope that she is not really gone from this world or that she might return. This clouds my head, making my vision blur as I concede to this new information.

Sobs now shake Mother's entire frame. As if battling it internally, she does not attempt to wipe the tears away. Instead, they run freely, bearing the severity of her words.

Just over his shoulder, I can see as Pa places his hand on hers, looking into her eyes. "He is not punishing us! You were just trying to do what was best for our daughter."

A sudden gasp brings her shivers to a halt. "Our daughter…" They are haunting, achingly beautiful words that convey a world of hurt.

MY FAITHFUL COMPANION

IT IS A PLEASANT August afternoon. The air smells of the freshly baked pie that sits on the windowsill. The cornstalks we pass on the way to church each Sunday have just begun to turn yellow, preparing themselves for the autumn harvest that is yet to come. The cherry blossom tree in our yard has become the source for my imagination and entertainment. Whether it is imagining up adventures to embark on or reading *Jane Eyre*, my heart has grown fond of this sacred spot. It is quite impossible for me to imagine the absence of this tree. I do not believe I would be nearly this sentimental about it if Pa had cut the sapling.

It took endless patience, but I have finally established my presence to the local bird population as friend instead of foe. A starling peers down upon me from the upper boughs as I crane my neck to return its gaze. I have begun to look to birds for inspiration, for they have mastered life in a way most humans never have. The starling has remained on a slender branch for several minutes; how does it ponder and observe with such tranquility?

Unimaginative people would assume that birds are incapable of the passion humans possess, but I severely disagree, for their manner clearly shows it. They have the capacity to understand their daily mission and achieve it quite flawlessly while maintaining a look of grace. Do they not raise families and provide for them? And yet they understand when it is time for their children to leave the nest. They accept that it is the last time they shall ever see their kin. I believe birds to be one of the most feeling of creatures.

Often enough I wonder if this is all a dream and that at any moment the sweetness of this new life might disappear, but no such thing has happened. The sunlight temporarily blinds my eyes as I hastily turn to the distant calling of my name. A brown-haired girl prances up the lane to where I remain at the foot of the tree.

"Hello, deary!" Nannie exclaims as she halts in front of me. The lace hem of her calico dress sways in the slight breeze. She tucks her hands behind her back, peering at the open book in my hand. "*Jane Eyre*, literature at its finest. I came to call upon you and see if you wanted to take a stroll? Although, I might just want to remain here in the cool shade of Scented Oasis!" Over the past few weeks, Nannie has ventured over to Aspenmoore many times, and one day she inquired about the cherry blossom's name. I responded that it had none. After a moment of hesitation, she dubbed the sapling Scented Oasis on account of its sweet aroma and general ambience.

"You have read my mind! We shall have to keep our walk short and only go to town and back. The heat is brutal on a cloudless day such as this!" I exclaim whilst abandoning the book at the base of the tree and taking my place beside her. With Pa working from dawn to dusk and Mother calling on neighbors or baking most every day, entertainment to occupy my racing mind has been limited. It does no good to fret about the coming school term, but I cannot help it when it catches me off guard! The first day shall be upon us in no time, which is a thrill and horror in itself!

Several quiet moments pass as we skip down the path, turn left at the gate, and head to town. A bird whizzes past as we step onto the bridge. My eyes gravitate toward the broken railing on the opposite side.

"What do you know about Francis Southerland?" I ask Nannie as we stroll arm in arm down the lane. The question has been pestering me for quite some time. Numerous chances for me to ask have arisen whenever Nannie has ventured over to Aspenmoore, but until now embarrassment has stopped the inquiry from ever departing my mind.

Nannie's brows furrow as her brown eyes search my face. I conceal my blush by focusing on the trickling water below. "Francis? Just about everything, really. My brother, Eugene, is friends with him. Francis excelled in school until his father died. Due to that, he had to drop out, then he got a job at the mercantile two years ago." *Francis works at the mercantile? I thought he was delivering the groceries as a favor to the Huxleys. Oh, goodness…* "He is exceedingly kind, not to mention rather handsome." My heart skips a beat as I bite my lip to hide the oncoming smile. "His mother is the town midwife. She often visits my mother and speaks of how she tries to convince Francis to return to school. Why do you ask?"

I reach up and sheepishly tuck a wisp of hair behind my ear, avoiding eye contact by any means necessary. "I met him a few weeks ago when I was working at the mercantile. I accompanied him in delivering the groceries. Whilst coming back from the Dawsons' place, I halted to peer over the bridge railing when it gave way in an attempt to sentence me to an early grave." The humor does not find her, causing me to resume a grim storyteller's voice as if reading a scene where the protagonist finds themselves in the climax. "I saw my sister, Florence…and Francis rescued me."

Upon mention of my fall, Nannie halts as if an invisible barrier lies before her, turning to look me in the face, her brows elevated. "Oh, how romantic—"

"Then he started asking all these insensitive questions! Can you imagine? The audacity." I grimace and march on ahead with my friend trailing behind me. "Normally, I am impartial to formulating an opinion about someone so early on, but how could I be so mistaken? Let us not speak of it anymore. What are the goings-on in Winfield? I have not toiled at the mercantile in two weeks. Mother says that it is too dangerous since the accident. The only social interaction in my life is church and seeing you. My mind was previously made to not fret about school anymore. Nonetheless, it is impossible, for I ponder it every available moment." At the end of the journey to town, we spin around and head back the way we came.

The breeze flicks a few locks of hair over Nannie's shoulder as she patiently listens to my rambling. Nannie is a truly kindhearted soul, my closest companion, and a fellow adventurer. I must admit, I was rather ambivalent about allowing myself to grow close to someone else after losing Florence and after Nora, Evelyn, Mrs. Jones, and Colleen absquatulated just as swiftly as they had appeared in my life.

The memories of my former life in Wyoming often resurface along with certain regrets and sentimental fondness. Sometimes it feels as though someone else lived through those moments and I was just there to watch them. Oh, how different my existence is now! It is both pitiful and a blessing, for it is exactly what I prayed for whilst simultaneously being the opposite of everything I wanted. Does it—grief, that is—ever leave? I have asked myself that very question countless times since May.

A sudden voice makes me jump out of my thoughts. "If I may? Not to be too forward, but is the reason why you are cross with Francis because of what his inquiry pertained to or is it due to the fact that *he* was the one who inquired?" My brows furrow almost immediately and the pair of us halt at the raising of my hand. Her amber eyes hide under long lashes before peeking at me, timidly awaiting an answer.

I ponder what she could be implying but come up emptyhanded. "What are you suggesting?"

She scans the landscape around us for several moments, then starts to twiddle her fingers. "Well…I do not know anything about your sister, nor would I ever directly ask in case it would offend you. I suppose what I am trying to ask is: are you annoyed because he asked about Florence…

or because Francis was the one to do the asking? My mother would reprimand me for saying this because it is inappropriate for young girls. Be that as it may, most of the town witnessed the moment between you and Francis Southerland while you were dancing."

A flutter of my heart and flush of my cheeks puts more into words than I could ever admit. Nannie, being the chum that she is, may as well be able to read my face as clearly as words on a page. Nonetheless, she simply nods once and continues. "Not to intrude upon your private feelings, but I believe you were quite taken with him—and he probably feels the same—the moment your eyes met. And that could be the reasoning behind your annoyance with him. I am partially surprised to have not heard about it! News tends to travel like wildfire in a small town such as Winfield. Then again, Francis is not a gossip, so I would not expect him to tell anyone of the private encounter."

"I…" My voice squeaks out in a pathetic tone as I attempt to piece together my now scrambled thoughts. Why would she say such a thing? Of course, the question was asked in all politeness, and I am in no way angry at her for simply proclaiming what she observed, but what prompted this proposal? I cannot in good conscience deny that there was something between us at the barn dance…Was it really that noticeable that everyone else saw it?

The seconds pass by with Nannie staring at me with catechizing doe eyes, and my lack of a response seems to give off an impression that what she says is true when that simply cannot be!

I clear my throat with a certain air of confidence and part my lips. "No, I do not feel anything for Francis Southerland. His interrogation was simply pitiless toward that private information about Florence. You are a good friend, Nannie. One day I will inform you about her…when I can move past the hurt enough to talk about her."

The corner of her mouth twitches into a half-smile, telling me to take all the time I need. As we stroll back down the dirt path through

Winfield's exquisite scenery, it seems as though the exuberant possibilities that the world holds for our friendship are endless. For all I know, Florence is watching from heaven this very moment, smiling down at this lifelong friendship I have been fortunate enough to find.

⌒

I awake on the first of September to a cold snap that gives the breeze a certain autumnal feel, even if summer was only yesterday. Despite there being no physical difference in the picturesque landscape outside the bay window, the orange sunlight paints the very façade of autumn.

I jump out of bed and rush down the stairs in my nightgown. The front door swings open and lets a burst of sweet air into the tranquil house. A titter escapes my lips as I raise the hem of my dress and step off the front stairs and onto the dewy morning grass. My right hand raises to the sky as the light grows to reach it within a moment. A pang of nostalgia strikes me as I recall this parallel almost a year ago…

"What are you doing?" I open my eyelids. Looking up at me is my older sister, Florence. She holds the empty milking pail in her dominant hand while using her right hand to shield the sun from her eyes.

"Taking in the scenery. Aren't the views just ravishing?" I gesture to the country around us.

The exhilaration and fondness of the first autumn glow vanishes as if stolen away. My grin falters as my arm falls to my side. Even the awakening chirps of nearby birds announcing a merry good morning do not reignite my fire. This internal affliction invariably steals my momentary exultation. Must I go the rest of my life being reminded of her at every turn?

⌒

"Penny for your thoughts, Pa?" A pancake sizzles on the skillet in my hand as I pour the batter. Pa has been standing in the doorway to the kitchen, focused on the scenery outside the window as if a thought is swirling around in his head.

I flip the pancake with precision. My cooking skills have vastly improved these past few weeks. Just this morning, there have only been two burned pancakes! Although Mother may take credit and say it was her expert teaching, I attribute it to the anxiety of school driving me to seek out any form of entertainment.

"Well, Bluebird, I've been thinking it is about time we do something with all this land." The heels of Mother's shoes click down the stairs, and within a moment she catches on to the conversation, as usual.

"Whatever do you mean, Albert? Surely not livestock! How ever could we manage that along with your job, Azalea's schooling, and all the work that must be done before winter?" I crane my neck to watch as she sends an approving nod my way after a careful inspection of this morning's sustenance.

A small grin touches Pa's lips at Mother's hasty response. "Now, Margaret, I'm not suggesting we buy a herd of cattle like the other ranchers around here. At least, not yet." His contagious smirk infects my face as Mother squints her eyes disapprovingly. "There is a small town about fifteen miles north—Carningsby—and Mr. Huxley informed me of a horse auction being held there this weekend."

Every muscle in my body tenses as I cautiously turn to face my parents. Mother's hands lie firmly on her hips, a slightly exasperated expression adorning her face. She ties the strings of her apron in an irked manner. Quite the opposite, Pa runs his fingers through his cropped hair with a coy grin. With their reactions affirmed, my own feelings are permitted to emerge.

"Oh, do you really mean it? In all truthfulness, I had hoped we would one day have a horse!" The spatula in my hand clangs to the tile as I dash to engulf both of them in hugs. Mother, being slightly disgruntled by the idea, partially accepts my thanks for the allowance of such a gift. "When shall we egress?" My smile is unconcealable as I bounce around the room in ecstasy. Suddenly, the thought hits me rather forcefully: how can we afford the upkeep of a horse?

As if my mind is an open book, Pa addresses the burning question in my pleading eyes. "Do not fret. We have money to spare. With the cold months ahead, work for decent carpenters has been plentiful. And Mrs. Huxley sent word through her husband that she will need your help at the mercantile these upcoming weeks." A side glance towards Mother reveals that she is no longer against the idea. *What changed? Did Pa convince her to let me return to work?* "Now that you are earning a paycheck of your own, perhaps you could chip in for your horse's care. The auction is on Saturday, so we must leave early that morning. We could even make a camping trip out of it and stay that night. As long as we return home in time for church, everything should run smoothly."

"Yes, Pa, of course! May I invite Nannie along with us? She is quite the whiz at dubbing animals or places. Just the other day, we were having the most challenging time declaring a title for that starling in the blossom sapling until she suggested Montague. You see, we are reenacting *Romeo and Juliet* by Shakespeare—Nannie has a book with all five acts—and the name appeared as if by magic! Is it not the most fitting title for a starling? Originally, I insisted that Nannie play Juliet—after all, she is the very embodiment of the character—but she asserted that the Nurse would be a more fitting role. I must say it is not as difficult as you would think for one to imagine trees as the rest of the characters. What a capital time we shall have!" Halfway through my jubilant skip up the stairs a voice calls my name.

"Azalea! Do not walk away from a conversation until dismissed. It is unladylike." Dusting her hands off on her apron, Mother takes over preparing the breakfast, simultaneously carrying on our discussion. "If you are insistent on this trip, then you might as well pick up a few supplies for school on the way." At the mention of school, my heart fills with a buzzing anxiousness. My feet stomp down the stairs, taking nearly two at a time until landing at the bottom in a breathless huff.

"Yes, Mother."

She strolls over to the parlor with a nod, disappearing out of sight for a moment while Pa and I exchange a quick expression of contentment. She then returns with a paper and pencil in hand. "Hopefully the store in Carningsby has some decent wool fabrics. You have already outgrown last winter's dress and most of…Florence's do not fit you just yet. Albert, be sure to ask the clerk for this amount. I cannot craft a dress with less than seven yards, especially if we want to include the material in the sleeves." Some may describe Mother as reserved or rigid, but Pa and I have learned to read her quite well. While the instructions are conveyed in a stringent tone, the glimmer of a smile is seen in the twitch of her lips as the shock sinks into my distracted mind.

The air pulls through my lungs as if breathing for the first time, like a dormant volcano that has been revived once more. Every day, night, or spare moment I have spent praying to God in the hopes that He would fulfill my greatest desire—finally owning a horse—flood my thoughts as if they have no room to be processed correctly. Faith is blind, deaf, and mute, yet we follow Him as dutiful servants awaiting that glorious moment when the veil between heaven and Earth is lifted. Despite my verbally unanswered requests, my faith and loyalty has remained steadfast, and it was not until this moment had I heard the voice of God. Although it may not be a literal voice speaking to me as if I am Joan of Arc, God is surely answering the prayers whispered in the cover of night since the tender days of my childhood through Mother's and Pa's actions. *Thank You.* My mind echoes with gratitude as a whisper responds: *You are most welcome, My child.*

I have never fully comprehended how one may sleep peacefully when such great things are just a few hours away. Last night, there was not a second from dusk to dawn when my eyelids were not open and my hands were not moving. My stomach has remained in knots ever since Pa told me about the auction.

"Do not worry, we will find you a suitable match," Nannie notes as the wind blows through my loose hair. Nannie's father was kind enough to allow her on the trip and provided a wagon along with a duo of horses for us to travel with. Despite the several weeks we spent traveling to Winfield, I have not grown accustomed to traveling in wagons. Every pothole and rock that one of the wheels hit sends us grasping for something to hold on to.

I clear my throat while tightening my grip on the wagon bed. The summer heat has yet to permanently give way to autumn coolness, making the air humid; the wagon has no cover, so shade is out of the question. "I am indeed quite thrilled with the prospect of locating my companion. Nonetheless, the apprehension inside me is inextinguishable! We have not been subject to luck on our previous travels. If only we could be there already! I hardly slept a wink, for my brain could not cease to invent new things to agonize over."

The twinkle of a smile is just visible at her petal lips and sunburnt cheeks. "To beguile some of the time, we can talk. Have you finished *Jane Eyre*? It puts *Wuthering Heights* to shame, does it not? I think you will enjoy Carningsby, it is similar to Winfield, except it is more of a livestock town and has an auction yard. You will see more of it during the harvest festival."

For most, if not all of my childhood, I have wished, prayed, and dreamt for the day when I may have a pet companion. Somehow, the fulfillment of such a long-awaited desire leaves an empty feeling inside my metaphorical jar of dreams. The same problem could relate to my friendship with Nannie; after several lonely years in Lorretta without a confidant and the loss of the few temporary friendships I have been blessed to experience, it is as if my subconscious expects Nannie to disappear or abandon me erelong. Her steadfast character says otherwise.

"Hmm? Oh, yes, it was quite a brilliant book. It reassures me that Charlotte was the better novelist of the Brontë sisters," I say quite distractedly while watching a bee tumble out of a nearby flower.

Pa clucks to the horses and our pace is hastened to an upbeat trot. The silence is filled with the melody of swaying grass and the occasional call of a soaring hawk.

Growing up seems to include a new world of difficulties and obstacles to manage. Rarely has a day gone by when my character, feelings, and future have not been affected or analyzed by myself. For example, perhaps my reluctancy to express unabated delight is due to my immutable grief or the philosophy of expecting disappointment in order to not be caught in a vulnerable state? These self-examinations are often wearisome considering they routinely go round in circles, ultimately lacking a confirmed decision on the cause.

⌣

Neighs and whinnies come from several faraway horses that await their turn to be marked with a red ribbon tied to their tail, proclaiming to everyone they have been sold. Pa follows close behind me, making note of the numbers of the few horses he thinks will be worth bidding on later.

My palms have met countless horses, but I have yet to feel a connection with any one of them. Each one is comparative in appearance, whether that be markings of stars or stockings, wide pointed ears twitching at each crunch of a footstep, and soft noses reaching out to catch a breath of your scent. However, how can I choose just one when there are so many possible contenders?

Bona fide cowboys chuckle and joke as one spins a lasso over his head. One of his chums holds his pointer fingers at the top of his head to replicate horns while he slowly gallops in a circle. The other cowboy casts his rope and tightens it within a moment of it falling over the "bull's" head. The glimmer of a smile on my lips lifts my spirits just as Nannie calls my name.

"Azalea, come look at this one!" She stands on the side of the wooden fence, waving me over. In a moment, I am beside her, folding my arms over the top fence board and setting my chin on it.

The horse, a lanky palomino with a golden-blonde mane and tail, munches on a mouthful of hay as we chat about it. My eyes glance over to the nearby information sheet that is individualized and pinned to each pen: four-year-old female, no name. Nannie comments on the mare's attentiveness as her ears twitch to us. I shrug as the animal swishes its tail at a fly. On the way here, I imagined I would feel a certain spark in my heart when seeing *the* horse. No such connection has been made. Should I settle for a specimen with whom I have no bond beyond that of a pet and owner? I desire a companion that will gallop across the field to be near me whenever I am within eyesight and possesses a wild spirit to match mine. This has started to turn into a hopeless venture and a waste of time!

"Girls, we ought to register for the auction," Pa calls over his shoulder as he starts to walk toward the registration table. My heart beats in anticipation with each step I take; the auctioneer's dragooning voice broadcasts over the endless noises, reporting the current price whilst a horse is paraded in a round pen. Bidding cards are raised constantly with growing urgency; one man in particular flicks his card up at each opposing offer until the moment comes when the price becomes so astronomical that nobody counters it. The gavel hits the block with a thunderous clap and the horse is taken to the back pen. After Pa signs a paper and collects our bidding card, we locate spots at the side of the crowd, near enough to see whichever animal is presented next but not too close as to suffocate from lack of space.

I start to pick the dirt under my nails as I gaze at an overhanging cloud. How beautiful it must be to look down and see the world from such an altitude! Surely, nothing else could compare to something so exhilarating. The hum of voices, distant neighs, and chirping of crickets seem a hundred miles away with my head in the sky.

A sudden gasp of, "My goodness," makes me jump out of my skin as my head whips to Nannie, who is on my left. Her brown eyes are wide in awe, her lips parted in shock. I follow her line of sight to the base of the salesman's stand where the round pen is. In my distracted state, I had not noticed the mustang bursting through the gate, dragging a man on the ground behind him.

The entire world quiets instantaneously, making my mind swirl at the sudden hush. My whole being is mesmerized by this animal as I peer around heads and shoulders to catch another glimpse of it. The man struggles to his feet, fighting against the horse's stubbornness to hold his tight grip on the rope and stepping toward the animal menacingly. Whispers and gasps of horror fill the audience as the horse rears up, thrashing its pitch-black hooves in the air.

The auctioneer cups his hands around his mouth to yell, "C'mon, Jerry! The beast too much for you?" The crowd chuckles at the joke whilst their eyes remain fastened on the display. "Let us begin the auction, folks!" Once again, his sunny disposition is an attempt to distract from the urgency of the situation.

I, however, am simultaneously horrified and delighted by this creature before me. It shakes its pale white mane and flicks its tail in a vexed manner, pawing its hoof on the ground repeatedly. The man in the pen pulls the rope tighter around the animal's neck and twirls the other end in the air. Its dapple-gray coat is resplendent in the sunlight, giving the impression that the horse is solid white.

My green eyes turn to Pa, who is currently observing his list of horses, their supporting and opposing qualities scribbled beside their numbers. His wide-brimmed hat shades his face from the sweltering heat. "Pa," I whisper just loudly enough for him to hear.

"Yes, Bluebird." He nods without taking his focus off the paper, crossing off another number before narrowing it down to three contenders. The pencil scratches the paper again.

My heart beats with a proclivity for this animal, increasing my urgency as the starting price is called out. "This is the one, Pa. May we please get this horse?" His head snaps to me, then to the animal trotting forcefully in the pen as the man runs behind it clucking. Pa's brows furrow, his lips purse, and his eyes narrow as if he trying to see every desirable or positive feature in this horse that I do. "It's perfect! The embodiment of the equine in my imagination. Please, I beg of you!" The only signs of his internal battle are the bite of his lip and stroke of his chin.

Not a soul is crazy enough to bid on such a creature, though the auctioneer tries his best to convince the audience to offer a bid with quips such as, "You, sir, look like a genuine cowboy who could break this fine steed," and, "Come now, folks, who will rise to the challenge?"

I clasp my hands together, raise them to my mouth, and plead for Pa to envision the potential this mustang holds. With a flash of determination, he raises his hand, the card held up for all to see. The auctioneer, not wanting to bear another moment of humiliation, shouts, "Sold," and claps the gavel down. My heart skips a beat as a soundless breath is exhaled from my lungs.

Whispers from nearby strangers do not go unnoticed. One woman standing a couple feet in front of us whispered to her friend "That wildie shan't break, let me tell you. They must be daft to buy such a beast." In this moment, I have made up my mind to win over my new companion, not by force but by earning its trust.

Once the bill of sale is signed and the amount is paid, the horse is presented before us.

"Good luck," the handler scoffs.

Wide eyed and cautious, I slowly raise my palm before the animal. His blue eyes gaze leerily at me, but he blows gentle breaths on my skin as if asking for a treat. The tips of my fingers gingerly stroke the creature's angelic coat as I stare at it, memorized.

"What will you name him, Azalea?" Nannie asks, in awe of the mustang.

It takes but a moment for the words to escape my mouth, as if they had been tucked into a deep part of my mind awaiting their chance to be brought into the world.

"Eye of the Storm," I say. The words give my heart a thrill. As I stare into Storm's eyes, I can feel it in my soul: he is mine and I am his.

Chapter 11

A VOID THAT GRADUALLY GROWS

THE BELL RINGS OVERHEAD as we step through the doorframe, a handsome hunter-green calico fabric in my grasp. My attention has not strayed from it since the second I found it in the store, even when it left my grasp so the clerk could cut the required yards.

Storm is tied at the back of the wagon, following us as we make our way to the edge of civilization. From the smidge of Carningsby I have seen today, a sparking sensation of pride comes from the fact that I reside in Winfield. In the few months we have called it home, I have grown rather fond of all that the town entails. What a picture it is to imagine me collecting wildflowers, occasionally glancing up to watch Storm grazing in the lush-green field, like something out of a novel.

I can barely look away for fear of ruining this pleasant memory-in-the-making. Every muscle in my body fights the urge to repeat his new name until he responds to it, to stroke his soft coat, and to write in my journal about every future adventure we may partake in. However, it would all be rather fatuous considering we have yet to build an incontestable bond and I have yet to stand in his general vicinity for more than a minute.

I cannot help but think of Florence. Ever since my fall into the river, my subconscious has returned to the pattern of torturing me with inquires related to her. Would she approve of Storm or comment how impractical it is to purchase a wild pet I may not even be able to get close to? In these instances, I strive to distract myself, as I do now while asking Pa if Nannie and I can go adventuring in the woods adjacent to our campsite. Pa gives his blessing and offers a warning not to stray too far, for it will be dusk soon. Nevertheless, these temporary fixes do nothing to diminish the eternal yearn I feel for her.

Twigs crack under my weight as I dash between the pines, suddenly halting. Around the sound of my beating heart is the crunch of hastened footsteps traveling behind me. Nannie arrives at my side in a flash. Despite our gasps for breath, with a nod we take off, racing through the trees until reaching a moss stump in a glade.

We collapse to the forest floor in a commotion of laughter and wheezing for oxygen. The underbrush is dry and brittle from the lack of rain. An aroma of pine sap lingers for a few breaths until a breeze whisks it away. Hair wrapped in knots from endless torment brought by branches and limbs sawed apart by thorny underbrush, I sit up with an idea brewing.

"Is this a forest or the enchanting hallways of a castle? Our dresses seem to be turning into lavish ballgowns before our eyes!" The ferns, only the height of my ankles, sway as I skip between them and spin, holding my arms out. How beautiful the canopies look in this light!

Nannie quickly catches on to my imaginative story. She too stands and claims a thin low-hanging branch as her possession, quickly fashioning it into a simple crown. With a giggle and a deep curtsy, I solemnly place the crown on her gleaming hair, which appears caramel in this light. "I crown thee, Queen Elizabeth of England." Forest echoes turn into adoring crowds cheering for their divine ruler. Something about this feels all too familiar. I shake the eerie feeling away and continue the fun.

Her chin lifts in confidence as the palm of her hand raises, sternly addressing the subjects who chant for God to save the Queen. "And you, Mary, Queen of Scots, will be my fellow adventurer. Shall we lead the troops to battle?" A pause allows us to survey our soldiers—who would appear as tree trunks to an unimaginative person. On the count of three, we charge, and our voices boom out, "For England and Scotland!"

After our heroic and prodigious victory in the Battle of Forestway, we embark on an adventure of finding "food" for two queens in hiding. Our fake shivers cease at the creation of a "fire," which the dull person would call a pile of broken sticks. The few pebbles in my hand are wild berries, which we eat by tossing them over our shoulders.

Nannie suddenly halts in front of me. I scramble to avoid colliding with her, looking around questioningly. "Azalea, do you know which way we turned at the moss stump? I do not recognize this part of the wood." The sweetness of the moment vanishes and is replaced by a foreboding one.

My head turns wildly as I spin around. There are no footprints nor familiar landmarks. We were foolish enough to not check the direction the sun was when entering the forest.

A fallen tree instills a speck of confidence in me as I exclaim, "I recall the sight of this tree to our left when we were running from that direction. Yes, I am quite certain! Follow me!" Trusting in my statement and relying on my skills of recollection, Nannie walks closely behind me. We abandon the "fire" and "berries" by the hollow base of the fallen tree.

Minutes pass by and there is still no sign of the forest's outer shell, Pa, the campsite, or civilization. The brush becomes thicker and more tangled with every step. Thorns clutch the hems of our skirts, forcing us to hold them out of reach. The last few minutes of light coat the wilderness in a tangerine color, declaring a nonverbal divulgence: when night falls, we shall have no hope of locating anything. Sweat drips from my forehead as I huff in defeat. "I don't know where we are! Nannie, I am terribly sorry for dragging you into this catastrophe!" Heat travels to my cheeks as tears well in my eyes. It is all I can do to turn away from Nannie's panic-stricken eyes.

A grunt sounds behind us, causing my blood to run cold as I gradually turn in unison with my friend. My breathing turns shallow as twigs snap.

From the thicket emerges an enormous obsidian bear. My body twitches and quivers in fear as we remain petrified, observing this lethal predator shuffling by, seemingly without noticing two young girls standing in its territory!

It lifts its massive head from where it had previously been sniffing the brush to where we are standing. In this moment, my heart ceases to beat altogether. Enormous menacing eyes gaze into my soul. Nannie clutches my hand, forcing me to the ground with her, just as the bear stands on its haunches to peer down at a late-afternoon meal.

"Tuck your knees to your chest." The clattering of my teeth and pounding in my chest fill my eardrums as I follow the instructions. "Hands over your neck," she whimpers as I squint through my eyelids to see the beast land on the ground, sending a quake through the dirt to us.

My whole body shakes uncontrollably. I say a prayer in broken increments while biting down on my trembling lip until blood oozes from it. The palm of my hand encases my mouth. My eyelids close tightly when I hear another grunt even closer.

Before I know it, my vision changes to the picture of the stagecoach robber's face as he wipes away a hot tear streaking down my cheek. Nails dig into the palm of my hand until purple crescent marks are left upon my skin. A bullet clicks into place when the gun cocks. Every whistle of wind, rustle of leaves, and chirp of birds are coerced into suppression with the bang of a gunshot.

"Please, no," I beg as he loads another bullet with a smirk. "Help me! Somebody, please!" My voice is on the edge of hysterics, shrieking the words as I cover my ears with my hands.

"Azalea? What is wrong?" a voice asks frantically through the darkness. "Tell me, are you hurt?"

I open my eyes frenziedly, hunting for the robber whilst expecting to be back at the stagecoach. But here I lie, sprawled out on the forest floor screaming over a figment of my imagination and a traumatic memory.

"It keeps happening. Why must my memories punish me?" Sobs rack my frame forcibly as Nannie looks upon me with her brows drawn together and her eyes wide. "For a while I assumed it had ceased, yet I am still haunted by the past! We were held at gunpoint and tied up to be killed when traveling to the city…two dead bodies that day. She had flashbacks too. I see her every now and then in my dreams." No soothing voice nor motivational words may pacify this. They had long since awaited to be unburdened from my inner conscious. Nobody but my family truly knows of Florence; Nannie has only heard her name a handful of times but never sought to ask about her, instead waiting until the moment arose for me to tell her, and Francis only overheard vague words spoken in anger.

I hesitate for a second as the tears choke me. "I thought I made peace with the world!" My voice cracks pathetically. "When will life move on from her death? I shall never be truly happy until it does…"

The last words come as a whisper, for I myself had not come to absorb this truth until it was said aloud! Nannie drops to her knees, sitting next to me on the ground. She takes my head in her arms and rocks me like a child. Words cannot comfort me—she knows this, so the pair of us remain silent in the pitch-black wilderness.

Her small voice speaks just above a whisper. "We must get out of here before the bear comes back. Come with me." I nod, feeling for her arm as she aids in lifting me up. Our elbows link up as we move forward into the unknown, leaving the pain of the past in our wake.

We walk until our feet become sore and blistered. To our dismay, we made several turns only to end up in the exact same place. Once enough time passes whilst wandering aimlessly, our hope subsides, our energy gradually wilts, and our legs buckle at the base of a tree.

Spiderwebs stick to my skin in an unyielding fashion. My finger-tips massage my scalp, which aches from minacious branches tearing and yanking at my hair, and a horrid mixture of sweat and dirt adheres to my skin. If there were a speck of sentiment left inside me, I would sob for what a horrid adventure this has turned into. Instead, I stare blankly, my back leaned against the mossy tree trunk. It is as though the vehemence that typically characterizes me has been drained without a hint of reoccurrence.

How have I come to be here? At dawn, I was fretting about finding a horse, and by twilight I have succumbed to the twisted, warping woods! My soft palms cover my face as I pull my knees to my chin. The humidity clings to me, refusing to release its unwavering grip.

Where has my ingenuity gotten me today, besides lost? More often than not, I feel as though every decision I make leads me to a dead end where there is a trapdoor below me, waiting to open and send me to rock bottom, and I am left calling from the stygian hole, biding time for someone to offer their aid.

My mind divagates from the subject as I hear a sonorous voice call out repeatedly. Could it be real, or is it just another creation of my subconscious?

"Azalea!" an echo calls. Breaths come from my mouth noiselessly. "Nannie!" This time, the call is even more desperate.

A newfound sense of strength rejuvenates me. I crawl on my hands and knees, feeling the ground for Nannie, whose breathing I cannot hear. Panic engulfs me as my voice croaks desperately. "Nannie! Where…are you?" A pang pricks my throat followed by a cough.

"Hmm," comes a mumbled declaration less than three feet away from me. I extend my arm in the direction of the voice, grabbing a piece of fabric on her sleeve.

"Wake up," my hoarse voice pleads as I shake her awake. She stirs multiple times before snapping to attention. Oblivious to where we are, she screams out my name, grasping my arm. I take her hand in mine and reassure her. "It's okay. I'm right here. We are in the woods; don't you recall seeing the bear?"

A long pause follows, to the point where I have to check that she is still awake. "I thought it was a dream," she finally responds. The weight of her disappointment is unbearable; although it was not intentional, her words make me feel at fault for the trouble we are in.

"Listen to me," I say forcefully while struggling to my feet. "There was an echo calling our name moments ago. It has to be my Pa. Our only hope is to find him by yelling. We cannot navigate in this twilight, so when we hear a response, do not move! He must come to us." Her pause is enough of an answer for me. "Ready?"

On the count of three, two ear-splintering calls come from inside us, followed by a momentary hesitation as our ears try to detect any sounds. Pa's shouts, closer this time, meander back to us. This "conversation" goes on until his last shout is a short distance away. I take off running, dragging Nannie behind me until I collide with Pa. A sigh of relief comes from his heaving chest as his arms wrap around us. It is as if a weight has been lifted from my shoulders, for this nightmare has finally ceased. For now, that is.

Chapter 12

THE WORDS WE DO NOT SAY

"Then we dashed madly toward Pa, not knowing what lay ahead or around the next bend!" My arms fly through the air as I reenact the story, adding in a few dramatic details. Afternoon sunlight leaks in through the window directly behind me, warming my back as Mother listens in horror. Her brows raise, only to plummet back down, and once the story comes to a resolution, she looks positively exasperated.

Her chair screeches against the floor, making me recoil from where I stand on the other side of the dining room table. Pa, in an effort to avoid the conversation, sought to "take care of Storm outside" and get him acquainted. Here I was under the impression that if the story was told with excitement and was somewhat enigmatic as to certain details, then Mother would handle it better. But after all, this is the second life-or-death situation in which her only living daughter has been in the past few months.

She huffs, putting her hands on her hips in an apoplectic way, and turns to face me. I expect her reprimand, hammering the saying of "think before you do" or "listen to your parents" into my mind until it takes. But in a surprise twist, it does not arrive.

Instead, she crosses the room and engulfs me in a bone-crushing hug. I stand flabbergasted for a beat, then choose to delight in the rare embrace. I am aware of how difficult it is for her to ignore my disobedience;

nonetheless, I am thankful she has. Being scolded for letting my imagination run free and disregarding Pa's instructions would only make me feel worse, for on the venture home my conscience constantly berated me. What feels like a lengthy embrace is a timespan of a few seconds. Once we break apart, Mother parades into the kitchen to prepare a delayed dinner, leaving me wondering what has overcome her.

⌒

Splinters of wood prick my palms as I hang off the side of the wooden fence. Storm blinks blankly at me as he swallows a mouthful of grass. Though this new pastime I've taken up over the past month might seem boring, it is actually quite thrilling! Who knew observing a horse could be so fascinating? I may be the only human being who finds that statement to be truthful.

"Mother thinks my dress shall be finalized in time for the harvest festival. Have I told you about that? I cannot recall. With all the goings on, we have not dedicated the proper time to sewing the garment. Nannie informed me that the livery is just beyond the schoolhouse, so come winter, when the snow is too deep for me to walk, hopefully I can ride you to school and you may board in the stable for the day. She said that is what most of the other children do in those scenarios."

Nannie's and my dilemma in the woods has brought us closer together. The near-fatal experience is something we now share in common. It is quite humorous, really, although it was not at the time. I have overcome a great deal of things since then. My head and heart have fully comprehended the fact that I must live my life for more than just the sake of existing. My grief has not vanished. In some ways, I fear the day it will but half expect that will never happen.

In the past month, I have ventured into town with Pa on a regular basis and resumed work at the mercantile. I have discovered that the same river in which fate had me fall stretches and meanders through Winfield, transforming in each spot. The river slims whilst wrapping around the bend in which the bridge—the same one I fell from—is located, goes through the woods and vacant meadows disguised as a harmless creek that would be perfect to dip a foot in on account of how shallow it is, then slows while remaining parallel to the dirt road that the Cassidys' house is located on, gradually turning and slithering to the front of the church! It is quite the sight to see the wooden-planked bridge in front of the beaming building with the tiny bell tower and wooden cross pointing upwards to the sky from where it stands steadfast on the apex of the tower.

The crunch of hooves and call from the postman distract my wandering mind, which rambles on about my town's beauty. "Hello, Tom! Would you like a carrot for your horse? I tried to bribe Storm with one, but he has not progressed." I became acquainted with Tom, the town's twenty-two-year-old postman, a few weeks ago when I mailed off two letters—one to "Rose" and the other to Russell St. Claire—and he inquired about Storm.

"Well, you'll get there, kid. Gentling a mustang ain't for the faint of heart!" My disappointed expression turns into a grin at the comment. It is nice to know someone believes I can earn Storm's trust. Mother and Pa have not offered their opinions besides warning me to "be cautious around that animal" every time I approach him, practically declaring their minimal faith in me. But Storm has calmed down a great deal. The wild look has left his eyes, and he no longer jumps the fence. "As for the carrot, Mare would love it." He gestures to the bay horse he is riding. Tom is very kind but unimaginative at best, considering he decided to name his horse Mare because she is a mare. Had he asked for my input, I would have generated a long list of unique but sensible titles.

Mare spots the treat in my hand like a hawk focuses on a mouse in the brush. Eager to taste the morsel, she stretches her head toward me.

"One letter for you today." Tom diligently hands me a faded white envelope.

Although it has been a long time since my eyes last witnessed the scraggly penmanship, I immediately recognize the sender's identity. My finger runs across the words "Miss Azalea Stanton" in a reverential fashion. Is it my imagination or do I hear my given name being spoken aloud by an angelic voice? In a second, images flash through my mind: the gleam of a gold ring on a chain, his lapis eyes smiling at me, his hand brushing against my cheek. To be honest, I have labeled the sender as a ghost from my past, someone who could not be easily forgotten but had to for the sake of everyone involved. Perhaps it is just human nature to desire something you cannot possess…

Before I can discern what is happening, the soles of my shoes are carrying me away and my voice is calling a goodbye to those I leave behind. Receding thumps from a horse's trot and a hearty farewell are hollered from the dirt path as I mindlessly travel up the lane, settling down against a fencepost. A cold breeze nips at my skin, sending a trail of goosebumps up my arms as I tug my sleeves to my palms. Exhaling a single breath that I was not aware was being withheld, my short nails pick at the triangular flap of paper on the back of the envelope until I am able to pull the note out. Softened by the touch of hands, it reads:

Dear Azalea Stanton,

First off, thank you for responding to my letter. I half expected you wouldn't…Second, I am sorry to hear about Florence. She was a true angel and has now taken her rightful place beside our Lord and Savior. Knowing you, those words probably feel like empty promises meant to soothe the loss. The only advice I can offer is to trust yourself. Time does not heal wounds; it is the help from others that makes it bearable. Some scars can last a lifetime.

Before you read further into this letter, I'm sorry for stirring up these feelings that you said would not go anywhere. The memory of you is in every campfire, every laughing moment, and every glow of the oncoming dawn. I have tried to turn my attention elsewhere, notice or spark some interest in others, but there has been no successful outcome. You have affected my life in every possible way. I've sworn to not mention it again, but you should know the reasoning for this letter is so that you are always aware of my intentions, and so I won't regret not telling you this.

Russell

A hand covers my gaping mouth as the note lowers to my lap. How is it he can read me so well? Unless…could that mean he is my soulmate? Why is it that in books the fact a couple is destined to be together is so plainly laid out, but it is not so in life?

If only…No, I cannot mistake flattery for something else! My conscience screams like a warning sign.

Oh, if only someone had gifted me that piece of advice a few months ago. It might have liberated me from a world of suffering! For a beat, I question whether to respond to Russell's letter for fear of further encouraging these particular feelings. That would be leading him on, and I cannot bear to toy with his heart, which he has bestowed upon me. But if I do not respond, Russell shall spend a lifetime wondering what has become of me, then possibly regretting ever sending this! Why must I come to a fork in every road? Is nothing straightforward anymore?

A nickering sound comes inches away from me as something softly nudges my shoulder. My head rotates gradually, making sure this is real before turning around completely.

The dapple-gray horse with whom I have tried for weeks to advance a connection—but failed miserably each time to the point where I questioned my decision in choosing him—is mere inches away. His soft white-whiskered nose sniffs curiously as his round eyes plead for the item in my apron pocket.

My right hand steadily pulls out the other half of the carrot I gave to Mare. I gently extend my arm through the boards of the fence so that he will have to move toward me in order to have it. His hot breath touches my palm as he accepts my offering.

"Have I ever enthralled you with the story of how I came to acquire this scar?" I hold my right palm up to show the darkened line across it. Storm swishes his tail while crunching on the treat. "Well, it begins with the story of a charming friend…"

Chapter 13

IN SPITE
OF IT ALL

One of the foremost pleasures in life is when you find yourself so enraptured in a book that when taking a second to look outside, you can see the world has changed—for that period or forevermore—in your eyes and your eyes alone. It is part of the reason I enjoy reading outside by Scented Oasis or at the bay window—because at any moment, I could have my attention removed from the words printed on paper and instead lifted to the beauty of Earth.

I have lived countless lives vicariously through hundreds of books. It is both a comfort and a source of heartache to my imagination, both something with which to entertain myself and a painful reminder of adventures I will never have the blessing of experiencing myself. Perhaps that is where my wanderlust has stemmed from. Winfield is congenial and homelike—which makes it the perfect place to return to after travels—but there is so much more to see outside the boundaries of the fence.

Maybe this realization is brought on by the adventures on which the protagonists venture, or perhaps it is the development of interests due to the evolution of my grief. I'm trying to fulfill my promise to Florence to the best of my abilities, but it's difficult to create a new life and leave behind the old one while the ghost of my past self still haunts me. It is liberating from a certain perspective to be able to know my mind and the reasoning behind my reactions. The circumstance, however, is like the breaking of glass; no matter how much I try to pick up the pieces from the event of it breaking, concealed shards shall always be left, waiting to prick me in a moment of naïveté.

I contemplate all this rather intensely whilst watching a wagon roll down Main Street through the window of the mercantile. How I wish I had brought a book to occupy the afternoon lull! The saccharine apple in my hand lacks a piece from the bite taken out of it. Once the dinner hour is up, I wrap the remainder of my sandwich in its handkerchief, tuck it into my pail, and then return to work. Setting the pail behind the counter, I take up the duster and begin sweeping the upper shelves.

It is hard to keep one's mind confined to the bounds of Earth whilst doing such tedious work. With the harvest festival less than twenty-four hours away, all of Winfield is wrapped up in the flurry of preparing their entries for the forthcoming inspection. Every oven door in town squeaks constantly as ladies check on their browning pie crusts. Livestock is herded from the fields, then brushed to perfection inside the comfort of the barn stalls. Patchwork quilts hang on clotheslines awaiting an accolade for the effort put into constructing them. Sunday bests are starched until stiff, then smoothed of imperfections. And finally, every buggy is washed and shined until scintillating.

Mother mailed in our entry information last week and has not ceased her effervescent conversation concerning pies, canned vegetables, and "Mrs. Peterson's prize-winning chickens."

The bell above the mercantile door rings out, jolting me out of my deep immersion in my thoughts. Gray eyes meet mine promptly as if I am the subject they have been searching for. A pang of remorse strikes me. How shameful I was to him after he saved my life. I never showed an ounce of gratitude! It is inexplicable how God can make a thousand things clear in just a heartbeat of time. Is he coming toward me? What shall I say? "Hello" is too rigid. *How are you today?* That does not seem right either. Is now the right time to apologize for my behavior? My conscience bashes my character like one would scold a child who just stole from the cookie jar.

A quick brush of a strand behind my ear and wave of my palm is all I can manage at the moment. Francis's eyes merely waver to me for the timespan of a heartbeat until his attention is directed elsewhere whilst crossing the room. Halting at the counter, he engages in a quick conversation with Mrs. Huxley, who coos in adoration.

My face burns furiously at my feeble attempt at friendliness, and I try to concentrate on my job. Yet my ear turns to eavesdrop on their discussion, which unsurprisingly and regrettably does not mention me. Out of the corner of my eye, I watch as Francis waves farewell and heads out the door. The bell rings out disappointedly as he departs without acknowledging my presence. A sigh drops my shoulders down, and my bottom lip throbs in anguish from where I was biting it.

Should I go after him and plead my case, telling him of Florence and the cause of my discontent in questions concerning her? Am I prepared to tell anyone about Florence?

Why am I so determined to achieve his forgiveness in the first place? I barely know him!

There is, no matter how much I deny it, a certain idiosyncrasy he possesses that makes the idea of him so clearly outlined in my mind.

I do not think of him in a romantic way…Of course not! How could you suggest such a thing! Nannie did mention something about a flirtation… not that it matters. Francis is an insensitive, heedless boy!

Undoubtedly, there was a kindling between us at the barn dance and at church, and he clearly made an effort to get me this job for undisclosed reasons…

You do not even know him! You are just abashed by the fact that he saved you and inquired about something personal. If you ask me, the reason you are hesitant is because repenting takes a great deal more courage than blaming him.

My eyebrows twitch as the theory is confirmed; how can Francis be the same person who I have characterized him to be when I have made no effort to actually know him?

The soles of my shoes thump across the floorboards, screeching to a halt to shout, "Excuse me for just one moment," at a bewildered Mrs. Huxley and toss the duster on the counter.

A ring sounds overhead, followed by the thunderous slam of the door. My braid whisks in either direction before I locate Francis rounding the corner. Before I can even comprehend my actions—or what words will fly from my lips when reaching him—I dash madly after him, pausing every few moments to call his name in the hopes it will make him come to a stop.

Huffing and puffing, I stand in front of his quizzical stare while gripping my beating heart. A stiff black cowboy hat shades his face from the light. He must have removed it when entering the store; I didn't even notice. "Francis, I—" My sentence trails off as our eyes align, both of us searching for some clue as to how the other person is feeling.

Where are the words when I need them? Here I stand, sputtering like an idiot after alerting half of Idaho in my plight to reach him! *Azalea Stanton, you cannot even express your contriteness!*

Without uttering a sound, he turns his back to me as I seek the right words to say. My entire chest feels like it is about to explode at the anticipation. Suddenly, my entire vocabulary spews out from my lips.

"Francis, I'm sorry! I wish to be a conscientious person who does the right thing, even if I am in the wrong. I am aware of my faults. You do not have to confirm them, for they are often scrutinized. I am pugnacious, belligerent, headstrong, and a thousand other horrid things! Please, forgive this dilatory apology and accept it, for I am terribly sorry." My efforts are brought to an end with a huff of breath, defeated by my own conscience. Francis spun back around to face me halfway through my hysterical outburst in the middle of Main Street. Luckily, no souls are within earshot.

"Well, that is axiomatic," he says, referring to the line of my evident faults.

I look around, flabbergasted for a split second that someone else in this town could actually comprehend that verbose outpour and respond in sesquipedalian speech equal to mine. Several moments pass in quietude—even the world seems to await a proper response.

"Are you attending the harvest festival?" He tips back the rim of his hat.

"Umm, yes I am." Is that really my voice? Since when has it contained such a flirtatious tone?

The glimmer of a grin crosses his lips at my response. Tipping his hat down quickly as if to shade the expression, he says, "I will see you there, Azalea." With that, the conversation is left on a cliffhanger, and we stroll in opposite directions, occasionally looking back at each other before disappearing from view.

Less than an hour after returning to work, the bell alarmingly announces a customer entering the store. I quickly note his darkly tanned skin and muscular figure, coming to the conclusion that he must live on one of the homesteads on the outskirts of sparsely populated Winfield. He has the expression of the sun: beaming with a welcoming radiance. Mrs. Huxley just dragged her oldest child into the back room after he shoved a handful of black licorice from the jar on the counter into his mouth. My ears are still ringing from the wails that shook the shelves as his mother scolded him profusely.

Nervously looking to the door behind which Mrs. Huxley had disappeared minutes ago, my palms begin to sweat as this boy—or rather young man seeing as he must be nearly eighteen years of age—saunters up to the counter I am standing behind.

"Hello, how are you today..." His deep voice trails off as he leans against the counter, waiting for me to insert my name into the sentence.

"Azalea." A dreadful pause follows as our eye contact remains stead-fast. "Stanton." Why does my voice sound unsure? Is this what an identity crisis feels like?

The corner of his lip turns up and a flash of white teeth leaves me dazed and blinded. "How are you today, Miss Stanton? I do not think we have met before. Roman Deighton." The sudden extension of his hand startles me, and for a few moments I stare at him quizzically. Realizing my delayed response, I firmly take his hand. Oh, he must think me an idiot! I mumble an apology, which is countered by a chuckle. "A few weeks ago, Mr. Huxley placed an order for some books under my name and I'm here to pick them up."

"Yes," I say, mindlessly staring before excusing myself to the storeroom. Notwithstanding the single window, the built-on room has a great deal of light. Three shelves line the wall with various items and notes placed on them. I scan each shelf twice before finally locating two hardbound books, one titled "Analytic Geometry" and the other "Cartography." I whisper each title as to remember them for later, as they are subjects that I have no knowledge of. I emerge from the room with the books and slide them on the counter toward Roman, who stands there grinning like the Cheshire Cat before scribbling his name on a slip to give to Mr. Huxley later.

"Are you…" His eyes stare with intensity that makes me blush intensely then look away. I clear my throat sternly to rearrange my question and bring forth the correct words. "May I ask what the books are for?" Another twitch of his lips and intriguing simper; my, he must be popular with the ladies, although I get the impression that this flirting is his genuine nature rather than intentional.

Putting his arm up to rest on the counter, Roman leans in, peering into my eyes. "I suppose you could call it a secret, but I'm studying for the exams come spring. Have you heard of Harvard University? No? Well, the entrance exams are horrible and difficult; making you learn every-thing ever spoken, written, or thought of! Winfield is great, but there is a world out there waiting for people like us to seize it before it runs away." He whispers the last line while gesturing with his hands. Could this be another to add to my collection of kith? He could be a raconteur with minimal effort; his voice is so mesmerizing and invigorating that even a boring topic could sound riveting.

Taking both thick textbooks in hand, he travels all the way to the door before turning around to face me. "We should talk again, Miss Stanton. Or should I call you Azalea?" There is that emphasis on "miss" again. Somehow it invokes something near to a laugh in me. No one has ever called me Miss Stanton before; Roman makes it sound like a pleasurable joke rather than a formal title.

"'Azalea' would be fine. It's what my friends call me." He gave me a smirk and a wink before the bell echoed his departure from my presence. How interesting indeed! I daresay Winfield is home to several young men who spark something in my heart…almost inflicting a swoon.

∽

For the rest of the afternoon, my mind wanders to the events of the morrow and the evaluation of what Francis's meaning was when he said he would see me there. Should it mean anything, or was it just a neighborly response? Just when I thought I was getting the hang of navigating my life in Winfield, something throws me for a loop!

"Azalea!" My mind snaps out of the submersion of pesterous thoughts to the source that has called me by name. A brown-haired beauty comes racing down the path to join me in my walk home from town. "My dear, you must be engrossed in thinking over something, for I called a number of times before you came to! Let us slow our pace so I may catch my breath." Interlocking our arms, we stroll leisurely.

Should I tell Nannie about my encounter with Francis? Or will she say something regarding the same topic as last time? Not that I am mad or blame her in any way for the inquiry, but it was rather embarrassing to think of a flirtation between Francis and me! A huff escapes my mouth at my own indecisiveness.

"Am I pestering you? Please, accept my apologies." Her pace suddenly slows as she takes a step back. Her eyes shine with hurt after misinterpreting my sigh to mean annoyance at her presence.

"No, dear friend, it is not you!" I exclaim rather abruptly. "Sometimes my infinite mind overwhelms me. I spoke with Francis today. It is the first time I have seen him since that day he rescued me. I apologized to him for my behavior, and his response was rather vague. I am not quite sure what to make of it."

My gaze drifts to the corner of my eye to read my friend's expression, which oddly remains unchanged as she says a simple, "I see," as if thinking it over. When I told her about Francis saving me after I fell into the river, without conveying the severity of the situation nor the encounter with Florence, she mentioned how romantic Francis's heroism was and I was less than pleased at the response. Could that have inflicted this hesitation? I suppose it should just be disregarded; oftentimes, I overspeculate and look for details where there are not any.

The silence in addition to my thoughts overwhelms me, so I continue to ramble. "That and the harvest festival keeps my head in the clouds. There were no such events where we lived in Wyoming, for there was a quaint population. Can you believe that tomorrow will be the seventeenth of October? Oh, how time has whizzed by these past few months." Despite my attempts to ward off the melancholia of the previous sentence, it still comes across as a longing for something, or rather someone.

"Well, the harvest festival is certainly a good occupier of thought." Nannie simply ignores my remark about the time passing—I assume due to her own lack of a response to such an observation. "It is more like a fair than a festival; for the past few years the quilting, pie baking, canning and preserve, and garden vegetable contests have remained. The main attraction is the horse races. There are two: the half-mile trek and the mile. Although, last year there was a swarm of grasshoppers on the track, so they had to cancel the mile race. The shorter one is more exciting anyway because you do not have to wait so long to see who will win!" The sound of laughter fills the sky like a heavenly chorus. "Oh dear, I nearly forgot! This is for you." She quickly jabs her hand into her dress pocket and unearths a piece of dark green velvet ribbon. "I came by the mercantile to give it to you the other day, but you had already gone home." Her explanatory sentence turns to gibberish once I lay my sight upon the ribbon.

Its softness is evident upon contact with my skin. "It is beautiful! Thank you, dear friend!" My hug catches her by surprise. Nonetheless, she welcomes it with open arms. *God, thank you for sending such a faithful friend!* "I will be sure to return the favor in the near future. Do not look at me like that! You have been so kind to me since I moved to Winfield. The least I can do is bestow some sort of gift upon you."

Nannie smiles at my gratitude but waves the suggestion away with her hand. "Nonsense. 'Every man according as he purposeth in his heart, so let him give; not grudgingly, or of necessity: for God loveth a cheerful giver.' We as God's people must follow His word and show it through heart and action. I thought of that handsome dress you and your mother made from that fabric we got in Carningsby the day of the horse auction; it and this hair ribbon will make a lovely pairing. From what I recall, they are exact in shade! Now I must make haste and return home. There is much to prepare before tomorrow's events!" After turning to blow a kiss, she disappears into the fiery autumn woods.

I closely admire the ribbon the rest of the journey home, imagining what it shall look like when tied in my hair tomorrow. A whiff of freshly baked peach pie travels down the lane, greeting any delightful neighbor who chooses to call on Aspenmoore and provokes the foreshadowing of the visitor and pie meeting on personal terms.

A flock of geese honk overhead as they form a V shape in the air, looking at their traveling companions for direction. Albeit an unpopular opinion, geese seem a great deal more romantical than swans. Mother once mentioned a ballet being based on the romantic story of a swan, giving me the impression of a captivating, elegant, and somewhat mystical creature. When the day came that I saw a swan, the creature was the opposite of what I had pictured. Geese are much more appealing to look at, and their devotion to their mate is heartwarming.

My green eyes turn from the wide-mouthed sky to Mother, who sits in the stained-black oak rocking chair. Whether enchanted by the brilliant foliage or swept away in some memory, her eyes stare into the distance without realizing my presence until I settle at her feet.

"Azalea, I did not expect you home so soon!" She scrambles to wrap the needle, thread, basket of square fabric scraps, and shearing scissors in an unfamiliar quilt.

My nimble fingers settle on a patch on the blanket, cream colored with embroidered flowers. Its touch is as soft as ever, holding a few precious memories in its stitching. "Florence's apron." I press my lips together as I begin to identify each square's origin. "Her daisy dress. The blouse with the coffee-stained wrist from that one morning she tried making tiramisu after she learned the word meant, 'Cheer me up.' That was the day I dropped Grandma Flora's glass flower vase down the stairs and wept at how cross you would be when you found it in thousands of pieces. She offered to help clean it up, and when my tears refused to subside, she pulled out the recipe box and found a recipe for tiramisu."

A gasp barely escapes as my fingers brush against black fabric, and I reach into my dress pocket to verify that the object in my mind is still with me. Unaware of when they began, I use the back of my hand to wipe away the hot droplets blurring my vision. A handkerchief appears out of thin air and is offered millimeters away from my face.

"It was supposed to be a surprise for tomorrow morning, though I am doubtful I will finish in time when there is so much more work to do!" Her fingertips lift my chin up as I place the hankie in my lap. Mother's rosy cheeks glisten with fresh emotion. "You have outgrown most of your old dresses and some of her clothes, the others seem wrong to wear, and we are in need of a decent quilt for winter. This way, we can keep a part of her possessions with us instead of locked in a chest waiting for the moths to get them. How nice it would be to win a shining satin ribbon for her."

Mother's slender fingers trace the patches as she speaks, her words unraveling like a poem as mine tend to do. The imaginary wall between us—whether forged by opposing personalities, general differences, or some unknown force—has cracked and weathered away, revealing the people who stand on either side. The pair are now forced to universally acknowledge that they are not quite as incompatible as they were tricked to believe by some illusion.

A single laugh escapes my mouth as I suck the corner of my bottom lip. "It is beautiful. Perhaps I can help finish it so that we may ready it for judging in the morrow, for Florence's memory."

"Florence's memory." Her gaze shifts to meet mine once more. "I'd like that."

It is a quilt made of warm hugs and laughter, of the sight of a breaking dawn whilst curled up in the rocking chair on the porch, of the scent of morning dew, and of the feeling of autumn chills. This is the blanket of cold shivering evenings when you need familiarity and comfort to wrap around yourself.

⌒

If only feelings or memories could be stored in glass jars, similar to how flowers can last an eternity if pressed. I often wish I could go back in my

139

life, not with the intent of changing the past but with the hope of reliving it. The contemplation of which year, day, or moment in my lifespan I would choose is without contention, as there has only been one particular time when life felt infinite and smiles never ceased. Reminiscing about "the good old days" never fails to cause my inner self to question what has changed.

Stroking the hunter green calico fabric does nothing to smooth the wrinkles. Had I listened to Mother and ironed it yesterday afternoon, then there would be no issue. The leg-of-mutton sleeves are slight and delicately puffed, and pockets have been sewn on the outside as requested. The buttons in the back are concealed by my flowy locks, and two pieces of fabric sprout from the waistline to be tied in a bow at the back. Just as Nannie predicted, the ribbon she gave me makes for a well-matched pairing.

"Darling." Mother stands in the doorway, eyes aglow and hands clasped over her heart. Outside the bay window, the dew settles on the grass as the empyrean above holds a splendor of violet, marigold, and turquoise. She takes a few steps toward me, bringing a lock of hair over my shoulder. My unconcealable pride gleams through each inch of my skin like a reflective glass within. "When did you grow up so much? Just yesterday you were a little girl climbing up the roof. What a beautiful young woman you have become."

Pressing my lips together at the memory of such a childish venture and simplistic time, I say in a low tone, "Thank you, Mother." My impromptu embrace seems to catch her off guard, but it is accepted with open arms. Her blossom lips gently touch my hairline as my eyes look to the rising sun.

Thank you, God, for bestowing such a joyful gift. I did not get too many of these experiences with Florence, even at the end—a time where all jealousy and differences were forgotten and we were just family. My vow to you and myself is to never let another moment go uncherished. Regardless of past actions, I will love my neighbor as myself.

Our warm embrace comes to an end just as quickly as it started. Mother strokes my cheek lovingly, then strolls out the door, the stairs creaking as her footsteps click down them.

"And when ye stand praying, forgive, if ye have ought against any: that your Father also which is in heaven may forgive you your trespasses." The verse floats into my mind as if whispered in my ear, almost like a clear voice quieting all thoughts and worldly distractions. I must forgive—not only because it is imperative to my survival, but also because life is a relentless battle until I truly lay everything at the feet of God. It's true: I must exonerate God, Florence, and myself from all blame for my sister's departure from this Earth.

For the first time in a while, I get down on my knees, resting my hands on the seat of the bay window, and say a proper prayer. For as long as I can remember, I have said a prayer to God before bed every night, but it in no way compares to this—comprised of asking for my family's and my health, happiness, and safety, begging to be acquitted for past sins, and expressing my gratitude.

RELINQUISH THE TROUBLES YOU FACE

Yesterday afternoon, Mrs. Fraser strolled up the lane just as the final stitch was sewn. Enraptured with our work, we did not notice the lanky woman marching toward us.

"So, this is the place where my daughter has been spending so much time!" Startled by the sudden yet friendly voice, I nearly jumped out of my skin, whilst Mother remained the picture of calm. The woman looks up at the house in complete adoration. "Mrs. Stanton, pleasure to finally meet you! Theresa Fraser, Nannie's mother. I've come to ask if your family would like to be our traveling companions to the festival?" Before that moment, I had yet to meet Nannie's mother. The resemblance was so striking that Mrs. Fraser seemed like an older version of my friend.

To a stranger, Mother would have appeared gracious and inviting, but someone who knew her true intentions of climbing Winfield's social ladder could see her hesitance in conjuring a proper response worthy of praise.

"That would be wonderful! Please do call me Margaret; we are neighbors, after all. Should you like to have a cup of tea? I must insist upon it after you walked all this way." An applause-worthy performance, to say the least.

So, they went inside like two old chaps. Later that evening, Mother informed Pa and me that we would accompany Peter, Theresa, and Nannie

Fraser to the festival at dawn, and their son, Eugene would be going with Southerlands. Pa said it sounded like "a fine idea," then retired to bed after kissing the pair of us on our foreheads. Just as I flipped to the next page in my book, with firelight as my only source of light, I witnessed the coy grin on Mother's lips as she lifted the rim of her teacup to take a sip.

Standing on the westernmost tip of Carningsby are the festival grounds, an absolutely breathtaking display of red- and white-striped tents the size of houses, hundreds of livestock organized in pens and enclosures, and triangle-cut fabric garlands hang above the entry sign, which reads "Carningsby Harvest Festival." My green eyes grow as large as saucers; what I pictured in my imagination in no way compares to the sheer brilliance of it all.

"Isn't it just the most thrilling thing you have ever seen? It looks like a great deal of people are here." Nannie turns to me just as our wagon halts in the shade of a tree.

Mother fastens her grip around the covered peach pie and patchwork quilt. Pa jumps out from the back of the wagon, then turns to help the three of us down.

The haybales, although hard to hang on to, are better than sitting in a jumbled-up heap on the bed of the buckboard. Taking Pa's hand, I jump down, landing awkwardly. Then I turn to my friend, who shares my appetite for adventure. Whether it be the starry blaze in my eyes or perhaps the general knowledge of my character, Mother calls out before the pair of us can reach a reasonable distance.

"Now girls, I trust you will be careful gallivanting about! Azalea, if it were up to me, you would be allowed the distance of a short leash, but your Pa says otherwise. Here is twenty cents. Pace yourself, dear, for that will have to last the entire day." She pulls the coins out of her petite purse, and they chime as they drop into my palm. "Do not forget to meet us at the homemakers' tent at one!" she yells after us as we madly dash into the fairgrounds—after saying thank you, of course.

A bell clings and a few claps sound. I catch sight of the display—a burly man has just won "The Hammer of Strength" and hands the prize off to a woman who tries to hide her blush by touching her fingertips to her cheek. We halt to cheer on a stranger who attempts tossing three rings onto empty glass bottles, then offer our condolences upon their loss. A group of young boys scramble over each other to snatch a bow tied around the neck of a goat whilst a small crowd encourages them.

Nannie spends five cents on the horseshoe toss as I jump up and down, clapping zealously. My hollers reach a new level when she is handed a prize of a metal pin with the words "You Won!" on it. I insist she pin it to her collar for passersby to look upon in awe. A waft of corn chowder travels on the zephyr, making my mouth water. Nonetheless, the tremendous line quickly diminishes my desire.

"My goodness, it's enough to make you dizzy!" I exclaim as we enter a tent to escape the brutal sunshine.

Blinking several times to allow her eyes to adjust, Nannie walks with a bounce in her step, pointing at a few booths we should loop back around to see. "Just you wait until the race at noon! Let me go see if that woman will loan us her pamphlet of today's events." She prances off toward the unsuspecting lady, clasping her hands and batting her lashes until the folded paper is handed over. Nannie skips back at her triumph. "How kind! She said we may keep it! Trust me, the draft horse pull is not as enticing as it may seem—just enormous horses being driven to pull sawed-off logs. Hmm…the rodeo is nearly the same time as the race. Which do you prefer? The race? Me too. In fact, I heard Francis has entered that filly he trained." As if burning coals, her eyes sear into my skin. I catch the sly twitch of her lips from the corner of my eye as we hunch over the paper.

Brushing away the blush from my cheeks, I flip a strand of hair over my shoulder. "Hush now!" I swat her arm playfully while a smile brims my lips. "I do not know what you mean. We like horses and perhaps races. That is the *only* reason we are attending it." Somehow, the mention of seeing him makes me want to rush to the racing grounds this moment. How strange…

A groan of "my goodness" distracts me; I follow Nannie's gaze to the corner mere feet away.

The couple's conversation leaks into ours as we involuntarily eavesdrop. "The weather is most unusual, wouldn't you say?" The lady attempts to run her hand through her hair but forgets that pins hold it up, and her fingers get stuck midway. What is comical to us is certainly not for the lady, as her face turns a shade of red. The man looks around the tent—hardly taking notice of the woman's misfortune—and returns to the conversation with a half-hearted chuckle.

"We've entered the informal matrimonial bureau," my friend mumbles under her breath, taking my hand and dragging me away. Nearly tripping over my own feet, I hasten along to match her pace. Before I may ask, the answer flies at me in another low tone. "All the ladies always come to one specific tent to pin down the eligible bachelors, although in the past it has normally taken place at the homemakers' tent so they may discuss crocheted doilies or preserves. Idle conversation bores me so!"

It isn't until now that I start to notice several couples conversing whilst chaperones stand a few feet from them. The involuntary memory flashes into my mind; the sight of the pearls glistening on Mrs. Jones's neck, the blush in Florence's cheeks as she concealed her smile with the back of her hand, sunshine gleaming on the pond with pink lilies and a breeze carrying the scent of fresh pastries. I push the flash of my previous life back into the past.

"Yes, let us leave at once," my voice instructs—mostly to myself—as the splendor oozes away from the previously hilarious moment. I take one last glimpse over my shoulder, verifying that the memories from the past are not following us.

Upon our immediate exit from the tent, a man gives a last call for contestants to join a foot race between young children. Leading my friend over as she stares perplexed, I call to the man just before he waves the starting flag, "Sir, two last participants!"

"What are you doing? We cannot race with skirts on! What will our mothers say?" Nannie gasps into my ear, loud enough for nearby onlookers to hear. Ignoring the comment and the possibility for utter embarrassment should a hem lift above the knee, I dig three cents for each of us out of my pocket, then place the coins in the referee's hand. Whether it be the money or just plain carelessness, he gives a nod of approval and gestures toward the starting line.

A mere twenty yards ahead is a long red ribbon held by two women; a quick scan verifies the fact that the five other participants are boys equipped in trousers. Releasing Nannie's hand, I clutch the sides of my skirt and prepare a readying stance, eyes wavering over to the man for the drop of a red checkered handkerchief. The hammering in my chest travels to my eardrums as the fabric is waved upward by the flick of a wrist, then whisked downward to announce the start.

Forthwith, my legs burn from the sudden dash in the beginning as I head toward the endpoint. A second's glance to either side picks out my competition. A boy no older than twelve shoots a glare at me as I get a few steps ahead. My friend is somewhere behind. If I had a moment to look back, I would, but the object of my concentration is the finish line ahead. My puffs begin to accumulate as I try to inhale and exhale pressingly. The whole display reaches a conclusion within a minute as I look down to see the ribbon collide with my waist and travel with me.

Nearly slipping from the sudden halt on the slick grass, I turn around to see the remainder of the contestants running to me with disappointed grimaces. All except my friend, who hollers indefinitely and provokes the audience to clap by widening her eyes at them until they get her meaning. Despite the less than stellar applause, my heart hammers with ecstasy. A shiny satin ribbon is shoved into my hand by the man as he halfheartedly shouts, "To the little lady for her victory." Then he shuffles away to comfort the young boy that finished last. My grin grows and my chest swells with pride each time someone points or whispers about the blue ribbon pinned to the right side of my chest; the feeling does not cease as we stroll about the grounds for the next hour.

The racetrack is enclosed by white fences on the inside and outside of the oval. We slowly wander over to the outer fence, claiming a place with a good enough view of the start and finish line to witness the action.

"Oh, darn!" I declare as a piece of popcorn falls to the ground. Opening my mouth as wide as possible, I say, "Another." Nannie munches on a piece, reaches into the half-empty container, and chucks a piece of popcorn up in the air. With much triumph, I lean at the last moment to catch the sustenance. A woman squints her eyes at me in disgust, then clutches her husband's arm tighter as they pass. I fight the feverish urge to laugh by chewing my bottom lip. Unable to control myself, a giggle escapes, lasting only a second because a kernel becomes lodged in my throat.

After a fit of coughs, I join my friend and the pair of us lean against the fence as the riders begin to warm up on the other end. A handler leads one racehorse around in constant circles as the jockey buckles on a helmet. Each jockey is adorned in black pants, a white shirt, and a black helmet; the only way to distinguish them from each other is the handsewn numbers of different colors on their backs. Their horses have saddle blankets that proudly show their numbers as well. Maybe I should sew a blanket for Storm; he might be more welcoming to that than a saddle.

"Should you like to know the line of prose I created earlier today? Luckily, I was able to borrow a pencil and paper from a vendor, or else it would have slipped my mind! Here, I have it in my pocket." At the nod of her head, I whisk out the small slip and comment before commencing. "Although I am a tyro in writing, it is a rather expressive interpretation of my thoughts. Here it is: 'If the modern-day world becomes overbearing,

I rely on the contents of my mind to remind me of who I am.'" My nose tilts up into the air confidently.

The less than stellar reaction of furrowing brows and turning to the distance as if contemplating makes me think the article should be condemned to the rubbish bin. "It is poetic… but whatever do you mean by that?" The hum of an incoming crowd fills around us as a substantial audience forms. The bleachers shade at least a hundred onlookers. I grow envious of the shade and their ability to sit in the benches but return to the conversation in order to defend myself.

"Look around." I gesture to the younger women all dolled up with their hair pinned in knots, ridiculous hats with yards of ribbon or handfuls of dyed feathers, and summer dresses that are much too thin for October and far too lavish for attending a horse race. I watch as my friend notices the men, who are adorned one of three different colors, their best trousers, and either a cowboy or bowler hat. "What similarity do you notice about the fashions, etiquette, and styles? Nearly every woman here is the exact replica of one another. The people are ubiquitous down to the conversation; it is as if a hundred mirrors surround one person and reflect their image perpetually until your subconscious becomes morphed to think that is what you too must embody. Your truest self lies on the inside and is comprised of your worldly desires, faith, thoughts, aspirations, and dreams. Therefore, by looking within, you will verify who you are at heart." Her brown eyes are like pools of honey in the sunlight as she scans the crowd in absolute confusion like a horse with its blinders taken off. "You cannot blame them, for it is the quiddity of human nature to be a follower," I conclude, reaching into the popcorn container, then throwing individual pieces from my hand into my mouth.

The coming minutes pass by in irksome silence. I suppose all quietude is irritating to me when prolonged by the person with whom I have been conversing. After all, silence is usually meant to bring a brutal death to a discussion. Perhaps Nannie is ambivalent about the subject. I often wonder if she views our gallivanting as childhood play—no matter how joyous, it is something I have been told you grow out of one day. And if so, then she will eventually accept the ways of society just as Nora did. Or this is simply the norm taught to her by her mother?

I huff out a sigh and scan the crowd; yesterday Francis implied that we would see each other here, but the day is half-gone and still no sight of him. Unable to hold off any longer, I pick at the dirt under my fingernails, a horrid habit I have put off for quite some time.

A boy with piercing gold and green eyes, a striking jawline, and midnight black hair characterized by its cowlick makes eye contact with me.

A winsome smile crosses my face as I wave my arm in the air above the towering shoulders and heads. "Roman! Over here!" Standing on the fence, back facing the track, clutching the board to achieve balance, I wave him over. This draws the attention of several others, Nannie included.

Yesterday—about an hour by the clockface after I had rushed to apologize to Francis—in walked Roman. We only talked for a few minutes—in all honesty, I had too much on my mind yesterday to contemplate the interaction further—nonetheless, there is something about him…

Today, we greet each other as if old friends, despite only knowing one other for the past twenty-four hours. Nannie's neck nearly snaps as she whips around, gawping at me. I step down from the fence once I notice Roman gliding through the crowd toward us, then turn to address my friend's odd expression. "What?"

"How do you know Roman Deighton?" For I moment, I question what the inquiry could mean. Did I misjudge him? Is there a reason why I should not be acquainted with the likes of Roman Deighton? I cannot recall a time when Nannie was left so baffled by my actions, except for when I told her I fell into the river.

The man behind her checks his wristwatch, which reads one minute until twelve. Now that a sizeable audience has formed, the once-gentle hum of voices has turned into an almost overpowering noise that fills the air. "I became acquainted with him at the mercantile just yesterday. Why are you gaping at me?" My laugh does nothing to diffuse her starstruck stare, which provokes me to squirm.

"Why, he's only the most popular older boy in school! Nearly all the higher-grade girls are moon-eyed over him. I've never even spoken to him…" The last few words are whispered as if a pitiful secret and said as if to remind herself of some desire. "I—Could you introduce us?" Before I can stop my oncoming snort, it comes out as a pungent criticism, which was not my intended reaction. "Please Azalea, I will never ask anything of you again!"

My comical mood falters as if I've been stabbed in the heart; Nannie, my kindred friend in all her altruistic glory, has never asked me for anything prior to this! How could I have been so horrible as to not return the favor constantly bestowed upon me?

Mother's voice from a distant memory seeps into my brain, quoting a familiar verse: "'Hereby perceive we the love of God, because he laid down his life for us: and we ought to lay down our lives for the brethren. But whoso hath this world's good, and seeth his brother have need, and shutteth up his bowels of compassion from him, how dwelleth the love of God in him? My little children, let us not love in word, neither in tongue; but in deed and in truth.'" Hmm, maybe Mother's teachings are not as obtrusive to my personality as I have always thought… Perhaps this apprehension is accredited to my progressive adolescence; more times than naught, my childish ways have been proved wrong.

Before I can come up with a response—due to my dumbfoundedness—Roman joins us at the fence's edge, beaming. "Hello, Azalea." Taking my palm in his, he kisses my hand like a proper gentleman.

"Hello." I nod my head with an inconceivable grin brewing. "This is my dearest friend," I say whilst gesturing to Nannie, who stares as if he is the most riveting thing on earth.

"Nannie Fraser. Yes, I have seen you in school many times! Pleasure to finally be introduced." Just as he had greeted me, he kisses Nannie's hand as the latter numbly stares. I would try to nudge her if only Roman wouldn't notice. *Say something!* my head shouts as I hint at her with my eyes. The scent of pumpkin and cinnamon wafts from some far-off source as her lips part, but nothing emerges from them.

Clearing my throat loudly enough to direct their attention, I say, "Look, the race is about to begin!"

Roman, a rather jocular and mirthful boy, says a humorous quip which sends both my friend and I into a fit of giggles. My eyes drift to the starting line, where the horses and riders await the firing shot, immediately noticing Francis, dressed in a uniform with the number three pinned to his back, staring at me with hurt shining through. The humor falls from my lips in a heartbeat, and embarrassment creeps into my cheeks as I notice my arm is looped through Roman's.

Chapter 15

THE SCARS THAT NEVER HEAL

ALL HALLOWS' EVE: black cats meow in their unlucky color, witches mount brooms and fly overhead, owls ask "who" at every being that dares to be out on such a night, Jack-o-lanterns with malicious grins glow in orange candlelight, and shadows dance as if alive. Alas, summer has surrendered itself completely to the mercy of autumn. It is surreal to see the leaves change color right before your eyes—a slow progression, yet no time at all.

The dreadful storm outside fuels our stories, lightning contributing to the overall effect. The fire crackles angrily as if discontented with the bounds of the hearth. The heat travels to where I lie with my stomach on the carpet, intensely listening as Nannie delivers the last line of her harrowing tale.

An eerie feeling sizzles through the air as a rumble comes from beyond the safety of the walls. Slicing through is the sound of my laugh, louder than the creak of the wooden stairs, which have no one walking on them, or the skeletal rapping on the window of the dining room. "You cannot plagiarize Edgar Allen Poe!" I exclaim before the pair of us burst into fits of giggles.

The endless tales, mostly concerning the genre of horror, have caused countless pauses in the making of a pillowcase, leaving the threads inconsistent lengths. I suppose the saying "idle hands are the devil's workshop" is true, for each time my work has ceased something has gone wrong, whether it be knocking over the bowl of popcorn or forgetting to add logs to the fire.

The scissors give a sharp snap each time the blades snip down, ending the threads that have gone astray. A yawn takes hold of me. I surrender my work, pushing it to the side and vowing to resume at some point, and settle on the carpeted floor with a pillow and quilt. For several minutes I attempt to fight against the grip of slumber by tracing the print of the carpet whilst listening to Nannie ramble on about the interworking of embroidery—a topic about whose origin I know nothing about. Catching my eyelids fluttering to a close, I contribute an occasional "hmm" or "yes, I agree" to the discussion. Nevertheless, my efforts are pointless as my subconscious is submerged in a vivid dream whose tranquil quiddity is vaguely familiar.

The zephyr ruffles my hair as I sit in the empty field of wild grass. Storm whinnies from his picket line, which ensures he is kept close. My eyelids flutter open, expecting to see the serene landscape without interruption of any being, but finding a far-off silhouette of a person and horse moving as one. A frowzy cloud devours the afternoon sun, darkening the sky as the stranger and I progress toward one another.

Long, coarse black hair tied in two loose braids and a feathered war bonnet become visible, and I squint and rub my eyes vigorously to confirm this is real. The sight is familiar, like an ominous dream I have experienced before, except this time we are cognizant of each other and comes as kith rather than foes. My heart is not pounding as much as I expected it would be when the day finally came when I was face to face with an Indian. I first became fascinated by the history of the tribes on our journey to Idaho; the terrifying stories told on the wagon train instilled fear in me, making me question whether the ghastly picture painted was truthful or a means to scare us away from tribes that wish to remain isolated.

The man's clothing is made of buckskin, his face adorned with darkly inked tattoos of dots along with a few images of animals. His feet are shielded by moccasins, and he is riding a Spanish Mustang. He, no more than forty years old, stares at me whilst angling his head high. Wrinkles adorn his face, giving the impression of what he has endured.

"You," the singular word emerges, seemingly questioning if I am a friend or foe, "have a way with nature. There is trouble within…Winona has joined the sky, leaving Lomasi." Tilting my head quizzingly, I follow his hand gestures as he repeats the sentence, this time pointing at me upon mention of Lomasi. Dark eyes shift past my shoulder, to Storm, who flicks his tail interrogatively at his two onlookers. "Wild, I see."

Surprising not only myself, I say in a dulcet tone, "We bought him a few weeks ago." He rides his horse bareback and bridleless—it's a wonder he can even maintain his balance—yet the creature acts calmly. "Would you mind indulging me as to how you have tamed yours?" I barely breathe as the stranger looks on sternly as if reading the world's unsaid thoughts.

Nodding his head multiple times before answering, he replies. "You must understand the horse as one, bond as partners, respect its ways." With that, his horse turns as if by magic and starts to trot, leaving me behind questioning what he meant.

"Wait!" I call, dashing after the pair of them until they pause. "May I ask what the feathers in your crown mean? The Noma people give special meanings in names, markings, and symbols, do they not?" The crown in question is adorned primarily in white-bodied and black-tipped feathers, but a small collection of them has been dyed various shades of red or brown. Handmade purple beads hang from woven strands of hair.

"White feathers are for battles we haven't yet faced." Reaching up diligently, he plucks an immaculate quill and bestows it into my care. "You have forthcoming battles, Lomasi. And others you are still fighting." I spin the feather between two fingers, examining its quality and meaning. I look up after what feels like a few seconds to find that the stranger and mustang have disappeared from view as if they were never truly there at all.

November: the month of crisp evenings, leaves shaken from trees that grow bare, the hooting of owls once twilight hits, the crackle of a fire whilst sitting on the sofa with a book in hand, crimson sunsets, and cinnamon bread loaves.

Each push on the swing brings me another inch closer to the higher boughs; the quick ebb and flow is relaxing. My fingertips reach up, plucking a leaf off the willow tree to which my swing is tied. Quickly, I tuck the frond in my pocket before gravity pulls me back down.

"Azalea! You are going to be late if you do not start walking!" Mother calls from the front porch.

Clutching either rope, I tilt back and raise my feet off the ground as I pull a deep breath through my lungs. The second shout of my name arouses me from the serene moment and sends me running toward today's events. Funny how just yesterday, my feelings about the first day of school were comprised of anxious excitement, and now that it's finally here, it feels like a dreaded weight that cannot be lifted. I met most of the girls at the barn dance, Nannie is my best chum, Francis and Roman happened along the way, and I have seen most of the other children in church; there shall not be many faces unknown to me. Just last week, we ordered schoolbooks, a slate, and a slate pencil from the mercantile catalog, with Mr. Huxley's assurance that every other child in my grade would have the same. Placing the items carefully in a small wicker basket, I tuck my glass water bottle and dinner pail beside them. Tying up my shoes that always seem to come undone at the laces, I grab a piece of bread and spread some jam on it.

Upon exiting the house—after rushing to grab the supplies—I take in an icy breath that feels like knives cutting me. Yanking on my gloves and buttoning the rest of my coat up does little; my teeth have already begun to chatter. If only I could ride Storm!

I blow a kiss to my pet as I pass him. He stares from the open Dutch window of the enclosed shelter Pa built after we brought my equine friend home. There has been some progression in Storm's training. Just the other day, I led him over to the nearby fence and used it as a step to hoist myself onto his back. Alas, Storm did not stand still for long, and I fell to the earth with a pathetic smack.

A few minutes into my walk—the majority of which is spent painting the picture of the landscape into my memory to have and hold forever—Nannie comes running up to me, her exhales coming out in visible puffs. "My goodness! Do you see the frost? I suspect the first snowfall will be any day now."

"Hmm," I mumble, bobbing my head twice.

Nannie returns with, "What is the matter, dear one?"

This causes the barricades in me to release the worries that have been burdening me like thorns. "Oh, I must be so far behind the class! And I will be the only new face, which is a terror and joy in itself." The knots in the trees seem to stare at me, questioning why I rudely awoke them with my childish cries. I press my lips together in an apology, and they turn away to resume their slumber.

Fixing her wool shawl, Nannie responds, "Not exactly. Last winter term was awfully disrupted with tornadoes, blizzards, and the rebuilding of the schoolhouse roof after a tree fell on it. We missed nearly five weeks last year! You have nothing to fear, for the older boys are arriving back as well; most help on their family's farms with the growing and harvesting, so the whole lot of them come for the winter term, then leave again in the spring." Holding her right glove in her mouth whilst tugging on the other, she mumbles the last few words. "There's an exam every April at the end of the school year. Things like spelling, recitation, penmanship, history, arithmetic, and the like. The teacher, Mr. Hasting—a horrid chap—determines everyone's level of study based on the previous year's exams. You weren't here for exams, so you're automatically in the grade level with your like-aged peers."

"That gives me some comfort. I only hope that the girls are not as bleak as they were during the barn dance. Phoebe in particular." Thankfully,

Mother convinced me to braid my hair, so when a strong wind blows over the empty field next to us, it does not toss locks into my face as it does for Nannie. "Would you like one of my extra hair ribbons to braid your locks?"

Gratefully taking the ribbon from my grasp, Nannie continues. "Oh, Phoebe's an interesting character; she can be abominably wicked sometimes, then pleasant other times. Did I use that right? 'Abominably', I mean?" Last week, after complimenting my extensive vocabulary, she requested I encourage her to use complex words. My beam is adequate praise, and she continues. "Thank you! Now to prepare you. When we arrive, Mr. Hasting will be standing inside because of the temperature. After we hang our hats and coats, then place our dinner pails under the bench in the cloakroom, he will inspect each individual. So long as your hair is tidy, face is clean, and clothes are not tarnished—all of which seem to be the case—you will be fine. Today he will probably reassess us or just review what we learned in the previous term. Here we are. Ready?"

The white building comes into view faster than I want it to. My hands begin to tremble as a few stragglers enter before us; nodding my head to convince myself I can do this, I follow suit and step into the warm space. Doing just as instructed, I remove my gloves, shove them into the pocket of my coat, put the latter on a peg, then join the line to be examined like livestock.

I am disappointed in the lack of décor; there is an old rug by the foot of the door, a blank blackboard up front, a quaint bookshelf on the wall, and two maps: one of America and one of the world. Besides those items and the supplies on the teacher's desk, the single-roomed schoolhouse appears the exact same as it does every Sunday for sermons. At the very least, there should be more for the students!

Mr. Hasting, not in the least what I imagined upon hearing of him, is a lean, near-twenty-five-year-old man with piercing eyes, an almost non-existent mustache, and a strident voice. A "horrid chap" indeed! He orders one of the youngest girls to go wash the smear off her cheek in the cistern outside, and when she refuses because of the cold, he grabs her by the collar and drags her to the door! My face falls and eyes widen as he dusts his hands off and resumes the inspection like wails did not rattle the windows just moments ago.

Once Mr. Hasting scans me and flicks his hand as a parting gesture, I look around for a seat as he calls for the class to come to order. Whether intentional, by coincidence, or per the teacher's instruction, the boys sit on the right side of the room while the girls remain on the left.

Come to find out, Nannie's chocolate hair is her hallmark amongst a sea of auburn, black, and shades of blonde. She ecstatically waves me over to the window side of the bench. I recognize Ophelia from the dance. She sits straight-backed on the aisle side of our shared bench. The teacher marches to the desk centered at the head of the room and pulls out a book, dropping it on the desk with a thunderous bang.

I shift close to Nannie, and we peer over a few heads at Mr. Hasting as he calls attendance by name. "Where are the younger children?" I whisper. Upon taking my seat, I took note of the fact that the two girls sitting in the row in front of us are the lowest grade and neither looked more than two years younger than me.

She leans in to respond, her eyes fastened on the front. "Around here it is custom to homeschool your children until the age of twelve."

The boys' side has three younger children, but given the low population of their species in the classroom, that is great portion! "Almost everyone here has known one another since age twelve?" Fear strikes like a lightning bolt. I am the odd one out!

"Well, Wilhelmina Koller moved here about two years ago, and John Taylor dropped out of school for a year to help the farm, so he's a grade behind us." Her shrug and pitying smile do nothing for my nerves. "Here!" she calls when her name comes around.

In a hushed tone, Nannie continues, "We are placed based on our grade level, so the older children sit in the back rows. At recess—or 'dinner hour'—the boys run outside playing games, the older girls sit quietly in that corner sewing, and *we* take the bench near the back window to eat and chat." The emphasis on "we" makes me question if she means the pair of us or the girls in our grade—which would be the ones I met at the dance. "Most of the older boys are sweet on us, like Roman, but the ones our age tease us nonstop or ignore us completely!"

After roll is finished, we recite the Pledge of Allegiance and the Lord's Prayer. Then Mr. Hastings explains our assignments. Our reading flies by, but the penmanship lesson is met with a few difficulties, especially when one of the youngest girls spills ink all over her sleeve. Then comes the long-awaited dinner hour.

Taking up our dinner pails, Nannie and I join the six girls from the barn dance, who sit in a circle on the benches in the back left corner. We're near the stove, which gives off a sweltering heat. Our spot is perfectly secluded, has a view out the window of the boys playing baseball, and is in close proximity to the warmth without being overbearing.

"I trust you all remember Azalea," Nannie exclaims happily as we settle down and turn to face the rest of the girls.

Phoebe raises an eyebrow at me smugly as the rest await her approval. "Azalea, is it? Yes, we do recall meeting you. We're talking of beaux; I do not suppose *you* have anything to add?"

A laugh escapes even though it was not meant to be a humorous inquiry. Why does that always seem to happen? "Not particularly! Although there was…" I trail off as several pairs of eyes implore me to continue.

Phoebe looks disgusted as Ophelia, who is munching on a tart, props herself up on an elbow and asks, "What?"

"Fifi!" is the response that quiets Ophelia's curiosity. *Is that her nickname? Why didn't she mention it?*

Lifting a sugar cookie to my mouth, I remain silent and focus on eating the treats Mother and I made the other day. Little stars are imprinted on them, and powdered sugar is sprinkled on each. Mother helped me make the dough, and I rolled it out, cut the thin cookies into circles, then stamped each one with the bottom of a glass. Rather brilliant, is it not?

The clearing of someone's throat breaks the awkward hush. I do want the girls to think positively of me, and it might appear rude if I withhold information, despite it being private. So I begin, "There was this boy named Russell. He saved my life, along with my sister's and mother's, during an unfortunate circumstance. He was quite handsome, and he gave me this ring." I untuck the chain with the ring on it that I just so happen to be wearing. Several "awwws" sound and someone pipes up, asking what happened next. "I never saw him again. Nonetheless, we do correspond even if an ember might burn in his heart for the idea of us." I blush feverishly at the end as the girls relish in the details of my once romance.

Henrietta Dawson, a short and plump girl with dimples, speaks up as a glare bores into her from a certain platinum blonde girl. "Do you love him?" Her brown eyes stare intensely.

"Goodness, no!" I practically yell out the answer, which alerts Mr. Hasting. He shushes me and returns to his book. A cold wave sweeps over me, sending goosebumps across my skin. Russell is a friend who I may have had a temporary dalliance with and nothing more. Henrietta's shoulders slump disappointedly as she chews her sandwich. Biting my lip, I try to think of something to divert the conversation to *anything* else.

Flipping her curled locks, Phoebe once again takes charge on the battlefield. "I heard the juiciest rumor, if you'd like to hear it. Well, if you insist! Mrs. Southerland—Francis's mother, if you didn't know," she casts a glance at me, shrugs a shoulder confidently, and resumes, "was over at my house yesterday. I overheard her conversation with my mother, and

Mrs. Southerland said that she was so taken aback by Francis's sudden desire to return to school that she 'attributed' it to the cause of one particular girl." Gradually, every pair of eyes follow Phoebe's gaze, which sears into my soul. A sweat breaks out on my palms. I wipe them off on my skirt, but the nerves do not dissipate.

Nannie, who before now was examining the split ends in her hair, takes notice of my standoffishness and jumps into the conversation. "Do not say such things, for they are falsehoods! How disappointed your mother would be had she found you peeping on a private matter said in confidence!"

Raising her alabaster brow as if shocked, Phoebe continues to spew gossip whilst nobody stops her, for they are her followers. "Where is your sister, Azalea? I haven't had the pleasure of meeting her at church; is she here at school?"

My blood runs cold and my heart beats out of my chest. I snap my head to Nannie, whose lips are parted, appalled at what has just been uttered. I stammer, trying to rearrange my thoughts into formable sentences, yet everything runs amuck and results in a jumble. Phoebe continues, "Mhm, maybe your family hides her away in *shame*. No, it's true, I have heard tales of such things! Fifi, shut up and let me speak." Ophelia clamps her mouth shut at the order, as the remaining audience gasped and turned to each other shocked at such a possibility.

Tears begin to well in my eyes as a fire ignites internally. I will not bear witness or sit by idly as this girl slanders my dear sister! "Perhaps she is a halfwit!" Phoebe cackles the snarky remark, and before she can let out another laugh, I stand, face aflame with fury, and smack Phoebe Peterson across the face.

The smack is not very loud, but undoubtedly painful based on her shriek. Clasping a hand to her swelling face, she screeches like a mockingbird, "Did you see that? She struck me!" A series of squawking noises emerge from the girls as they rush over to comfort the sobbing girl. I stamp off to the cloakroom, roughly yank my coat halfway on, and slam the door so hard the windows rattle.

I could run home, but what good would that do? Exhaling a profound quantity of air, I plop down on the last step of the stairs leading up to the door. Less than a second later, the door behind me squeaks open and out walks my friend, who is understandably flustered. Crouching down next to me, she peers into my face as I turn away to hide my tears. Before she can say anything, I gruffly murmur, "Go back inside. I wish to be alone right now. This is not how I pictured my first day of school eventuating to, and I would rather not be weakened by someone watching me cry."

Wrestling with her leal nature and the urge to comfort a struck-down bosom friend, she sighs and obeys my wishes. A pang of guilt aches, and though I rub my side to rid myself of the agony, it is ceaseless. Mother will be terribly disappointed when she hears of this! Why can't I keep my temper controlled? Sure, Phoebe said wicked things, but how horrible of me to strike her!

After what feels like hours, a thump lands near my feet as a sequence of scoffs sound. Lifting my head from my arms, which are wrapped around my knees, I spot the white baseball a mere foot away from me.

Roman jogs up, stopping a considerable distance away when he notices me. He is equipped in a fur-lined jacket, a gray cap atop his head, and earmuffs. "Come now, throw it back!" Perplexed by the offer, I grab the object and look to him for direction. More laughs come from the group of boys that stands in the triangle field. Pursing my lips ambitiously, I swing my arm back and let the ball fly to Roman's gloved hand. Every murmur and scoff is hushed, leaving stupefied expressions in their wake.

Walking the rest of the way up to me, Roman's imploring gaze is unshakeable. Shrugging to the boys behind him, who stare vigorously, he says in a low tone, "Why don't you come play? No, really! The boys will not mind, given you are fast around the bases." My nod is enough of an answer as I am led to the starting plate and handed a bat. I slip off my shoes and throw them to the side with an air of confidence.

The sun peeks out from behind gloomy clouds to watch. Out of the corner of my eye, I catch the girls crowded at the window, pointing against the pane at me as the boys hit their gloves and shout. Everything melts away in my mind as my eyes focus on the pitcher. Caught off guard for a moment when I see that it's Francis, I tighten my palms around the bat.

Less than a second later, the ball and bat collide, sending the former soaring through the sky and the latter falling to the ground as I dash over each base. Yells of "here, here" and "throw it, man" whizz past my ears. My feet touch the first, second, and third base as my teammates howl for me to make it home.

Just as the ball hits the mound, I slide onto the base, reaching out my arm as an extra precaution. The momentary silence is stabbed by victorious roars. A hand appears before me, pulling me out from the crowd of people patting my back.

Roman draws me into a momentary hug before joining the boys; my blush dies when Francis's lingering stare conveys a thousand words. I tug on my shoes and tie the laces haphazardly as the bell dings in the tower, calling us inside. Whether it be my victory or the frosty air, my rosy cheeks shine as I follow the crowd that rushes inside. From the moment I crossed the home base, I wanted to tell Nannie of every thought pounding through my heart.

Turning to tell her now, I find Ophelia blinking nervously and my friend on the other side of her with crossed arms and a sulky expression. Surely, she is not mad about me playing with the boys. Or is it because I demanded she go back inside when she was trying to be friendly?

"Ragamuffin. Only little children play sports. How immature," a whisper says from over my shoulder.

Someone says, "That girl's got moxie," loudly enough for all to hear, including Mr. Hasting, who slowly rises from his chair and saunters around the room, his watchful eye missing no small detail.

"Azalea Stanton." I nearly jump out of my skin! My "yes, sir" is not satisfactory in the matter of improving his lemon-sour frown. "To the front of the room. *Now!*" Ophelia, shaking more than me, turns to me with eyes like saucers; I start to notice most of the class mirrors this as I step forward.

As I walk to the desk with my head held high, everyone's attention follows. Why does Nannie seem to have tears brimming in her eyes? Turning my chin to face Mr. Hasting, I see he has a sneer at his lips. He draws a thin broken branch from the top drawer of his desk.

A laugh almost escapes my lips, instead coming out as a wheezy breath, as I'm tickled by the thought of what he'll do with a branch. Not a single soul shares in my humor. Instead, several girls huddle together with hands covering their gaping mouths, boys are frozen like a picture, barely daring to twitch, and Phoebe Peterson's smugness makes me want to slap her again. A whisper in my mind makes me wonder the reason why she is pleased as of currently. The question is soon answered as Francis jumps up, knocking his books on the floor on the way to stand in the aisle.

"Sir, she did not mean to. We teased her and forced her to play!" His urgent tone worries me. *What is about to happen?*

"Sit down, Mr. Southerland. There will be order in my school. Girls do not play roughly, and I will not condone the striking of another student!" My heart thumps irregularly. Pa once told me a story of when he was young and got whipped in school. The branch in my teacher's hand seems to become more like the birch switch in that tale. Every previous emotion melts off my skin as the realization hits me like a bullet: this is a punishment.

With a glare and a nudge from the end of the switch, I gulp, turning my palms up hesitantly. I wipe the petrified shock away so no one may read me, then replace it with a stony look focused on the door without meeting anyone's eyes. My legs shake violently as each inhale prepares for the searing pain to come.

The slicing whistle of air travels to my ear just as the switch makes contact with my palms. An ear-splintering scream releases from my mouth, causing me to lose all sense of propriety. Mr. Hasting's glowing eyes convey enjoyment as the whistle sounds repeatedly. The pain from each slash barely sets in, sizzling my skin, before another one comes. Clamping my lips down tightly only muffles the whimpers and makes the teacher that more determined to inflict pain. I feel the stings travel up my arm in response.

By the time it is almost over, the agony is so overbearing that when I open my eyes, water blurs my vision. I can no longer feel the switch as it lands one last time. Many of the girls, even some of the older ones, have their faces covered in their hands to be blind and deaf. The ones who do not are hysterically sobbing.

My humiliation continues as I am forced to stand on the recitation platform for the remainder of the day, including the grammar and spelling, history, and geography lessons and the chore assignments. It is a guarantee that after my whipping, not a single soul paid any mind to the things being taught. When I can no longer bear their pitying looks—for all but two people in the room sent them—I bite my lip until the metallic taste of blood fills my mouth.

I don't examine the results of my lashing until the dismissal bell rings and Hasting and I are the only ones left. As if I've been forgotten, he pays no mind as I fetch my coat, basket, and pail, then slam the door.

My eyes catch the sight of dried blood that trails down from my wrist to my pinky finger, but I disregard it in case Hasting happens to walk out and see me examining the cuts. Fixing my disheveled hair, I show no remorse. Half expecting Nannie to have waited behind, I am sorely disappointed to find the vacant scenery in my face.

One thing that did not escape my view whilst standing on the platform was Francis and his rambunctious ploys to attract the attention of Hasting. He chatted with the people around him loudly and purposefully broke his ink bottle by knocking it onto the floor—the stain on the wood was rather significant—yet he was not minded nor punished as I was for committing a lesser offense!

As if reading my thoughts, Francis appears from behind a tree and joins me as I march home. The silence is daunting, something I never suspected would happen. Impotent to the force of my fury, in part from the aching pain and pounding headache from battering notions, I halt, slipping while turning to Francis. He happens to catch my arm whilst trying to steady me, and my cry echoes through the woods.

"Let me see it." The calmness in his tone is enviable as he cradles my left arm and pulls back my coat sleeve. This morning I adorned one of the dresses that belonged to Florence. Neither one of the long sleeves were pulled up for the whipping, so now several small cuts and tears have ripped through the fabric. Behind that is my throbbing skin that is dotted in lashes in various places—some of which have dried blood in them and others which will probably bruise in the coming days.

Repulsed by the view, I turn my head to my other shoulder. Francis's hand feels so comfortable holding mine as he checks the severity of each cut. Spasms cause my arms to twitch as he comments, "None too harrowing nor possible to be infected so long as they are cleaned. Are you all right? It was rather grisly." Opening my eyelids when he began to speak, I am shaken by the importance in his pupils.

"Umm, yes. I best be getting home." His hand gradually releases mine, causing a chill to travel along my skin. Turning away and marching onward, I leave him standing on the path as I take the shortcut home. Thankfully, the sky has turned back to dreary, and a drizzle begins. Balmy unclouded skies would be unendurable at a time like this, for my beloved thoughts of the first day of school have been soiled to the point of no return.

A scorching rage toward Hasting—he is no "mister" and deserves no respect of mine, so I shall refer to him as that from now on—sizzles like a crackling bonfire. Nonetheless, I will abide by his preposterous rules to avoid another punishment and that's all! Why is it that every desire of mine is surreally dispirited when finally achieved? When the green-eyed monster was killed at last, my sister left. Traveling west has been characterized by grief and hardships relating. I finally have a horse of my own but I cannot ride him. The only real friend I have is Nannie, but I have upset her. And now school is tarnished by the calamity that has taken place! It wasn't supposed to be like this. Is God bestowing strength by sending trials to make me impenetrable? If so, where is the endpoint of the treacherous tunnel?

I sneak through the house, creeping up the stairs and only breathing a sigh of relief when I arrive at my room. I strip off the dress and begin to hastily sew up the more sizable tears on the sleeves. Mending has never been my strong suit, but it has graciously improved, nobody will notice unless up close. I tug the dress back over my head and button the back up with the help of a mirror. This morning I was in such a haste to get outside that I neglected the pile of dishes. I quickly snatch a rag and start tackling the chore, hoping that the heat in my cheeks has subsided. Less than ten minutes into washing, Mother walks into the kitchen.

"I didn't hear you come in." I crane my neck to see her pressing a hand to her chest with a smile. "How was school, dear?" she asks, tossing the freshly cut carrots into the pot on the stove. How can I respond without telling a falsehood? "My, it is turning into a real downpour out there." Hands on her hips, she peers out the window where the brumous clouds are relinquishing their floods. A pin sticks out of the knot at the base of her head, and she attempts to fix it without having to redo the entire hairstyle, buying me time to think.

Distraction—that is my key to survival. I grab onto that rope, pulling the conversation that direction with all my might. "Is it?" I ask with fake curiosity. "Just an hour ago the sun looked like it was going to come out." *Quick, say something else!* my brain yells, scrambling for something, anything. I hardly notice Mother next to me, placing the cutting board and knife next to the workload. Both my sleeves are rolled up. Comprehending her close proximity, I turn my arms over awkwardly so the undersides cannot be seen.

But her eyes travel down to my hands, forthwith finding a cut at the top of my wrist—just what I was striving to circumvent. "What is that?" When I try to pull away, she clutches my arm. Although her touch is gentle, it hits a nerve and I issue an involuntary cry, releasing the plate in my hand. It smashes to the floor, erupting into numerous shards. She does not pay any mind, instead taking both my palms in hers, gingerly turning both of my arms over. Her posture stiffens and muscles go rigid at the display. A heavy feeling weighs down my stomach as she fans her fingers out against her breastbone. "Who did this to you? Tell the truth!" Like a mother bear protecting her cub, she roars the words.

Pa, who was sitting in the parlor, comes barreling into the kitchen upon hearing her yell. I stand ossified in fear as his green eyes travel from the broken plate to my forming tears and quivering bottom lip, to Mother's exasperated expression, finally seeing the marks upon my pallid skin. A coldness hits him in the core.

"Mr. Hasting…the teacher. Today." Even though it's as low as a mouse squeak, both of my parents can hear it.

"Why didn't you say anything?" Mother's gasp inflicts intolerable pain on me as I break down sobbing, finding comfort in her arms as she holds me up.

Breathing in gasps, my sentences come as somewhat inaudible gibberish. "I…wanted to…you'd be cross. He's an insufferable man…to treat me so! Playing baseball for less than five minutes! And…Phoebe said horrid things…What else was I to do?"

Pounding steps make me dab feverishly at my eyes as Mother yells, "Albert?" A break in my sobs comes just in time for me to hear the front door slam.

Mother has me hold my arms over the bowl as she sponges each cut. Once the medicine stops stinging, she covers my skin in bandages from elbow to palm. Supper is dreary, the two of us sipping flavorless soup as our minds ask where Pa is.

⸏

Mornings are typically a comfort, the dawn of a new day bringing hope despite past mistakes. Today, however, is an exception, for the rage has not subsided in any of us. My throat feels like sandpaper as another swallow of corned hash scrapes down. Pa massages his bruised knuckles.

The radiating pique creates an elephant in the dining room. Part of me wants to vow to never return to that schoolhouse; the other half argues that by doing that Hasting would be granted the satisfaction I especially do not what him to receive, and my education—which is already lacking in some respects—would suffer.

Two kisses are placed on my forehead as I journey to school, numb of all feeling. Dark circles, puffed cheeks, and frizzled hair is not my preferred appearance. Nevertheless, my frowsy mien cannot be restored.

I purposefully arrive last. Even if I am a reticent person, I wish to snatch the temporary contentment from Hasting's face. A twitch of a grin comes as I do just that; walking in when everyone else has already been inspected, pledged their alliance to our country, uttered the prayer, and class has been called to order.

No tongue in the room can keep from wagging as I toss my coat on a peg, saunter up to my seat, manhandle my books defiantly onto my desk, and perch on the bench. Hasting's shiner does not escape my notice, for it has red hues and has caused his eyelid to swell shut. Pa's bruised knuckles suddenly make sense.

Nannie continues to sit on the aisle seat, and at dinner when the girls retreat to the corner, Roman calls for me to join the boys eating at their benches. Shrugging a shoulder, I parade to the other side of the room, take a place next to my friend, and talk as the lively introductions are passed around amongst the older boys.

Come to find out, there are four older boys, most of whom are seventeen or eighteen; one who has been held back is nineteen but he declares his withdrawal will come at the end of the winter term. There are three boys my age—Francis, Eugene, and John Taylor—and three younger boys. While this may seem to be a tidy sum, when compared to the population of girls (which is a substantial sixteen), it is low. Also, a drastic difference is their attitude toward one another. The girls are purposefully separated by grade. Each of the girls' groups have a different place in the classroom to which they isolate themselves, whereas the boys socialize together and go as one crowd outside or sit together on the benches whittling, chatting, and eating. Certainly not what I would have expected, and the dinner hour is already much more pleasant with them!

When Hasting calls everyone back to order, for nobody dared to play outside due to the frosty cold snap, laughter overtakes the room.

Searching for what seems to amuse everyone, I spot a calico bonnet on the boys' side of the room. The person wearing it turns around to high-five the boy behind him. My grimace is unavoidable, as is an eyeroll, as Francis taunts the teacher, asking if he'll get out the switch.

Phoebe's declaration that I am the reason Francis returned to school—suggesting some flirtation or even infatuation—angers me now more than ever because he is trying to stir up trouble in order to divert Hasting's attention away from me. He walks over to the front row on our side, sitting down and crossing his arms as he slouches, breaking several rules that have now been chalked up on the blackboard after yesterday. In a moment, I snatch the bonnet from his head, throwing it to the floor.

"Leave well enough alone." I whisper the deadly caution as someone whistles at our interaction. The incline in his head brings me no assurance, for the smugness does not disappear even after he travels back to his own seat.

A beat of my heart makes me want to smirk at his valiance, but I crush the feeling like a bug under my heel.

Chapter 16

I ABSOLVE THEE

NEARLY A WEEK HAS GONE went by, and I have yet to speak with Nannie. Just as I'm collecting my pail in the cloakroom, ready to join the boys on the benches for dinner like I have been doing, Phoebe prances over, her platinum blonde curls bouncing as she skips up to me.

I mumble under my breath, grabbing my dinner pail and turning around to find her vicious eyes boring into me. "Hello, Azalea." Humph! It would almost sound affable if it had not come from her mouth. She tucks her hands behind her back, rocking on her heels and blinking at me.

The eerie feeling that this is some ploy creeps over my shoulders. "Is there some subject you wish to address?"

"As a matter of fact, Nannie has sent me over to speak with you." A quick peer over her shoulder verifies the statement. Nannie immerses herself in a book after meeting my gaze. My brow raises for Phoebe to continue chattering as my arms cross defensively over my torso. "She says that she will not speak one word to you until an apology is made. And that it is rather rude of you to not concern her feelings."

Apologize! Her feelings! The audacity. What have I got to make amends for? What wrong have I caused? I doubt she is this upset because I got mad at her or slapped Phoebe. The latter certainly had it coming after speaking that way. Nannie does not even like Phoebe—unless she was lying—so why would she send her of all people to be the peacemaker?

"You tell Nannie that I have done no wrong, and if she continues this childish fight, then she's....she's..." I scramble to think of something. "Then she's being pertinacious and pig-headed! Quote me!"

Marching off to join the boys once more, I stop in the middle of the aisle, contemplating where to go. I notice Roman's eyes focused on me, unwavering.

"Azalea!" a polite voice hisses. It takes less than a second for me to find the source, and my eyes nearly bulge out of my skull at the sight of Daphne Dawson flickering her thin fingers at me to come join the group.

Daphne is the oldest girl in school; therefore, the other three eighth-grade girls look to her for leadership. From what I have observed, the older girls do not speak to nor invite the younger ones to sit with them under any circumstances—another reason why this public invitation catches me off-guard. Strawberry blonde hair frames her diamond face, which stares at me with imploring eyes as I settle on an empty chair next to her. Wind blows through the microscopic cracks in the floorboards, and with the stove a distance away, a cold creeps in.

"Hello." My goodness, I sound like a lost child! Clearing my throat and starting again, I say, "Azalea Stanton." The inclination of a head or quick handshake from each of the girls is greeting enough.

"Where are my manners?" Polite laughter travels around the small circle as Daphne speaks. "My younger sister, Pearl Dawson—she's supposed to be in the seventh grade, but her score was sublime on last exam, so Mr. Hasting moved her up—Elspeth Augustine, and Magnolia Taylor." Each girl smiles at the announcement of her name.

I shift my weight in the chair, waiting for instruction. A hushed word reaches my ear, and every head in Phoebe's group snaps down when my neck turns. I barely catch Phoebe's face contorted with rage, then notice Nannie's clenched jaw—they are jealous of me sitting with the older girls!

The green-eyed monster seems to be in the iris of every beholding girl in the room.

My neck turns back around at Daphne's honey-toned whisper next to my ear. "Do you happen to have any particle to share? We split our treats each lunch so everyone gets one: gingerbread, pan-dowdy, et cetera. You don't? No problem, you may offer my Saratoga chips. It's no bother. The girls will not mind if I 'forgot' to bring something this time." She slips a tied handkerchief into my hand as small portions of everyone's dinners are broken off and distributed. I untie the hankie to find two handfuls of thinly sliced potato chips, which are divided evenly amongst us. My gratitude cannot be put into words but is conveyed by an affable grin, returned with a wink from Daphne.

As the conversation builds, partially led by me, I quickly come to the conclusion that the atmosphere is appreciably more cordial than that of Phoebe's group. The hour ends much too soon. Our smiles fade and tears from laughing too hard are flicked away when Hasting returns to teaching. Shortly after the clock chimes four, everyone rushes for their coats as the first flurries sprinkle from the overcast sky. Hasting stops me just as I head for the door, pulling on my gloves—one of which has a coffee stain on it from this morning.

"Miss Stanton, you are in charge of filling the coal bucket." Wrapping a scarf around himself, he sternly exits the schoolhouse. So, this is his way of punishing me: by giving me chores?

My grimace is seen by the only other person in the building, who just so happened to escape my eye until now.

Francis tugs on his cap, giving me a tilted smile that strikes a nerve inside me as he says, "The coal is in the supply closet, around back." I snatch the empty bucket from beside the stove, which grows cold, marching toward the door without giving him so much as a side glance. "Let me get that for you." He holds the door open as I walk past him, our gazes frozen to each other until shattered by a purposeful cough.

Roman stands at the foot of the stairs, wrapped up in a fur coat, arms crossed as he stares with a curled lip. My blush is imminent. Francis's glowering look is well matched. My eyes flicker between the two of them and for a second a silly thought crosses my mind. *Surely, they are not…no! Well, maybe?*

"I'll walk you home. Where are your books?" Roman says. Never in all the time I have known him—albeit, I have not known him for long—has Roman been anything less than welcoming, but there is a new emotion shining through. Almost possessive of me. My goodness, is he jealous of me talking to Francis? It is all I can do to stop my mouth from falling wide open at the realization, which is verified by his sullen glare directed at the brown-haired boy holding the door open for me.

I am truly stunned for a moment, contemplating how to go about remedying this issue. In all honesty, Roman's stares gave me an inclination that he wants more than friendship. How do I go about this? "I…umm. Can I speak with you for a moment?" As soon as I ask it, both boys take a step forward. What a mess this is!

I walk down the slippery steps as I speak, taking Roman's offered hand at the end. "I will see you tomorrow, Francis." He gruffly nods, closes the door, then strides past us and around the corner. My gaze involuntarily follows him until he is out of sight. When I turn to face Roman, I notice his hand still touching mine and his eyes squinting at me as if trying to weed out some sort of feelings I may hold for Francis—which is completely absurd.

Briskly snatching my hand away, I begin my impromptu speech. "I need to make something clear to you; you have been a gracious friend over this past week or so. And I have enjoyed our time together…but I feel like *this* has to come to an end."

What I had expected to be a pained reaction turns into a joyful one, leaving me perplexed. "You said that perfectly! I feel the same way."

The resulting silence seems to mock me. I respond with a confused, "You do?" Before I know what is happening, he begins to lean in. His face is dangerously close to mine…

"What are you doing?" More than a shout but less than a yell. The plan in his head, which I guessed just in time, is struck down by the meta-phorical knife in my words. Running my fingers through my hair, I try to revise my plan. Straightforward it is then; this mirage must end. "That is not exactly what I meant by 'this!' How do I…" A deep inhale and breathy exhale clear my jumbled thoughts. I open my eyes to see Roman's face shining with hurt; why must he look at me like that?

I break the silence once more. "Listen—" He starts to murmur some words filled with love. "Please, just listen." I wait, holding up my palm until the only sound is the wind in my ears. "You are sweet, true-blue, and kind-hearted. I just cannot reciprocate—"

"You do not feel the same way for me as I do for you," he mumbles. My heart breaks, slowly at first, then all at once in those few words. My silence is enough confirmation. It is all I can do to keep from looking at him directly. Instead, I massage my temple delicately as if to cure a headache.

Giving up in a moment of weakness, I observe the gradual compre-hension as he bites his lip, frowns, then turns his back to me. His broad shoulders rise and fall multiple times before he gathers the courage to face me. By then, I have started to regret my previous actions that invoked the illusion that I could love him.

"I am sorry." Four syllables, three words that convey his pain, anguish, and apology. With that, he takes my gloved hand, kisses it gently whilst gazing into my green eyes as if searching for a chance, then shuffles away into the ebbing cold.

A voice screams internally, causing me to massage my temple once more—this time due to a real ache. *Is there something wrong with me? Am I incapable of love? Why must these pesky thoughts be so intrusive?* I stomp off, confusion clouding my judgement as I resume the task given to me by Hasting. A part of my heart holds a sense of annoyance that Roman, someone I thought I could have a long-term friendship with, is discontent with that and would rather not speak with me again because his feelings are not reciprocated.

Come to find out, the supply closet is a small addition on the back of the building. At first the door is jammed—causing me to unleash all my frustration out on it—but after a few tries it flies open, throwing me against the floor. The bucket clatters as the wind screeches, slamming the door closed as soon as I am out of the frame. I groan, rubbing my shoulder as a cough diverts my attention.

Nannie, brow raised and arms crossed, leans against the singular window in the compact space.

Stumbling to find my balance, I stand with the aid of a nearby chair. "What are you doing in here?" The space is a mere six feet long, four feet wide, and maybe eight feet high, home to dusty books and supplies piled up against the wall, a crate filled with coal, a broken desk and chair, and now two girls glaring evilly at one another.

"Francis told me you wanted to talk to me; I waited in here while he went to fetch you. You took an awfully long time." Her voice is characterized by irritation as the sentences fly at me like darts trying to pierce my skin. "The door was jammed, so I could not leave. Did you not hear me yelling for help?"

Wiping the dust off before settling on the chair, I listen carefully before responding. "Francis never—" Is that why he was opening the door and being friendly after I was rude? How could I have been so gullible? What right does he have to interfere in our problems? What an exasperating boy!

For now, there is a more pressing matter. All my anger melts like snow in the summer heat, replaced by throbbing pain. "Why have you ignored me this past week?"

Her dark eyes blink several times, scanning the space. "Originally, I was mad that you were infatuated with Roman."

What is going on today? First, Roman tries to profess his love for me, and now this? "*Me* and Roman? Not in the least; not for me, anyway." My scoff seems to confuse her further.

"I saw you hug him after you scored a homerun. Then I thought it was silly to be wrathful over such a thing. Phoebe said she would explain everything to you when I was telling the girls. She said you called me 'pertinacious and pig-headed,' then declared your love for him!" From the moment I attempt to speak up, she holds up a hand and speaks louder until reaching a yell that makes the Earth shake. "No, Azalea, I do not want to hear whatever lies you have to say!"

Now she's yelling at me! Exasperated, I return with the same volume, staring Nannie down. "Love? I said the former only because I was enraged. For that, I apologize, but everything else is a lie." Nannie squints her eyes at me before rolling them and turning her chin toward the window. I whip around and start to walk out but the door does not open when I turn the knob. Using all my force—and my desperation to get out of here—I try to yank the door open but once again nothing comes of it. "Phoebe spews countless falsehoods; you didn't think for a moment that my 'love' for Roman could be another one of them?" Phoebe has played us like a fiddle; for the life of me I cannot understand why. Is she threatened by my friendship with Nannie, is it out of pure boredom, or does she hold that much hate for me?

"I—" Wisps of hair frame her face as she searches for answers. Her crossed arms become less tense and her brow furrows. "Azalea, I am so sorry. I should have trusted you and talked to you sooner! You are my closest friend and I believed Phoebe's word. I am gullible and stubborn without reason. Ever since that day at the fair I could see that Roman was taken with you. For the longest time I hoped that he might look at me that way."

Using her sleeve, Nannie wipes her cheek while turning away from me. I'm the first person she has ever told this to; I can hear it in her scattered words and sense it in her hesitation. I suppose everyone has a hope chest filled with their utmost desires. There are the ones that have never been spoken aloud besides in prayer, the ones that sprout from insecurities, and the ones that have formed from envious thoughts. Although dreams may fade into memories—some forgotten over time and others labeled as childish wants—our human nature compels us to seek what is beyond our current possession.

We could talk until we're blue in the face, analyzing everything, but what would be the point? "Forgive and forget?" I ask with a shrug. She gives a solemn nod, holding out her pinky finger to seal the promise.

Believing we are stuck until morning, we quickly devise a plan to use our coats as blankets and call for help when day breaks. Hopefully Hasting will arrive early and hear our shouts.

Nonetheless, the faulty plan turns out to be unnecessary, for just as the sun begins setting, a pounding sound comes from beyond the door. Exchanging a curious glance, we back away to the corner as the pounding becomes louder until the previously steadfast door bursts open, Francis standing triumphantly on the other side.

Something about his foolhardy grin draws up every last drop of anger inside me. Stamping up to him, remaining mere inches from his exquisite face, my voice booms out before being caught by the wind and carried away. "HOW DARE YOU! You lock us in here for what? The audacity—"

The humor in his tone refuses to die despite my ear-splintering shouts. "It is jammed, Azalea. The door is bigger than the frame. Always has been." My eyes travel with his to the corner of the doorway, where he stands pointing up.

As I open my mouth to once again declare this was his plan all along, Nannie zips past the two of us, twirling in the frigid wind while exclaiming, "We are free, at last! I had best get home before my family starts to worry."

Nannie galivants off down the path. Francis insists on walking me home, and I am in no position to refuse, for he will just do so anyway. It is quiet up until we reach the lane leading to Aspenmoore, when I put the puzzle pieces together.

It begins to grow dark as we halt at the fence line. A cloud races by overhead as the flurries turn into unique snowflakes. "Tell me the truth. Did you plan for Nannie and I to become locked in the supply closet?"

He tucks his hands into his jacket pockets, his muscles tensing ever so slightly. "Yes. Azalea, do not be cross, but I felt compelled to! You two had to sort out your differences. Yes, I noticed your quarrel." How can he read me so well, better than anyone else? The growing anger in my cheeks drains as he unknowingly answers my inquiry. "I stayed behind for a while, then pretended to find you both. I had figured you would come to the realization that I had a hand in it, only I hoped—as I do now—that you would not yell at me."

My jaw remains unclenched as I sort through the facts. He stayed behind? So, he witnessed the exchange between Roman and me? And Francis knew about the fight with Nannie. He must have been observing me, and then put together this scheme. I do not know what to make of it all! Should I yell or thank him? He rocks on the heels of his cowboy boots, waiting for my decision, perhaps expecting the former over the latter. Instead, I hug him abruptly, finding comfort in his arms and superfluous benevolence.

⤺

Once I enter the house, I explain to my parents that Nannie and I were locked in the supply closet, leaving out the how and why. When it is all said and done, Mother settles by the fireplace with her embroidery, turning to me to ask, "Azalea? Who was that handsome boy who was walking alongside you?"

Fighting the blush that sizzles on my skin, I respond coolly, "Francis Southerland. Why ever do you ask?"

A smirk twitches at the corner of her rosy lips as she threads the needle and avoids eye contact. "Oh, nothing. I simply noticed the way he gazed at you…" My heart skips a beat at the words. I open my book, trying to hide the emotions playing across my face, and find myself unable to concentrate on the printed words.

Chapter 17

THE OCCUPANT OF MY THOUGHTS

"I STILL CANNOT FULLY COMPREHEND that Phoebe would do such a thing!" Nannie exclaims as she takes a cookie off the plate Mother brought up moments ago. Just outside the window, the fields are coated in blissful snow due to the latest blizzard that has swept through town, leaving school out of the question for the coming days. Despite her mother's worrying that she would catch her death, Nannie refused to let a few feet of snow separate us. Since we reconciled, Nannie and I have been spending more time together to make up for what we lost during our quarrel.

I reach over from my desk to grab a gingerbread cookie, fresh out of the oven, off the ornate plate. "She has held on to this vendetta against me since the moment I arrived. The reason why is beyond my knowledge," I mumble around the crumbs in my mouth, surely looking very undignified whilst doing so. We sit in the garret, which has been dubbed "Esteridge Haven" after I proclaimed it was not romantical enough to refer to such an intimate place as "the garret."

My eyes glance over to the thin postcard Mr. Huxley handed me yesterday, with the words:

Dearest Azalea,

Our condolences and prayers for the loss of your sister. How I wish I had the chance to meet her! My apologies for the delayed response.

Materials are scarce, and I wanted to send all the news at once instead of several short letters. My husband and I have adjusted nicely to the untamed Arizona territory. We have established a small hotel in the nearest town. There aren't many guests, but it is wonderful to call something our own, at last!

With love, Rose

My attention goes back to Nannie as she walks over to the window to stare out at the snowdrifts. "My mother says there are three reasons why someone would be envious of another person: they are threatened by you, they desire something you possess, or they hate themselves. That may apply to this situation with Phoebe." A pause follows as she twirls a lock around her finger. "Have you thought about entering the contest Mr. Hasting talked about?"

I flip through one of my textbooks looking for the last familiar lesson; with school and church postponed until after the snow stops, I can finally have time to catch up on learning. "The oratorical contest? I am not much of a writer or public speaker." *Where did we leave off in Macbeth?*

A chuckle diverts my attention like a bomb going off next to my ear. Nannie turns away from the window to look me in the eye. "Nonsense! I see you scribbling in that book every spare minute."

Lately, I have sat at the desk up here in Esteridge Haven to write in my journal. Most of the entries are letters to my beloved Florence. Despite the fact that she will never read them, it brings me comfort to find a secluded place to write them. It is as if I'm speaking to her once again. The leather-bound book lies nearby, almost intimidating in this moment. "That is quite different. Those are just scribbles of short fiction and thoughts. I could never assemble a campaign to win a competition based off oration!"

With much maternal instinct, she strolls over and kneels before me. "Dear, when it feels scary to jump—because the sharks circle or you have been bitten before—that is the moment you must let go of your control and fall. If not, then you never progress, forced to remain on the edge for the rest of your life. Step outside of your comfort zone, and something spectacular might happen. After all, fear and anxiety aren't things we inherit—they are things we learn."

"When did you become so wise?"

A charming grin responds. "It comes with the territory of being friends with Azalea Stanton."

Whilst The Maidens are in the parlor engaging in a quilting bee, chatting about stitches and the blue ribbon Florence's quilt won at the harvest festival, I am tucked away in Esteridge Haven trying to scratch out something to present for the contest. The rules are simple: each school declares a winner, their piece moves on to the county level, and if awarded first place there, then it progresses to the final state level.

The troublesome part is creating a worthy piece. There must be fifty stories I have authored in my lifetime, none of which I had any intent to share with anyone else because they were for my personal enjoyment. When I write, my thoughts are well engaged. My thinking is less direct and reaches further into my knowledge—uncovering things that I had no idea I knew. There is also a certain state of mind in which one must be to write, and if you do not obtain it then there is no point, for they will just be words on a page instead of a story. Your heart aches purely with inspiration to the point where you can feel it; only a handful of people will ever come to understand the attachment between a writer and their creation. The elocution portion is not a challenge; each Friday afternoon we have a spelldown followed by the recitation of a poem, both of which take place before the entirety of the class.

The true meaning of these crumbled up, inked-stained pages is the fact that the theme for the contest, "Imagine a world with or without boundaries," feels like a lock whose skeleton key has been mislaid.

Everyone is ecstatic in the days leading up to Christmas Eve. After numerous failed drafts and unceasing renditions, a final speech was produced. Hasting has required everyone who is participating to arrive at the schoolhouse early to prepare for the contest. Nearly every family in Winfield will pile into sleighs and travel through the dust of snow fluttering down to witness a select few pupil's speeches.

A snowflake lands on my palm delicately. Less than a second later, it succumbs to the heat of my skin, resulting in a droplet that trails down my arm. "Looks like it will be a white Christmas." The words roll off my tongue as I stare upward to the hazy clouds. My breath clouds in the frosty air as I tug on my white cotton wrist glove, an early present from Pa and Mother, taking in the joyfulness of the day despite the nipping of Jack Frost. "If only we weren't preened and equipped in our Sunday Best; we could ride toboggans tied to sled runners like the children do in town!"

"Hmm. Well, wearing a dress has never stopped you from doing something before."

"You know me too well! If my heart were set on it, I would; notwithstanding, I possess no toboggan nor sled to try the experiment. Dear me, I'm so timorous. Do catch me if I faint off the platform! About a month ago, I could barely write this speech, but one afternoon while I was tucked away in my cozy haven, mulling over the prompt lead to a burst of words that when pieced together created the perfect response. I was terribly afraid that changing my speech at the last minute would be my undoing, but I believe this variation outweighs them all!"

Upon arrival at the schoolhouse, I quickly locate my seat amongst the fray and find a posy of red tulips before me. Turning to the nearest bystander, which happens to be Ophelia, I ask, "Ophelia, did you see who put these on my desk?"

Staring up at the ceiling, noiselessly mouthing the words of her speech, which is written on a paper before her, she loses focus when addressed. "Indeed, I did. But I vowed not to speak a word of his identity." Her eyes sparkle, the skin underneath them wrinkling from her lifted cheeks, and a smile brims at the corners of her lips.

Who would gift me a flower, on Christmas Eve no less, whose meaning is based on true love and devotion? Roman has remained cordial and at a distance for some time. Surely, he wouldn't…Could there be a secret admirer I am unaware of? I laugh internally at the thought and dismiss it, although it remains in a corner of my head, waiting to be brought about again. "May I inquire why Phoebe calls you 'Fifi?'"

"Well, that's simple." Perhaps terrified I will pester her with questions until she cracks, her shoulders ease as she faces me, radiating a confident energy one as nervous as I would be jealous of. "Phoebe assigned us nicknames. Mine is Fifi, Henrietta is Etta, Wilhelmina is Wila, and Catalina is Nina."

"And you like that, being called Fifi?" A shrug is her only response. "Then why condone it?"

"I suppose I never thought there was another option. Sitting with the lower grade is mortification. The seventh-grade girls normally spend dinner hour reading, which makes conversation fall short, and the older girls won't even speak to us. That's another reason Phoebe was so furious when you were invited into their group! Daphne and Pearl don't even address Etta and Nina in school, even though they are all sisters! You know, I really admire you, Azalea. You've got a good deal of ideas and use all those fancy words when you speak."

Who knew the timid girl who never says more than two sentences at a time would have so much inside her just waiting to be released? Mind boggling to say the least. I guess you cannot judge a book by its cover! Before I can utter a word of gratitude, Hasting instructs us to move so the benches can be rearranged.

An hour later, the clamorous sound of an overabundance of voices fills every inch of the room. Hasting strung up a floor-to-ceiling curtain where his desk once was so the remaining presenters can wait their turn behind it. John gave a short squib that made the audience cachinnate, but his perplexed expression led me to believe that was not his intention.

I peer over Phoebe's shoulder to see Francis walk through the curtain and onto the platform with aplomb. The judges—most of whom I recall seeing in church—sit on the front two benches, scribbling on scorecards. One in particular, Mrs. Alder, can only be described as a resolute woman who is not easily impressed.

Francis gives a canorous speech to the crowd, his voice reaching every attentive ear in the room. Not once did he divagate from the theme or falter in his presentation. In the end, the thunderous applause all but crowns him the winner, for it was a meritorious speech.

Phoebe shoots a poisonous glare at me. The reason as to why is soon revealed. She begins practicing her recitation, her inaudible mumbling soon changing to clear words. "My imagination is a cruel and wonderful place." It takes less than a second for me to realize the familiarity, for they are the exact same words I had memorized until a week ago. My face falls flat as she wears a coy grin like the Cheshire Cat.

With the audience still reeling over Francis's brilliance, I brisky pull her out of line and to the side of the curtain. Eyes gleaming like red coals, I whisper with venom, "Where did you get my speech?"

"You really should not leave important papers on your desk for all to see…and use." Oh, if only I could slap her again! What a low-down dirty trick! "What will the judges think when you go on—after me, mind you—saying the same words as the predecessor?" A momentary pause the she continues reciting from memory. "A world without boundaries. Could it be a dream or does it exist here in some medium?" She easily notices the sudden shift in my expression; the corner of her mouth twitches in question at it. She doesn't know I switched my speech. Even though my previous draft—the one she is about to perform—is well-thought and direct, it does not amount to much in terms of leaving a lasting effect, thus the need for the change. For once I am grateful for vacillating; it has finally come to my favor!

"You stole my speech, and everyone will know it…" A mulish expression crosses her face seemingly about to retort my accusation, hesitating at the forth coming threat that is on the tip of my tongue. Would marching on the stage this very moment, claiming that Phoebe stole the preliminary version of my speech, cause too much of a fuss? Would it even be believable? Mother, Pa, and Nannie witnessed me practicing those very words; they could attest to the fact that it belongs to me. Should I demand she confess to purloining it when the contest is over?

My green eyes gaze between the curtains, where there is a sliver of space for one to look past the stage and to the audience. Mother, gloves off, brushes a wisp of hair out of her eyes and folds her arm around Pa's. Lately, we have grown a great deal closer. The cause of the magnetic pull could be attributed to a number of reasons.

I think that my being jealous of Florence and having every speck of attention delivered to her clouded my judgment. But Mother has only ever had her daughters' best interests at heart. Since we were young children, she has aimed to protect us from every obstacle by preparing us ahead of time. The insistent desire for Florence to find a husband was to save her from challenges that many unmarried women face in today's world and to save our own family from poverty. From the dawn of time, I was envious of my older sister—her beauty, talent, personality, and a thousand other particulars—but now, I have become my mother's daughter. Each spring a tree sheds its seeds, waiting for saplings to sprout like a mother bird watches its children disperse into the world; similar to those scenarios, I am the apple that does not fall far from the tree.

Would Mother let the offender walk free? No, she would test their conscience and deliver the moral of the story; therefore, no matter how much I want to follow my own way, the pragmatic route demands to be taken.

"I will not breathe a word of it," I say. Properly astounded, her eyelids blink several times before catching a glimmer of hope. "Nevertheless, I hope you have not abandoned the moral compass that God gave you and that it may point you in the right direction. Thou cannot bite then wish to not be bitten."

The ensuing silence is incongruous with the clamor of everyone behind the curtain and the general hum of the audience conversing to fill the void. Could this be the olive branch to a futile feud? The horizontal wrinkles disappear from Phoebe's forehead. She attempts to conceal a smirk by pressing her lips down, purposely failing in her efforts to hide it as if trying to aggravate me further. My blood has only just stopped simmering, and here she goes striking the match yet again! With a toss of her locks, she marches onto stage, delivering an articulation that has lost some of its vigor but does not sound as half-hearted as I had imagined it would if she had felt guilty. Turning the other cheek has only resulted in that one getting struck too. So much for taking the high road…

In the midst of Phoebe's scheming, I completely forgot the fact that I am to speak after her. The butterflies in my stomach turn to bees, stinging profusely as I shakingly inhale. The time I have been waiting for is approaching like a runaway train, and all I wish to do is dash in the other direction! A wave of panic sweeps over me, rattling my bones. *Is that lump in my throat nerves or vomit?*

Kerosene lamps light the room to a dim hue of glowing gold, like a ceaseless sunset through the windows. My eyes scan the words on the page, trying to make sense of what is written. *Imagination…exiled to a world…My goodness, why is my handwriting so illegible in this moment?* A provisional lull settles as I walk through the parting middle of the drapes. Tucking a lock of hair behind my ear, I take one last glance at the wrinkled paper. Slashes are patterned along the page, crossing out the words I decided not to use. A pound in my chest brings the realization that I had stopped inhaling for a few moments. *Is this what a heart attack feels like? No, you are being overdramatic! Say something, the judges are watching!*

The internal conversation does not motivate me as much as I hoped it would. Nannie holds two thumbs up from where she sits next to my parents, both of whom beam. For the first time in a while, Mother has styled her hair with ringlet curls. At times like this she embodies the image of an older, grown-up Florence. Sometimes I look back on life in Lorretta; when compared to Winfield, it all feels surreal and intangible. How could I have imagined a year ago that this is what God had in store for us? How could I have imagined that the end of one story would bring the inception of another?

Fear is a strange thing; it is overwhelming and petrifying in the beginning, and once conquered, it vanishes, leaving behind a ghostly feeling. It also comes at the queerest of times! The fog that previously muddled my thoughts has been blown away by powerful lungs, bidding its farewell and leaving a void in its wake.

What now? A million things can happen before a minute ticks by. While it might seem like I have been standing on this platform for a century, in reality, barely thirty seconds of time have passed.

A trickling feeling tickles down my spine. Here it goes…

"My imagination is a cruel and wonderful place." The dramatic pause is just how I envisioned it: *enrapturing*. My gaze travels amongst the crowd, grabbing hold of their attention as if the sentence was screamed in their faces. One pair of gray eyes, barely visible in the darkness, gleam as if a fire's gentle glow shines through them. *Why is Francis gazing at me like that?* "It whisks me to beautiful places I have only ever read about in books—then reminds me that I shall never experience adventures as wild as those. They are not just plain words on a page, but worlds that have been created and imagined. Regardless of the jubilation reading brings, the greatest heartache lies in the fact that I can never truly reach these places nor bear witness to these adventures. I will never meet the characters who are bound in prose and sheets of paper. Here I remain bound, exiled to a world which *we* cannot escape. The only thing we can do is dream of different places.

"There is a barrier between you and me; the 'and' is not the only thing that separates those words. A world without limitations; there would be no difference between me and you, and we would coexist under the shared label of human. Life and death would not separate us, and I would have her back. I suppose we stay within these invisible lines that our minds have created because what lies beyond—ourselves, our mind, and life itself—puts us in a paralyzing fear. A comfort zone is a lovely place, but nothing really grows there. I miss my daisy-girl. She brought light to a world of darkness, but now she is just out of reach. After all, the only thing more powerful than life is death. If I had it my way, there would be no veil between us, and our worlds would be the same." Equanimity flourishes with every second that ticks by. Hand gestures, a dramatic pause, eye contact; in a grand total of five minutes, I run through my edifying speech and use a portion of the public speaking tactics we learned in class.

A terrifying second passes where everyone is paralyzed; chests stop heaving air, muscles become tense and rigid, even the flames in the lamps stop dancing as if suddenly aware they are inanimate objects. The chilly haze settles like fog, bringing trickling goosebumps to the spines that are arched from sitting on the edge of their chairs.

Like a clap of thunder, the applause ignites. An impetuous sound, somewhat familiar yet frightening, with deafening hollers and penetrating whistles. Incapacitated and flabbergasted, I stand erect before the crowd, which has progressed to a standing ovation. My mind puzzles at the sight of Mrs. Alder's rosy cheeks being kissed by the light and the small smile on her face as she jots down notes.

The first step off the platform nearly takes me out; however, a hand materializes before me, steadying every imbalance. I relinquish my need for control and loop my arm through Francis's, mindlessly following him to a nearby bench. Nannie's dark hair blends with the shadows toward the back of the room, but I find her smirk directed at me. A warm feeling sizzles in my cheeks as I bite down an imminent grin.

Hardly moving a muscle, I peek over to Francis as he settles down next to me, snatching my gaze away when it meets his. Instead, I direct my attention to Daphne as she takes her place on the platform.

The speeches begin to fade into the background, jumbled up as if nothing more than an echo down a winding tunnel. Francis beams and claps loudly at the end of each presentation, plucking my heartstrings like guitar cords.

The gentle hum of conversation strikes as the judges deliberate to compare scores. I can barely breathe as Mrs. Alder steps forward, rotating with flamboyance and fanning herself with a white card until her presence is observed and a hush falls.

A soundless room is more intimidating than an obstreperous one. Fully aware that my hand is intertwined with Francis's, I chew my bottom lip apprehensively. "And the runner-up is…Francis Southerland with 'Boundless Subconscious.'" A round of applause shakes the room. *Francis got second place? Whose speech could have possibly beat him?* "The winner of the Third Annual Winfield Oratorical Contest is…" Holding up the card and squinting as if it's hard to read, she hesitantly announces, "Azalea Bree Stanton with 'Earthly Ties.'"

I anticipated the hypothetical occurrence that if a miracle happened and I won, then I would be jumping for joy. But here I sit, awestruck and obtunded as cheers fill every available inch of the room. Unsure of whether to laugh or cry or both, I shakingly accept the medal.

The loudest of them all are Pa and Mother, a duo in seventh heaven. How I wish this moment could be captured, so that one day in the future I may look back on it with fondness!

As if sent down to Earth by God himself, Mr. Huxley lifts a handheld Kodak camera—I recognize it from the mercantile catalog—to eye level and takes a photograph of Mrs. Alder shaking my hand as I hold up the medal placed around my neck. Is this a dream? It must be, for something as immaculate as this could only happen in my subconscious!

Chapter 18

EVERYTHING I'VE WISHED FOR

THE WORLD IS PEACEFUL as children awaken and dash down the stairs to the foots of fir trees decked with popcorn and cranberry garlands. Birds nestle in the nooks of boughs, deer venture out into the stillness, and bears hibernate in cozy dens. The only things disturbing the tranquility are the jingle of sleighbells and our animated laughter.

I clutch the fur blanket to keep it from slipping away as my eyes water from the wind. Eugene and Nannie sit opposite of Francis and me, and Mr. Fraser drives the horses up and down the snow-coated roads at our request.

The cutter we're riding in is what I picture Father Christmas's looking like—minus the bag of goodies and reindeer. Curved runners, a driver's box at the front, two loveseats facing each other so its occupants may chat without having to talk over their shoulders, and a rounded back.

"I never got to congratulate you on your win! You are a literary luminary," Francis calls above Nannie's laugh and the continuous jingle. The four of us wave at passersby heading to the Christmas church service. Every soul that dares to venture out in such frigid temperatures is bundled up in thick coats, knitted mittens, and laced-up boots that leave firm prints in the snow.

"Thank you! Your piece was a surefire winner, everybody thought so!" I clench my teeth at the rigid conversation. Since last night, I am unaware of how to converse with him. His zealous clap followed me to the platform and echoed around the room long after the others had quieted. Even with the swarm of people crowding around me, offering their sentiments on my speech, my gaze did not waver from the boy standing across the room sending a coy grin my way. The ardent stare breezed into my dreams, causing a queer emotion when I awoke this morning. It is as if he makes me nervous for some unbeknown reason...

He clutches his black Stetson, a completely nonsensical choice of headwear, to keep it from taking flight. "What is next for Winfield's authoress?" The title makes me grin sheepishly, even though it has a rather nice ring to it. I am at a loss for words—how often does that happen?

Nannie leans forward, almost falling off her cushioned seat while filling the void in the discussion. "I propose that she submit a handful of stories to various magazines. They pay handsomely—you could have a regular stipend once a few are published and afford college in no time!"

Nodding thoughtfully, Francis declares it a brilliant idea, making Nannie smile broadly and sit back with satisfaction. "College?" he asks with a playfully raised brow. Whether it be the icy wind or the battling of a blush, I feel my cheeks turn rosy.

"One of my many aspirations. That is, if I can find one out here on the plains that accepts women." I fold my hands inside my mittens to keep frostbite at bay, focusing on the landscape as I speak to avoid look-ing at him. "Perhaps, one day, I might author a novel. Every book has an impact on your life—how you act, your view of the world—and makes you realize who you truly are. And if it does not, then did you truly read it? I simply adore the fantasy that my hypothetical novel may achieve that for a stranger I have never had the pleasure of meeting."

I pick at the dirt under my fingernails. How odd that Francis has that effect on people, making them admit their deepest aspirations, ones that might not have been discovered by the beholder, with a simple imploring look. He does have a certain ambience to him that would make one trust him before being properly introduced.

"And what of your ambitions?" My voice is sweet like molasses as the question is delivered with a "pray-tell" glance. His gray eyes remind me of the dewy fog over a meadow on a chilly March morning—mysterious as if hiding the gateway to numerous secrets, while simultaneously impossible to ignore and not appreciate their natural beauty.

As if it is confidential information, he leans forward to say in a hushed tone, "I believe both higher education and a view of God's creation are the key to unlocking success. I pray both are in store for me. And one day, a girl who would love me wholeheartedly."

To be frank, I can hardly focus on what he is saying due to his close proximity. Is my heart even beating right now, or has it ceased entirely? Although, I did catch the last sentence and give a gradual nod while grinning. Nannie's eyes flicker between the two of us, making me blush deeper and wave away the observation that is brimming at her lips. Francis catches sight of the little interaction, exchanging a knowing look with me, then starting up a conversation with Eugene about horses.

As their conversation progresses, my friend and I lean forward synchronously. She takes a hand out of her mitten and brushes a loose strand under the hood of her burgundy cape. "Dear, if you do not mind me saying, you seem a tad shy."

The fur from the collar of my coat tickles my face. "I do not mind your observation, for it is true." A quick peek confirms that the conversation with Eugene has Francis's full assiduity. "Words have left me completely! About all I can muster is a response that attributes temporary entertainment! My usual voluble personality has utterly vanished." Words said in whispers are those most heartfelt. It is as if God made that tone of voice to expedite the process of letting your heart be opened and your emotions flow out.

She reaches over and grasps my hand. Even through my gloves I can feel the heat of her skin from the warm ceramic bottle that she holds to keep from freezing. The morning sun scorches a sparkle into her brown eyes, glimmering with slyness as she whispers, "Luckily, I have the remedy to fix the awkwardness." Before I can raise a brow, my friend turns with an air of confidence and exclaims loudly as if the angels in heaven should be invited to chat, "Francis, did Azalea ever tell you about her mustang? Oh, he is handsome, indeed! You break foals, isn't that right? If I recall correctly, it only took a few months for you to train that racehorse from the harvest festival. Well, maybe you could aid Azalea with Storm."

My blood freezes as if we have just entered the arctic. A bashful grin comes gradually to Francis's face as he looks to me for confirmation. I stare blankly, aware of how many pairs of eyes await my answer.

"Yes." My voice cracks, but I quickly talk over the moment. "Yes, that would be of great help! Storm is quite fickle at times. I daresay we are one and the same," I say as if admitting a secret. Eugene and Nannie chuckle as the corner of Francis's mouth twitches at the joke.

The sound of sled runners slicing through the snow fills the pause between us. My nails pierce into the palm of my hand as each second endured in quietude mounts tension onto my shoulders, which are already weighed down by the heavily insulated coat.

"It would be a pleasure to help with the venture."

That is all? He turns back to Nannie's brother, picking up where they left off. My gaze follows him, too stunned to think of a response to such a vague answer. I whip back to face my friend, as the idea was hers—which I am most grateful for, although it did not go as planned. Her jaw is unhinged as she shrugs her shoulder with a pitying look as if to say, *Sorry I could not be of more help.*

"Maybe some afternoon this spring, if that is convenient for you?" I ask.

"Very well." He says amicably over his shoulder. What just happened? One moment I am the object of his interest, then the next he gives a short reply. It is as if we have swapped roles; I am now the chatty character, and he is the shy one! Boys are mysterious creatures, all right…

Less than a month later, I am dashing across a barren field half past tea-time, waving an opened letter in my hand. The snowdrifts have frozen over, making a delicious crunching sound each time my heels step down. However, it is not as enjoyable when my heel catches in a hole and almost sends me tumbling down the slope, a whirl of wind swirling my loose hair around my face and trying to distract me from the task.

"Unhand me at once!" I yell, tugging my boot out of the hole. "That is more like it. I see you have a sense of humor, Jack Frost."

Once I reach the house, my knock is muffled by the sound of laughter from within the walls. The small prints leading up to the door glow against the dark wood porch that has been swept of all snow. A wreath on the door decked in holly berries and a gorgeous red bow, as well as skinny candles in each window, give the impression that the holidays—despite what the calendar says—have yet to end. Footsteps from within lightly thud up to the door, swinging it wide open without hesitation. Nannie's hair is braided and pinned up into a crown around the circumference of her head, her skin that once was tan has now begun to fade back to pale. Her naturally curled black lashes bat a hello.

"Azalea, dear! Come in this moment, before the frost bites! We were beginning to fret that you were not attending the party. We would be lost without our guest of honor," her sweet voice sings out, ushering me into the entryway of the spacious home, then gesturing to the row of Adelaide boots where I can set mine. A flood of water is pooled around the shoes from the melted snow. Hanging my coat on the hook, I follow her down the hall, past the wide staircase, and into the parlor twice the size of the one at Aspenmoore.

I have come to realize that each room I have encountered in Nannie's house is papered in expensive and ornate wallpaper. The first time I saw her room, I asked about the paper depicting a gallant scene of the countryside characterized by green fields like rolling waves, trees swaying in the wind, and puffy white clouds in a dawning sky. She responded, "My mother is a collector of all things British: decoration, furnishings, manners, customs, cuisine—the list is endless!" Then she went on to explain their twilight ritual of washing her locks with New England rum, brushing for seven minutes by the clock, applying oil, then braiding it for the night.

The parlor is no exception; after all, the overabundance of decoration surprises any guest that enters the room. A tête-à-tête chair, circular velvet sofa, and a wingback chair sit together near the crackling hearth. The walls are covered in Currier and Ives print wallpaper portraying a scene of a city viewed from the air—with a snaking river cutting it in half, steamers releasing puffs of smoke as they go either way, pointed roofs and towering church steeples, and rural land in the distance. An assortment of paintings are hung up around the rectangle-shaped room, a grandfather clock ticks in the corner, windows with heavy drapes sit along the front side of the house, and a table matched with chairs holds trays of food, all making the room rather sumptuous.

Whether by the splendor of home accessories in the room or the preparation for a party, my jaw opens with a pop, and I am left speechless as girls rush to me. This morning, I felt rather silly to be wearing my go-to-meeting clothes, considering my birthday is tomorrow and not today, but seeing my friends adorned in their gowns makes a smile brim and my heart swell.

Ever since the older girls first invited me to sit with them, the sixth-grade girls have been friendlier, and in the time since the oratorical contest

I have had the pleasure of getting to know them better. Henrietta and Matilda have remained loyal to Phoebe, disgracing my "modern" ways and ideas in mostly nonverbal ways. Nonetheless, in a diplomatic act I have extended the olive branch by inviting them to the party. A good deal of that came from Mother forbidding me to exclude them, for they would tell their mothers and it would cause a ruckus among The Maidens. Ophelia, Wilhelmina, and Catalina have fully welcomed me and even abandoned the nicknames Phoebe assigned them, which caused the latter to stomp off at dinner hour one day in a furious rage.

Due to the former dictatorship, I had to explain to them that I am by no means a leader and wish for a new self-government, and everyone involved in the matter agreed to the proposed. Perhaps in Phoebe's mind I staged a coup d'état, as she seems disgruntled lately. Pa always says that politics are a messy business when they go beyond giving your opinion. Mother takes the traditional approach that only men should have input on the subject.

An arm loops through mine, bringing me back to the cozy parlor. "Mother is having Anneta make us New England fare for supper!" Anneta, whom I have only met once—and in that time she did not say a word—is the Frasers' maid. "In the meantime, we have your favorites: chocolate squares, bite-sized ham and cheese sandwiches, candied fruits, and more! Catalina, do you mind passing the tray of macaroons? Thank you! Azalea, you must try one. They are unlike anything I have ever tasted!" As she speaks, we gradually travel to the table and take the two empty seats next to each other. All the while, the paper fastened to my palm is the elephant in the room.

Finally, when I can no longer stand the anticipation, I stand and declare, "Very well, but first I must announce…it has happened!"

Nannie slams her hand down on the table in utter shock, making poor Anneta jump and drop the simmering teapot she was carrying into the room. The stain near the middle of the carpet is evidently spreading as she rushes to collect the shattered porcelain then tasks a hankie with mopping up the mess.

Nannie's squeal of delight remains unmet as the others' eyes flicker between us for some indication. Phoebe's eyes, however, sear into my soul. Raising the paper above the tablecloth for all to see, I proclaim, "The editor of *Magazine of Verse* wrote me a letter saying my poem has been accepted for publication!" I pass the article to my eager friend as numerous pairs of eyes follow, each holding a different emotion.

With the clearing of her throat, straightening of posture, and a shift to the edge of her chair, she begins, "It reads: 'Dear Azalea Bree Stanton, we write to inform you that the submitted poem titled 'The Sum of My Subconscious' has been chosen for publication in *Magazine of Verse's* spring edition. The edition will be mailed to you once published. Included is your copy of the poem and your payment of one dollar. We hope to see more of your work in the future. From, The Editor.' May I?" With a nod, she reads the words of my creation for all to hear.

"Somewhere, there are honeydew meadows with blue forget-me-nots.
They are plucked by soft fingers,
Pressed between the pages to make their beauty last.
What is that sweet smell, you may ask?
It is the smell of green meadows and wild grass.
It is the scent that surrounds my childhood.
Light cascading from the canopies, birds swoop past as if I am nothing more
than a figment of my own imagination.
The tapping of rain on the windowsill has not vanished from my memory, but the nature of the world echoes my name.
My life is the compendium of it all.
When taken from it, I am nothing but a withering flower."

As Nannie reads, I observe each expression that plays out along the round table. Phoebe, as I expected, looks like she has eaten raw lemons and is twisting her napkin menacingly. Catalina appears to be tasting every single morsel of sustenance without actually taking a bite. There she goes, sticking her finger in the side of the cake and licking whipped cream off it—oh, how Mother would scold me if I ever did such an unladylike thing! Ophelia is the only one, apart from Nannie, who is interested. Wilhelmina and Henrietta—Matilda has a head cold, so she was unable to attend—have folded their napkins into different shapes, failing tremendously whilst calling them "swans." Nonetheless, I applaud them.

My kindred spirit—Nannie—is truly my twin who has been lost in time, for she notices the lack of attentiveness promptly. Her wandering eyes look to me for confirmation. The luster of my excitement has dimmed like a dying flame.

She returns the letter to me, and I fold and tuck it into my dress pocket. Addressing it is not preferable, but ignoring the fact that none of my "friends" care is far too painful. Before I can make a decision, the flow of conversation picks back up.

"Did you notice those shabby dresses that Elspeth Augustine has started to wear? I daresay the waists have been let out so far on the rest of them that they won't fit any longer!" Phoebe comments as she takes a bite of a macaroon to hide her devious smile.

Honestly, the way she speaks is ghastly! From what I have heard, Mrs. Peterson is no better, practically the town gossip—reminding me a great deal of Miss Hackenberry, one of the ladies we met in Brockschmidt. A great many of the Winfield mothers are so starved for gossip in a town of this size that they will search for a speck of scandal on an otherwise immaculate being.

Back at Christmas, I gave Phoebe the chance to come clean, thinking that allowing her the opportunity to behave conscionably was the proper thing to do. However, I was proved wrong, as she never spoke a word about the speech that she 'napped from my desk. Not a soul knows besides the two of us. In a way, I feel tarnished, as if I helped her cheat. But now that so much time has passed, who would believe me? It is not like it matters a great deal anyway— Phoebe was fuming when I won.

"Elspeth is perfectly lovely; you would know that had you ever been invited to sit with the eighth-grade girls." While I did not intend to be spiteful, my words certainly sound that way. If only there were not an audience of five others in the room to bear witness to the words escaping my mouth, as the reactions are far worse than if it were just the two of us! If only God made a way for humans to reach out and pluck said words from the air; that skill would be a great help in this time of need!

The halcyon days between Phoebe and me have long since vanished. She tosses her locks, putting on airs about how when she is that age her waist will be no more than twenty-three inches around and anything more is disgraceful.

Ophelia, most times the conciliator in soothing Phoebe's and my arguments, suggests a game of Blind Man's Bluff. A chorus sounds, praising the idea as each girl jumps up from the table.

The previous conversation vanishes immediately from everyone's minds except mine. The fact of the matter is Phoebe and I are magnets that repel each other, two utterly different characters when concerning morals and general personalities, interests, and etiquette. A resolution will have to come someday—the sooner the better—but for now I must brush it away, for nothing would be more impertinent than wasting the effort put into the party by not enjoying it.

Chapter 19

WHERE THERE'S LOVE, THERE IS PAIN

Time. It is what we crave, what we wish we could reverse, and what we feel we have control over when, in fact, humankind bends at the face of a clock. How could I have known the metaphorical clock was coming to a stop? How could I have known on that November morning of 1893 when I climbed up on the roof that Florence would only be with us for one more Christmas, New Year, and birthday?

These holidays feel unusual without her, memories of last year resurfacing on days such as this. It is only when I look back on memories with the fondness of yesterday and that I wonder if time is even real. The very thoughts running through my mind can be recalled in a heartbeat, but with the recollection comes the fact of how many years it has been since then. Am I a person frozen in time whilst the world passes me by? Is the world spinning so fast that we have no hope of catching up with it?

Fifteen years old, how strange…At midnight on January twenty-ninth, I tip-toe down the stairs, carefully avoiding the creaky ones that would wake my parents. As I do most every birthday, I strike a match, think of a wish, and blow out the match at the exact minute of my birth, 12:27.

Happy birthday, Azalea, Florence's honey-dew voice breathes into my ear—or at least I imagine it does—as a puff of smoke trails into the air. There is something melancholy in my manner as I travel back up the steps and climb into bed. I turn my cheek over to the other side of the pillow, trying to find sleep, and my skin touches the spot where tears have fallen.

〜

"It does not feel as though I am older," my voice calls out over the crunch of our footsteps as Nannie and I walk arm-in-arm. After Mother and Pa presented me with a dazzling cake, which we ate alongside an array of pancakes for breakfast, Nannie raced over so that we could partake in a birthday stroll.

The sunlight sparkles along the mounds of snow that are piled along the hills. "I suppose the new title takes some getting used to each year," Nannie remarks.

A sudden jolt at my side and tug on my arm nearly send me backwards. "Dear heavens, what was that for?" I exclaim. Nannie tightens her elbow around mine as her face explodes with excitement. Like me, my friend has a touch for the dramatics.

The flash of a dimpled smile perplexes me. Before I can determine what could have possibly stolen her attention so viciously, she remarks, "Perhaps I should travel over to Aspenmoore later on, as you are preoccupied as of now." Now it is my turn to stare in astonishment.

"Preoccupied? Whatever are you saying?" My inquiries are met with a wave and a coy grin as she traipses off through the trees to our right. "Wait, dear! Where are you going?" My voice wraps around the trees that have snow covering one side of their trunks.

The only reply is an echoed, "You will thank me later!" Her words invoke even more probing questions rather than delivering me an answer as to her hasty departure.

A throb of pain echoes in my chest as I am left utterly alone on a chilly winter morning, forced to walk home in unwanted placidity. A huff escapes my lips as I tuck my mittened hands into the pockets of my coat.

"Azalea!"

I tense at the voice that yells my name as wind sweeps over the blanket of white. I feel the blood draining from my cheeks. Whipping around, I spot a tall boy walking with his shoulders tucked in as if the cold has gotten to him. There is that Stetson hat again. I wonder if there is some sentimental attachment, considering he can always be found wearing it. Nannie once mentioned that Mr. Southerland passed away two years ago; perhaps it is a memento from his father.

"Francis?" Suddenly Nannie's rush to get home makes perfect sense. I hurriedly smooth my hair, which the wind has taken the liberty of undoing. Taking the exclamation of his name as an invitation, Francis hastens his pace before halting in front of me.

Those sensitive eyes look into my soul, reading my every emotion in a way that makes me squirm. Similar to the prowling clouds of a thunderstorm, his eyes seem to hold a thousand thoughts that turn dangerous if not expressed. "How do you do?" His voice cracks from the bitter cold that travels on the occasional gust.

"Very well," I say, scanning the landscape for some distraction or excuse to dash away; there is nothing but barren fields covered in white dust. "And you?"

"Hmm?" he asks inattentively, as if the question has yanked him from some pressing matter. "Oh, yes."

Biting my lip, I bob my head slowly as Pa often does when he is talking to someone and cannot think of a reply. A minute passes in utter silence; I notice Francis shoving his hands further into his pockets and rolling on the heels of his boots.

"Well, I better carry on home." A singular laugh sounds from me, and without so much as a speck of humor, it falls away. My goodness, isn't this a pitiful sight! Trying to avoid any more of this incommodious colloquy, the fast crunching of footsteps echoes my getaway—that is, until Francis begins to trail after me.

I shy away from his touch as his hand brushes my arm, and we stop once more, facing one another. "Wait! I am glad we have run into each other. I wanted to talk to you about…" His eyes search beyond my shoulders as if attempting to find some topic off in the distance. "Your horse."

"My horse? Storm?" Nothing, not even if he got down on one knee and proposed here and now, could have caught me off guard more than the mention of Storm as the circulatory of a discussion.

Nodding profusely, clearly relieved that the reticence has evanesced from both our minds, he says, "Yeah…you mentioned needing help training him back at Christmastime. Well, I know it is not spring just yet, but I could come over some afternoon." His stare, though persistent, almost appears abashed, as if he mustering up every ounce of confidence to propose something so simple.

I blink several times as my eyes adjust to the sudden blinding rays of the sun as it erupts from the discourteous cloud that blocked it from the Earth. "I did not think you cared about it. At least, that was the impression you gave when the idea was mentioned." My *response sounds rather haughty coming from my disdainful lips. Perhaps I meant it to sound that way. After all, Francis has a way of aggravating me to new heights with things as unostentatious as taking my hand in his, which he just so happens to be doing right* now.

"Do accept my apologies. You are…" He searches my eyes imploringly. "I do not know how to act around you. One instance your fury is directed at me for unbeknown reasons, then the next we act like chums!" Dear heavens, is he always this straightforward, or have I just now observed it? There is no doubt that we share a mind; vocabulary aside, even our actions are analogous! Here we stand in the middle of the road as Jack Frost sends one chill after another down upon the pair of us, him sincerely holding my mittened hand in both of his as if it is a wounded turtledove.

I stammer, trying to think of some retortion or explanation for the erratic behavior I seem to have around him. In my short existence, I have become acquainted with numerous kindred spirits, but not a single one amounts to the identical connection in personality, process of thought, desire for secret aspirations, or depth of imagination Francis Southerland and I share. Why is that? Why do his actions have such power over mine?

Interpreting the lull as the death to whatever idea may have arrived in his mind, Francis drops my hand and slumps his shoulders. Giving a halfhearted smile—if it could even be called a smile, for it seems to just be a lifting of one corner of his lips—he turns to walk away, traveling a small distance before I locate what to say.

"Should you like to visit Aspenmoore? Mother shall say I am terribly rude if I do not offer you an invitation; therefore, I am offering." The only sound in my ears is wind. "What if I told you that today is my birthday?" I hardly notice that I am fidgeting with my hands.

"Then I would say happy birthday." A surge of happiness comes within at the playful rejoinder. "And that I would be honored to accept the invite."

As we walk toward Aspenmoore, I imagine the trees gossiping heinously to one another, bending to catch a look at the couple as we stroll past, too distracted in the engulfing conversation to notice anything else. Birds peer down from where they soar above to comment on the pair and how well matched they are, even if they are oblivious to the fact themselves. The wind sends a gust my way, causing me to clumsily trip, only to be steadied by Francis's arm. The river, coated with a thick layer of ice this time of year, secretly chuckles and claims to the rest of the wood that the credit lies with it for bringing the two together that summer's afternoon.

⁓

The front door swings open, revealing Mother wearing a welcoming grin that fades away at the sight of her daughter standing next to one of Winfield's most pulchritudinous young men. Pa's yell from the parlor asking who is at the door does not stir Mother as she stands aghast with one hand on the door frame and the other on the knob.

"Hmm? Oh, yes, do come in this instant before you both catch your death from the cold! I was just asking Albert what had become of Nannie and Azalea; those two sure can get into some mischief." Mother rattles on as snow is stomped off at the mat and coats are stripped off to be hung on the hooks. She shakes her head in a matronly manner at the word "mischief" whilst waiting to lead us into the parlor, treating me like a guest rather than her daughter who has lived in this house with her for several months.

Abandoning us in the hall, most likely to run ahead and warn Pa, Mother disappears in a heartbeat. Francis runs his fingers through his short brown hair, making it more unruly rather than manageable. Noticing my amused laugh, he sets his cowboy hat atop my head. A chuckle sounds as it drops down to cover my eyes, temporarily blinding me. However, before I can so much as breathe, a hand brushes against my cheek for a second, lifting the rim of the hat up to reveal a twinkling gaze.

It is as if the world melts away, leaving the two of us in a trance where eye contact cannot be broken and words cannot be spoken aloud. Gradually, he lifts the palm of his left hand to my cheek again; I lean into the small embrace. Warmth fills my skin as my heart ceases its natural rhythm. Humorous expressions fade into serious ones. *What is happening?* I am paralyzed by fear as he leans in.

Suddenly, Francis halts, immediately correcting his posture and assuming a causal guise. Curious at the sudden change in his manner, I follow his gaze over my shoulder and find Mother standing a few feet behind me with a knowing blush.

It feels as though a bucket of icy water has been poured over my head, leaving me drenched. The blush is contradictory to the potential statement that nothing was going to happen had she not walked in. Nonetheless, something was going to happen—Francis Southerland was about to kiss me! And I was about to let him!

If only I could just faint dead away and be buried on that hill over yonder just so that I would not have to relive the moment when my mother interrupted Francis and me! Speaking of Francis, there is no doubt he finds the encounter comical based off the beguiling smirk as he steps in front of me, shading my red face from Mother, who appears on the verge of an explosion of laughter before she disappears from view.

"You *two* can go on into the parlor with Mr. Stanton while I put on the tea." Despite not being able to see her, I can envision the playful sentence being spoken with raised eyebrows and a knowing air.

I snatch the hat from my head and place it on a hook, shooting it a dirty look as if it invoked this ordeal. Just when I think things cannot get worse, Francis shoots a boyish grin my way, causing me to giggle as the pair of us step through the parlor archway. Pa is absolutely ecstatic, jumping to his feet, throwing his book onto the seat, and taking great strides to reach Francis and shake his hand.

"How are you, Francis?"

The gruff handshake is met with a blithe, "Very well, sir."

"You are staying for supper, aren't you? It is my little girl's fifteenth birthday today, so Margaret has prepared a feast."

I would never have extended the invite to Aspenmoore if I had known this much embarrassment would be in store! Francis peers at me out the corner of his eye, and I cover my face with my hands to hide the growing flush of red. "It would be a pleasure, sir, to attend such a momentous occasion."

I spend the rest of the day in Francis's presence, which I have come to find is oddly homey and peaceful.

We spend a great deal of time in the garret as he reads a few stories I scribbled down when it was too frigid or the snow was too deep to venture outdoors.

"It is too flossy or grandiloquent?" I ask as he gently sets the papers on my desk. He leans back in the chair, looking out the window behind where I sit on the other side of the room. The more distance, the better; I seem to lose all levelheadedness when in close proximity to him. When he and Pa were going on chatting like old chaps, I could not help the flush in my skin as the scene of Francis leaning in replayed on a continuous loop in my mind.

The floorboards creak as the wind outside blows against the window-panes, disrupting the quietude. "Not at all. The plot is subtle, protago-nist's and antagonist's relationship simple and not overly complex, and the ending sublime—although a tad melancholy." Constructive criticism at its best; every word is genuine, praising enough but not to the point where it comes across as fake, as some overly enthusiastic ones tend to do. I stare down at my unruly nails, shying away from the persistent gaze.

"Is that from her?" His sudden question catches me off guard; I gaze up to see Francis nod his head to a handwritten note pinned to the slope of the gable ceiling, hanging a few inches to the right above the shabby desk.

The realization hits me like bricks thrown mercilessly at me. In the past, the inquiry would have caused me to shrink back into myself, but I am not as mercurial as I once was. Nonetheless, I was raised to not be a prevaricator.

"Yes, it is from Florence. She wrote that letter to me the day she was diagnosed, perhaps knowing that a goodbye cannot be said only one time or in a few words." My vision blurs, and I hastily use my sleeve to mop up the tears before he can see. "There is a confidential fact that I have been withholding." The admission escapes before I can ponder it.

"I have never known you to keep secrets."

A glimmer of a smile comes to me despite the oncoming relinquish-ment of something that has torn at my subconscious the moment since it happened. "I had an encounter with her—Florence—that day you saved me from drowning in the river. I never told anyone what happened…The place looked like what one would envision as heaven, positively ethereal. And she looked like one of God's flowers dressed in immaculate white.

My heart aches for her presence every morning and every night. Does that ever go away?" His eyes have never looked more clouded than they do now. Have I struck some chord and brought up something too personal? "I—I figured you would understand or at least have something to comment because…"

The solemn voice speaks out from across the room. "Because my father died?" Staring at my hands as I pick the dirt from underneath each fingernail, I give a brisk nod of my head, unaware of his reaction or whether he even saw mine. "Some think that grief is an ailment that is remedied by time, but even a broken door hinge does not magically start up again after a handful of days or months have passed. It is like a scar that has been left on your heart, forevermore evoking the same emotions felt when they parted this world. It does not evanesce, nor do I believe *you* want it to." Somewhere in between the short set of dialogue, he traveled across the room to kneel before me, wiping away a tear from my cheek with his thumb.

I throw myself into his arms, and his embrace tightens around me as I sob hysterically at the impromptu speech he so artfully articulated. It is only now that I have come to fully comprehend the end of *Wuthering Heights* when Catherine says, "He's more myself than I am. Whatever our two souls are made of, his and mine are the same."

⤶

We spent the rest of the day gallivanting around outside, reading books in the nook by the hearth, having lengthy chats that encompassed every viable topic about which we are knowledgeable, and attending an effervescent supper comprised of laughter that continued long after the stars replaced the sun.

When Nannie later ventured back over to Aspenmoore, she caught a glimpse of Francis and I tossing flour at each other in the kitchen and buoyantly proclaimed that she could hear her mother calling for her—even though it would be impossible to hear from this distance and despite the fact that she had just arrived. She announced her departure so loudly that I heard it over the convulsions that had overtaken the pair of us coated in white.

A smile has been permanently fixed on my alabaster face ever since Francis kissed my hand after bidding me farewell 'til the morrow. Rolling my lips, I pretend to be fixated on the book in hand, but I soon realize I have been holding it upside down.

Mother's nimble fingers tie a knot at the end of her thread, and she begins to suture up a wound made to one of Pa's shirts.

A pop sends embers flying up the chimney as Mother's voice states gently, "Mr. Southerland is a very nice young man." Raising an eyebrow, I peer over the edge of the book—now turned the right way so the paragraphs are legible—to observe her expression. I catch the glimmer of a mysterious smile whilst she remains focused on the task upon her lap. Prior to my query as to what she is propounding, the causation of her precursory statement is revealed. "You two are a well-matched pair, like your Pa and me. Having things in common, amongst other attributes, is the perfect foundation for marriage."

"Mother, do you even hear the sentences that are escaping your mouth? Me and...me and Francis? How absurd." If a meteorite had crashed through the ceiling and landed in our parlor, I would not have displayed a different reaction!

Dead serious with a hint of joy sparkling in her pupils, she holds eye contact as she speaks in a matter-of-fact tone. "Azalea, you are fifteen and have long since grown out of the phase of thinking marriage is avoidable! Although, no daughter of mine should be married before she is eighteen, mark my words." Is that a "mark my words" that I will marry him or that I will not be married before turning eighteen? Oh, what does it matter; I am not ever, in the entirety of my existence, getting chained to someone!

"Mother, stop it! I am not planning a wedding any time soon, and neither should you," I exclaim defiantly while setting my book beside me on the sofa. Thank goodness Pa is not a part of this discussion, or else it might be ten times worse considering how fond he is of Francis. He even addresses him as if he is one of the men who work alongside him each day! "What brought on this notion?" *Not that I want to know*, the voice inside my head whispers.

Setting the shirt she is mending in her lap, her icy blue eyes stare at the glowing fire before meeting my leer. The sight of a brimming smile and dancing eyes shocks me to my core, leaving me utterly flabbergasted. What has come over her? Does the topic bring up memories of Florence for her as it does for me? "Not once in the eight months since…Florence died have I seen you smile the way you did tonight when you caught Mr. Southerland observing you at the table. Not once since last May have I heard such hearty laughter come from your lungs—even though the kitchen floor that I scrubbed spotless yesterday is now sprinkled with flour. We have finally progressed past feeling guilty for living without her. It is nice to see you living again, dear."

Living again. As if the piece of me that died with her has finally been laid to rest. I press a palm to my chest until I can feel a heartbeat, vigorous and whole, through the fabric of my dress. Have I finally woken from the slumber that has engulfed me since last May?

Chapter 20

LOVE IS THE CENTER OF THE UNIVERSE

I DO NOT BELIEVE WINTER to be dull nor depressing, as some unimaginative people might. In actuality, I find it to be a rather glorious aspect of nature to breathe in the chilly morning air and observe the stillness of it all. Nonetheless, spring is the one depicted in poetry: blush-colored roses, lush grass swaying in the zephyr, chirping chicks dashing after their mama. Every color appears to bloom several shades brighter after the winter lull.

The end-of-year examination is on the tip of every wagging tongue in the Winfield schoolhouse. The only trouble Hasting has given me since the first day of school is the occasional prejudice during the weekly spelling bees. Last Friday, Matilda was tasked with spelling "liquefy," whilst I was given "abecedarian"! I suppose it is inconsequential now, as Hasting did not get to experience the satisfaction of seeing me lose. Instead, he had to shake my hand—which he did in a lukewarm manner with a grimace—when I was the only student left standing.

A parade of shoes sound on the steps as the crowd of children emerges from the pearly white building, awaiting the moment they get home to pore over textbooks in anticipation of tomorrow. Spring's gentle breeze tickles my skin as I stroll under the shade of the trees, enjoying the feeling of being alone.

This morning, when I walked over to the Fraser's house before the dew had even settled on the blades of grass, Mrs. Fraser proclaimed that my friend was suffering from a headache, adding that, "It is likely due to the squinting and horrible posture of studying. Mr. Hasting should not put all this pressure on a yearly exam that most students pass." Therefore, I am a solitary creature on this Thursday afternoon!

It is rather difficult to remember the last time I had this temporary peace. Tranquility is enjoyable every once and a while, but far be it for me to become a hermit; after all, thoughts alone would drive me to lunacy if they were not hashed out! Bluebunch wheatgrass makes a delectable sound when the wind rushes through it like the shushing of a mother trying to put a babe to sleep.

A blood-curdling scream makes me stop dead in my tracks. A flock of crows disperses into the sky above the canopies.

Clutching my books, I hesitantly step closer to the trail that cuts through the petite cluster of trees near the path to the schoolhouse. A quick glance over my shoulder verifies that the rest of the children have dashed home, leaving me staring wide-eyed at the edge of the lane. A shaky breath whistles from my chapped lips as I begin to walk down the short trail. Not many people travel through the tiny woods. For the most part this path is useless, considering it only connects two roads that are not far apart and arrive at the same destinations. Similar to a tunnel where you can see the light at the other end, I can see the opposite end and Mr. Koller's field with green sprouts of corn seed.

Sudden darkness engulfs the grove, and my common sense abandons me as my mind thinks of sinister forces; in reality, the likely cause is a cloud shading the sun, as the turquoise sky is filled with tufty pillow-shaped puffs today.

My gradual progression halts when labored breathing leads my eyes to find the least likely of candidates for the shout.

"Elspeth Augustine?" A rabbit shrieks and scurries off somewhere nearby. The girl to whom I referred to tosses her light auburn locks, which have fallen from the messy bun at the back of her head, to return my stare.

"Azalea, you have to help me!" Her eyes are pools of tears, her dress stained to such a degree it looks like she has been rolling in the dirt, and her face drenched in sweat regardless of the cool temperature. Elspeth's brown freckles stand out on her pale skin, which almost looks a shade of green.

A thump comes as I toss my books aside and kneel down on the ground next to her. "Okay, okay. Umm, how did you get here? Hasting—I mean Mr. Hasting—said you could go home early." What can I do to get rid of that quiver in my voice? It seems to worsen her condition. "Please do not cry! Here is a hankie." Rattled by the sudden sobbing, I yank out a crumpled handkerchief from my pocket and offer it to the hysterical girl hunched over on the forest floor. A squirrel chitters along a fallen log, chattering to the other woodland creatures about the display.

"I need to go," she stammers before blowing her nose, a movement which causes more cries of anguish. Is she in physical or mental pain? I know she is shy, but now, especially if this is something serious, is not the time to withhold information! Elspeth sways once before falling back to the dirt with a grimace.

"You are in no state to walk home! I…I'll think of something." My gosh, I am sweating to the degree she is! "Help! Someone, please, help us! Anyone!" My lungs scream the line several times until it turns to screeching; nails on a chalkboard would be a more pleasant sound.

Matthew 7:7-8 says, "Ask, and it shall be given you; seek, and ye shall find; knock, and it shall be opened unto you: for every one that asketh receiveth; and he that seeketh findeth; and to him that knocketh it shall be opened." There is no doubt in my mind that God has impeccable timing, but in a panic such as the one I am in, the reassuring sight of Francis

Southerland whistling whilst strolling by proves that God does answer prayers.

Like a madwoman, I stand with wobbling legs, scream as loud as my voice will let me, and wave my lanky arms. Properly startled, he jogs over, perhaps reading the urgency in my manner. It strikes me odd for a moment that he would be traveling home on this path. His family's farm is in the opposite direction. This lane connects to the main road that goes past my house and into town. This way will take him twice as long; I should know, as I once calculated how much time it would take to get from school to his house—for no other reason besides general curiosity.

It has been nearly three months since my birthday, when Francis tried to kiss me and Mother commented on how well-matched he and I are. Even though I would never admit this aloud, I have replayed that day in my head, wondering if Mother is right. There have been inconsequential encounters between us since then, such as competing against each other in the debates or passing by one another on our way out of school. Now that the weather is warmer, the boys have resumed their games outside during dinner hour. How I long to galivant around with them, playing ball or running without shoes just to feel my feet in the dirt! I doubt Hasting would punish me with a whipping after Pa gave him a shiner, but I would rather not risk making an enemy of my teacher.

It feels as though I am seeing Francis for the first time since January. His skin is slightly bronzed, sleeves rolled up to reveal rippling muscles, and eyes still soft to the harsh world. Whether it be the fact that my voice is hoarse or simply the sight of him, the air seems to have been whisked right out of the confines of my lungs!

"What is—" The upturned corner of his friendly smile seems to be a force of habit. The more time I know him, the more I comprehend that being hospitable and cordial is in his nature. "Elspeth?" I missed his reaction, but judging by the aftermath, it was the same as mine.

"The pain is getting worse!" she screams out, clutching her stomach, which I am just now realizing is curved.

Strange how fast the human brain can work; in the timespan of ten seconds, hundreds of ideas, solutions, and observations can be processed. My furrowed brow slowly unknits. Phoebe once mentioned something about Elspeth back in January. What did she say? The egocentric voice yammers in my mind, *"Did you notice those shabby dresses that Elspeth Augustine has started to wear? I daresay the waists have been let out so far on the rest of them that they won't fit any longer!"* I had defended Elspeth afterwards, thinking Phoebe was telling falsehoods like she has been known to do—after all, the girl is quite the spinner of yarns—but the rest of the girls came to notice the same thing. Gaining weight is not uncommon, especially in the winter months, but Elspeth started letting out the waists in her clothes as if covering something and often skipped schooldays or arrived after dinner.

Gracious Lord in heaven! Clasping a palm to my unhinged jaw, I turn to Francis, who avoids my gaze and bends down to be eyelevel with the girl. He knows? How does he know? Unless…no…well, maybe… He is rather excellent at hiding his expression. Is he deploying that talent now so that Elspeth is not as petrified or horror-stricken as she was when seeing my face? Why was Elspeth waiting here, on a footpath that almost nobody uses, with Francis strolling this way? My goodness, I feel faint!

"May I speak to you for a moment?" Writhing in agony, Elspeth peeks open an eye to see who I am referring to. Her paisley dress, hiding the small bump at her stomach, is tarnished beyond belief.

Barely a second before he can find his footing, I grab hold of Francis's arm and begin pulling him along, battling a blush at the strength that nearly forces me backward. Coming willingly, he follows behind me until we reach a mossy stump a mere seven feet away from the mother-to-be. Whilst every moment is important in an event such as this, I need answers! And reassurance that this is not something he is capable of…

"Did you know she is…" There is a fine line between being rude and asking a personal question that has a distinct possibility of offending someone. I, however, do not locate that line and just sound flat-out rude.

If I could take it back, I would, for nothing could be worse than witnessing this. Scoffing, turning away, and angrily running his hand through the short hair, he takes a breath, then faces me straight on. "You really think I am that kind of person? Azalea, you know I would never… My mother is a midwife for crying out loud; I can see the signs when a girl is pregnant!"

My query was not a simple question; it was comprised of distrust in his character, and that is why it was rather rude. Nannie once said that Mrs. Southerland is the town midwife, no doubt her son has aided in many house-calls.

Too stubborn and remorseful to apologize, I exclaim haughtily, "Now is not the time for this!" Shooting one last blazing glare as if I am the one who has been defamed, I march to Elspeth as tears are squeezed from the corners of her eyes. "We have to get to a house; the sun shall set within the next two hours." Wrapping my arm under hers, I attempt to lift her up. Elspeth pulls away at the worst possible instant, and the pair of us succumb to gravity's pull and flop to the ground, knocking the air right out of my lungs.

"No, I can't! I won't!" Is this an eighteen-year-old woman or a five-year-old child? If only I could scream, *You are having a baby!* I would, but now does not seem the time for it. She clutches my wrist as I regain balance and stand. She sends an intense glare at me. "No one can know of my impropriety. Nobody!"

Winfield is notorious for its gossip, and with the boredom of the winter months faded, a scandal of this degree would be retold to any forthcoming generation or visitor to this small town! Do her parents—or even the father of the child—know? Assuming by the severity of her demand, I would guess not. Mother has always taught me not to judge others' sins no matter the degree, because the devil has whisked away many lambs from God's flock and it is our responsibility to welcome them back with hearts of gold. Prayer is the key to almost any obstacle, which is why in this moment I wish to get on my hands and knees just to ask, *God, send me a sign to help carry this girl to some safe seclusion!*

As if possessing the ability of empathic accuracy, Francis rushes to the other side of Elspeth, tucks her arm over his neck, and sends me a nod. Strange how the Lord has been answering my prayers quite literally today; if only it could always be like this. I have never considered myself to be burly, and this instance reassures that fact. I stumble under the weight draped over my shoulder, biting firmly on my bottom lip until the metallic taste of blood drips onto my tongue.

"We can take her to my house. My mother will see to her and the baby." The quiver in his tone verifies the fact that he is shouldering most of the burden. My gaze drifts from his to Elspeth's twisted face. I doubt she even absorbed Francis's words, for her previous defiance has not reemerged at the suggestion. *Was this your plan, to have a baby in a grove so nobody would know?*

Lightheadedness overcomes me as the world spins rapidly. "No." The word steadies the swaying. "No, Aspenmoore is within sight of the main road; by the time we arrive at your farm, it will be too late. We shall send for your mother after." After we reach my abode—assuming we are able to carry her that far—or after the baby comes? Hopefully Francis will not think too much of how I know the distance to his farm…a trouble to fret over some another time. There are more pressing matters to attend to!

By the time we stumble up the lane to Aspenmoore, our necks are scorched from the rays on our backs, my hair ribbon has long since fallen out and unraveled my locks—causing me to become so pestered by it, I internally vow to chop them off—and Elspeth is vociferous. Each sob shakes my eardrums and stabs me in the heart. Shutting my eyelids for a second, I am transported back to last year.

A human's preconscious mind is convoluted and peculiar. Oftentimes it takes all my willpower to remember my sister, but this current state is like a black hole engulfing me. I need something or someone to hold on to, to pull me back to the present day instead of a downward spiral into the past. Why are relics of a bygone time so taunting? They cannot be forgotten nor buried; in lieu if that, they resurface from the abyss of one's soul to grab hold of you like metaphorical hands.

Thankfully, a "dear heavens" arouses me enough to turn my chin up and catch the sight of Mother lifting the hem of her Sunday best skirt so it will not catch underfoot as she screeches all the way to us. A pin comes undone, releasing her hat to the pollen-coated grass. "Albert! Albert, come quick; something dreadful has happened!" Her voice echoes for miles, alerting half of Winfield's flora and fauna to the display of two children carrying a girl through the front door.

The sparkling front porch, which was swept this morning before I traipsed off to school, is now spotted with the soleprints of filthy shoes. I can barely squeeze the air out of my lungs to say, "Parlor," and tilt my head in the direction of the room to the left. The pair of us shakenly drag the now-unconscious Elspeth through the archway and hoist her onto the sofa. Collapsing in a heap on the carpeted floor provides momentary relief. Mother gallops into the house, searching wildly for the patient, whose cause of illness is unknown to anyone but Francis and me.

"Azalea!" Finding the space between a whisper and yell, she feverishly waves me into the hallway. Catching sight of Francis snatching an old newspaper out of the kindling bucket by the vacant hearth, he beings to fan the young lady draped across the sofa. Blue eyes search mine for any indication as to what plagues Miss Augustine. I had not thought this far in advance; Elspeth was absolute in her demands that nobody know, and I am not to be made a perfidious person, yet how can we aid her if nobody knows what is wrong? Materializing from thin air, equally startled, Pa appears at Mother's side, properly confounded at what is happening in our parlor.

"Send for Mrs. Southerland. We are going to need an experienced midwife." My resolute voice cracks.

A pop sounds as Mother's jaw drops and her face grows pale. Pressing her fingertips to her temples, she mutters inaudible sentences, ogling the ceiling and clasping her hands. Pa does not even flinch. He merely slips past us and snatches a wide-brimmed hat off its hook as he dashes out the door. A puff of spring's gentle breath sneaks through the open door and whirls through the house. A solemn mood settles on its inhabitants.

When twilight overcomes the once-brilliant day, all hope starts to wither and wilt away as if a flower without the resolution to grow. When Francis's mother finally arrives, Elspeth's screams become ingrained in the wooden floorboards. The women of the house shoo Francis and me outdoors, claiming that the house is "no place for children."

Crickets chirp like the strings of a bow being tugged across violin strings, a piteous melody. Less than thirty minutes ago, the line of dusk had just begun to pencil the horizon, and now stars are like diamonds on black velvet. How many hours has it been since we brought her home? Counting on my fingers, I reach a perilous number that even in my inexperience seems much too high. I push my palm down on my chest, begging the hammering to cease for a short time. However, my pleas are ignored and the pulsing continues.

She is fine. Mother and Mrs. Southerland are attending to her every request. There are not more capable hands in all of Winfield that could be trusted with her wellbeing!

I suppose that is true, a whisper admits to the voice of reason. Still, the momentary relief is not enough to satisfy the jumble of nerves in my stomach. To occupy my racing mind, I twirl a blade of grass around my finger, my back laid against the earth.

"Remarkable, isn't it?" Craning my neck to see what the voice beside me is referring to, my attention is led to the sooty night sky. "Regardless of the interval between us and them, those lights in the distance seem as close as ever. Do you think mankind could ever acquire the knowledge to understand how they operate? If Galileo could do it over two centuries ago, surely, we can too. Or maybe we already have…Imagine something that historic not being shared to every viable individual." What may sound hopeful out of context gives the impression that these are lost dreams being conversed over for the first time.

In the portion of discussions in which we have partaken, Francis has never mentioned the details of his aspirations. Part of me refutes this claim, for surely he did tell me about them on Christmas after he made an inquiry of what I shall do next with my writing—Nannie suggesting I submit prose or poetry to magazines and me mentioning the possibility of authoring a novel. I can almost recall repeating the question, *"And what of your ambitions?"* The flirtatious query causes a blush to resurface to my freckled cheeks. What did he say in return? I rack my brain before arriving at the answer; *"I believe both higher education and a view of God's creation are the key to unlocking success. I pray both are in store for me. And one day, a girl who would love me wholeheartedly."* But there was nothing correlating to future career ambitions, just a yearning to tour the globe, attend college, and find love.

The endless internal discussion becomes stale as the severity of the situation returns. I can imagine myself a world away, perhaps in an enchanted forest where the trees tell the tales they have witnessed in their perennial existence. I would have a capital time befriending every creature in sight, for they would view me as friend rather than foe. Nonetheless, my body cannot travel along with my mind, and eventually I must return to whatever situation I was trying to forget. Heedlessly, a sigh comes from my lungs, attracting Francis's attention.

"What is wrong?"

"*What is wrong?*" I repeat the question with puzzlement, whilst flying into an upright position to face him. He tilts his head with a look of perplexity. Can he honestly not read the situation; is he incapable of feeling any emotion tied to perturbation? "It is taking longer than it should. Why hasn't there been any word on how Elspeth is? I—" The lump in my throat has grown to such a degree that I choke on the sentence, threatened by oncoming tears. Defeated and tired of agonizing over every little thing, I lie back down and mindlessly watch stars winking at me mischievously. Is his silence an affirmation to my worries, or is he biding time while he mulls over what I have said?

"Do you ever stop fretting to just exist?" The rather brusque reply pricks me. His eyes are focused on the sky as I stare at him blankly. Is that a hint of annoyance or simply the tone he uses when telling something truthful?

I begin to pick at the dirt beneath my nails, a stubborn habit that has yet to cease. There was a time when Mother's constant worrying would drive me mad due to how obstreperous I was heretofore; now it seems that I am simply a reflected image of her in that respect. When did I convert from the person who would jump off the cliff without a note of warning, to the one who would stand petrified in fear, forevermore remaining on the edge?

In a decided manner, I force my heart to rest, the fidgeting to desist, and the stress to vanish like the darkened moon has behind a cloud. "Of course, but after that second has passed, the subject that is pestering me finds its way back." My laugh is lonesome and overshadowed by the buzz of twilight. The grin falls from my lips as I peek from the corner of my eye at Francis. How sullen he looks; I suppose meeting an earnest topic with a joke does nothing to diffuse the mood.

The chirp of crickets fills the lull between us. No matter how many times I peek at him, Francis remains stretched out on the grassy carpet of the Earth, hands folded over his torso and eyes lost in the heavens. There has been something bothering me since January; I guess it is now or never…

"Francis?" My small voice, somewhere between a whisper and a mumble, travels to his ear and breaks the tranquility.

"Yes, Azalea." Like a parent who has just scolded a child, the tone of disappointment is similar to a sprinkle of salt on sustenance—untraceable by sight but so bitter you can taste it.

My palms begin to sweat as I focus on a dark cloud engulfing a portion of the diamonds hanging in the sky. The moon hides its face as if embarrassed by the couple lying a foot apart, diverting their attention to the heavens in order for the unfeigned conversation to appear causal. "Do you remember my birthday? And afterwards, when you stayed for supper?"

"Quite vividly. I relive it nearly every night before I go to sleep." His response is quick but hushed, spoken as if by a delicate narrator of a fable that has a profound underlying meaning or moral.

My pulse halts at the statement, which contains something so personal. How does he do that—share intimate information without discomfiture? I take it we are no longer at variance with one another. "Why is that?" Every word and movement are deliberate for the reason of concealing a greater meaning.

"Because I wish to dream of you." Not once in my fifteen years of life have I ever heard someone speak of me this way. From the second we met, Francis saw right through me; disregarding countless faults, reading me like an open book, and knowing me better than I know myself. I would not be surprised if he could possess my mind and predict every thought or action before it happens!

Gray eyes meet mine. Despite our distance from the house, there is a hint of lamplight that travels across the backfield, lighting up a sliver of his face. A soft expression clashes with his sharp jawline, which appears more defined in the veil of shadows versus the subdued illumination. My heart counts the seconds as they pass; my lips part as if some response may come of it, yet the silence remains untouched.

His voice intervenes. "What were you going to ask?" Why is speaking in a whisper more romantic compared to other tones?

"Hmm?" Engrossed in my observations, the foregoing topic vanishes. Here it goes…all formality or subtle hints are dropped at this simplistic line. I do not wish to be a cunctator; therefore, I shall no longer impede this matter by addressing it. It has invaded my mind like a swarm of bees constantly buzzing until I am driven mad! This is the endpoint, the destination at which we have arrived, and we now have three options: we can bide time whilst waiting to make a decision—leaving the pair us of bewildered and left to guess at the other's mindset—go our separate ways, or move forward together. "I was going to ask if you remember…when you were about to kiss me?"

The silence is deafening. "Why do you want to know?" A coy grin appears as he runs a hand through his hair.

"Can you just answer the question?" I hide my face in the shadows so the crimson color I feel in my cheeks will go undetected.

He pretends to search his mind for several minutes, stroking his chin and shrugging his shoulders playfully; the quietude of a spring evening is shattered by a honey-dew answer. "Yes, Azalea. I remember every moment spent in your divine presence, no matter how insignificant or uneventful it may seem." He has a way of making unornamented sentences sound like poetry.

Is there a suitable response to that declaration? What do I say in return? A heavenly body winks at me from above. "Can we have a redo?" I take a gander at him, finding that his gaze is already set upon me. The demand, or rather request, is so spontaneous and serious that it causes Francis to hesitate. To my surprise, he jumps to his feet—my startled expression follows him as I prop my elbow up to watch whatever is about to take place—then extends his hand to me. "What are you doing?" I ask, properly surprised by the paroxysm of his manner.

"Asking you to dance with me. Don't look at me like that!" he exclaims with a chuckle. "We can pretend this world does not exist—just you and me." The corner of my mouth turns upward and warmth travels through my fingers at his touch as our hands intertwine.

"But it does exist," I whisper, abandoning my imagination for a moment to be realistic, which I must admit is quite unusual for my character.

Placing my other hand on his shoulder, Francis responds in a matter-of-fact tone, "It need not for a moment if you let it fade away and grab on to me to keep from falling." *And what if I have already fallen?* I am not bold enough to say the words aloud. Just hearing the echo in my head is enough.

Contrary to the barn dance—where our first encounter took place nine months ago—there is no upbeat fiddle that swings like a pulse beating, no swift moves of dancers, no audience to stand on the sidelines gossiping about the couple lost in one another's gaze. There are only the fireflies and dash of lamplight as the steps of the slow dance are spontaneously invented, fortuitously known by the two of us. Somehow the simplicity contributes to the unalloyed gambol.

This is a place where I feel at home, where every tedious human fault that I possess or thing I wish to alter are stolen away with my permission. Every few moments, Francis spins me around, causing fireflies to rise up from the grass and light the way. At times, a minute can feel like a century, whilst in other circumstances it passes as quickly as the exhaling of a breath. This is one of those situations when your heart begs and pleads to remain here forevermore, because for once this self-imposed purdah feels infinite. This is the comfort I have strived for and dreamt of for months, a place where the burdens of the world cannot take hold of me. It is not the same as when we were matched together at the barn dance; for instead of an upbeat fiddle, there are imaginary piano keys dancing along with us. Instead of two strangers, we are something more…

When the imagined melody ceases and the pair of us are left wondering what comes next, I say with a laugh, "Why did you do that?"

"Do what?" A playful shrug contradicts his previous response. I bite my lip and tuck a wisp of hair behind my ear. Reading my mind once more, he raises his eyebrows and catches my gaze. "Ask you to dance?" The flash of a nod says it all. With a chuckle, he turns to look into the distance as if formulating an answer or possibly biding time. "Because…I intend for this to be a memory that will not be consigned to oblivion for the rest of time."

I furrow my brow, trying to find what he meant to articulate in the statement, only to receive an answer a moment later. The palm of his hand cups my face, hesitating for a moment. Just as I wonder what he is about to do, his lips collide into mine.

My heart rate accelerates, pounding like a war drum as we part, remaining an inch away. I peek from beneath my lashes at his face, which is erupting in a grin, to verify this is not a product of my immense imagination. Every inhale is flooded by the smell of homemade soap with a hint of pine; the aroma is hypnotic. For a second it feels as if I have forgotten how to breathe normally, internally hyperventilating as my outer expression is radiating gaiety. The kiss was like a black hole sucking me in as everything was relinquished, gravity failing under his touch.

A wave of warmth sweeps over me as we place a distance between us. What does this mean? Are we…am I part of an "us"? I have been rendered speechless by this person before me; who knew the boy I danced with nine months ago would be the one who just kissed me!

I meet Francis's eyes despite the lackluster light. They are searching for my reaction because he has waited for this moment, perhaps since the night we met. He couldn't…or could he? Does Francis love me, or have I misinterpreted his fervent gaze? A rush of adrenaline pulses through my veins, initiating my fight-or-flight response. Do I wish to stay and fight the fear that surrounds whatever this is between us, or does vulnerability frighten me too much to find out? I cannot abscond to an inner haven so that I may contemplate this further; there is an unpremeditated discission to be made. I suppose this overanalyzing is congenial, for it seems to be a pattern I have practiced to perfection; eventually it terrifies me to the point I sequester myself from whatever has frightened me. Due to the million things dashing through my brain, I don't know whether to laugh or cry! One thing is for certain: Francis is my nepenthe, straight out of Homer's *Odyssey*.

"Azalea?" I jump at the sound. Mother's voice wraps around the house, echoing from the front porch. Why does that tone—shaky with a single crack that would grow if anything more was uttered—make me think the worst has taken place? A chill ripples through me as I turn back to Francis; why must his face convey so many emotions? In the short time I have known him, his every movement has been precise and expression carefully processed, but now that has evanesced, leaving everything unfiltered.

I half expected to be halted by a declaration or some explanation as to what just happened; alas, nothing ever goes according to the plan contrived in my head. As I turn the corner and locate Mother's face, everything falls away like a withering flower. When is the last time she looked this disheveled? My gosh, one would think she has walked through the fiery depths and back again based off the weary longing in her crystal blue eyes.

"Mother?" Sounding more like a lost child rather than a fifteen-year-old girl, I halt for a moment before taking so much as a step closer. "What has happened?" Panic fills my voice as I shy away from her touch. Comfort is not something I wish for if treacherous news lines the horizon!

"Azalea, I—" She casts her sight to the darkness, shying away from my perilous leer and pressing a palm to her rosy lips. My stomach twists and curls painfully as footsteps softened by grass come from behind me. Wisps of hair frizz at the top of her head, and a lock of hair has come unraveled from her bun. As she turns back to me, I catch a glimpse of a tear trailing down her cheek before it is feverishly swiped away. "It is best if you hear it from Mrs. Southerland." My brain feels muddled as I step through the threshold of my house, feeling more like a stranger than an inhabitant.

Stopping once more, I scan the dining room to the right and the parlor to the left. Mrs. Southerland cradles a wailing newborn wrapped up in a blanket in her arms. Sensing a missing presence, I start to ask where Elspeth is but pause midway. I divert the course of my inquiry after coming up with a viable explanation as to where Elspeth is—she must be resting upstairs. After all, she just had a baby! "Where is Pa?" Was the reason Mother shed a tear because she was overcome with emotion? It has been a whirlwind night, after all.

Why does Mother stare like I have just asked a senseless question? "Your Pa went to fetch the pastor, but they are too late." Through shaky breaths and momentary pauses, the sentence comes out in delayed parts, contributing to my overall confusion. Something is wrong, something is terribly wrong! What has happened? Why does the house feel so empty when the joy of new life should fill it? Possible outcomes swarm my head like a hive of angry bees shouting and buzzing to disarray as Francis and I are corralled into the parlor by Mother's outstretched arms. Her delicate hand hardly touches my shoulder as we make our way through the archway and stand stone-faced while looking for answers.

My eyes travel to the newborn in Mrs. Southerland's arms. "My gosh, is something wrong with the baby?" I exclaim, clasping a hand over my chest as Mother often does. A peculiar look is exchanged between the two women, as if they share a secret that should not be divulged for reasons unbeknownst to me. Why else would they require the leader of our church?

Prior to anything more being said aloud, Mrs. Southerland takes the reins of the conversation. To my terror and surprise, Mother becomes overcome with emotion and settles down defeatedly in a chair in the nearby corner. "No." Why does that singular word make me think a piece of dreadful news is coming? "No, the baby is perfectly healthy and well. Miss Augustine has…"

A hush falls over the house. Even the baby has stopped crying. Gaining control of her emotions, Mother uses a hankie to dab at her tears, then takes the newborn out of the midwife's arms and whisks it out of the room, cooing and shushing along the way.

A prickle stabs like needles along my skin as I guess where this is going. The beating around the bush, the change in ambience as if this is a graveyard, and the mention of the pastor; I have pieced together the broken object to find the result missing a vital role.

It has happened again. "She is dead, isn't she?" I ask, my voice halfway between a lethal whisper and a heart wrenching scream. A solemn nod confirms it. How did I not see this beforehand! I ignored the blaring alarm in of my head warning that something ghastly was about to take place and that I should not allow myself to grow accustomed to certain people who try to get close to me. The room spins and sways as I fall to my knees, half expecting and hoping that someone might rush to me and help bear the heartache; alas, one peek at Francis shows he is paralyzed in fear as he runs his hand over his mouth. *Dear Heavenly Father above…*

My insides coil as nausea takes hold but is pushed away as quickly as it was brought forth. "What…*was* it? What has happened to Elspeth?" I look through blurry eyes coated in tears to find Francis's mother struggling with the news herself.

"Her heart wasn't strong enough. If she had involved me in the matter beforehand, there might have been hope for preventing this." Is everyone in the medical profession so impersonal? At least the lines on her face show genuineness.

Elspeth, the quiet observer in the midst of a busy school room, wrapped up in the small circle of the older girls, with a shy smile on her face—gone in a matter of hours. She was the same age as Florence, and just like Florence, she was taken away when there was still so much of life to experience, aspirations to fulfill, and ambitions to follow.

When does this curse end? Is it when a breaking point is reached? Here come the persistent questions that never locate an epilogue, a book whose pages are repetitive and pretentious at best. Did she disclose any information regarding the baby to her parents or at least the father of the child? Who will nurture and raise a baby whose parentage and linage are obscured and erased? When dawn emerges, what will become of the memory of Elspeth Augustine? Notwithstanding her efforts to avoid the tarnishing of her family's reputation, will she succumb to scandal? How do you conceal the birth of a baby and the death of a young girl on the same night without a correlation being realized?

My lungs begin to struggle as the sensation of hands tightening around my neck strengthens. Air. I need to escape from this suffocating conversation and this horrid place! Stumbling to stand without aid, I dig my nails into the archway and shuffle my way to the door, tossing it open to the chilly air that seemed so romantic mere minutes ago.

Nearly falling down the narrow steps, I collapse after a couple yards, sitting on my hands and knees as my stomach heaves. The sour taste of grief causes me to retch, spitting until my mouth becomes dry. The hoarse sobs come out of nowhere, strengthen with every gasp until I'm hyperventilating. *Maybe this is all a dream?* The thought is squashed like a bug under my heel. *Stop it! This is life, comprised of sorrow, masked by scenic landscapes and crude beauty, and filled with humans who are blind, deaf, and mute to the world's true nature. I cannot keep doing this, all of this! How can I make progress when one small setback forces me to hit rock bottom? It feels as though I have been beaten with a whip: each time it is pulled away, my flesh is ripped open and bleeding out. God, please instruct me, how can I exist in this world without being struck down by every painful thing?*

A voice, internal in some ways, speaks with clarity and gentle force, bringing everything to a hush. *"Fear thou not; for I am with thee: be not dismayed; for I am thy God: I will strengthen thee; yea, I will help thee; yea, I will uphold thee with the right hand of my righteousness."*

When the words die off, the crickets and numerous creatures of the night resume their chatter, going on as if they were not just rendered silent for a minute. I am not declaring myself the next Joan of Arc nor some religious prophet, but God has spoken to his followers more commonly than most admit.

"Isaiah forty-one ten," a mouse-like voice squeaks. I realize now I must remain steadfast. Running from my problems shall not remedy them; instead, I must face them head-on, don the armor, and march into battle, wielding the sword of strength once I find it within myself. Nonetheless, I cannot continue this infinite pattern. I must not go from one extreme or the other. Love is a virtue that I may no longer be able to give so freely; everyone I give my heart to leaves me in some form or another. At some point I have to protect myself. Pulling in a deep and quaking breath, I regain my balance and stand.

Hearing the thudding sound of running footsteps from over my shoulder, I turn to find a breathless Francis screeching to a halt in front of me. Gray eyes search mine as I come to a conclusion: *this, us,* or *we* cannot happen. Whatever *this* is—or was—must be laid to rest before any heartache may become of it. Death is too excruciating to encounter time and time again. I need not think the names on the gradually expanding list of those who have departed from my life. The fact of the matter is that I do not want to fret over something happening to him or us if we are romantically involved! Which is why I must vow to never be with Francis Southerland. We are incapable of being so much as friends, for his continuous presence would only influence me to change my conviction. I have to do this…regardless of whether it is what I truly want.

"Azalea?" Filled to the brim with agony, I tuck my chin into my shoulder, but he marches up to me, cupping my face in his hands despite my reluctance. Guessing the notion inside my head, he declares, "What about everything that just happened?"

"The only thing that 'just happened' was a girl dying from something preventable! As for us, assuming that is what you are really referring too, that was a mistake!" The glimmer of hope ceases to shine, and his face turns to stone. Once, in Brockschmidt, my family and I went to an art gallery where there were statues made of marble. Prior to that experience, I had never witnessed such beauty at the hands of mankind. Faces hand-carved and weathered by centuries of being carted around the globe to be admired or criticized. Analyzing such graceful and subtle beauty with minimal emotion, I came to find the expression "stone-faced" complex and undescriptive. It is only now that I have come to fully comprehend what the saying means; sometimes you can only understand the definition of the word when it is shown through an action.

"I—I think we are better off going our separate ways." My impetuous response is met with a stumble as he releases his careful grip on me. There was once a bird—Vireo—that was abandoned at a young age in the hayloft of our barn in Wyoming. I nursed and cared deeply for him, but when it was time to part ways, something inside of me forced me to relinquish my grip and let him go. Is that not what they say, that if you truly love something then you must let it fly free, and if it is truly meant to be in God's will it shall come back? Is Francis using that same tactic here, on me?

"Azalea." He gestures his hands wildly, and I grimace at what comes next. *Do not say the words aloud. How can I leave you if you do?*

"Please do not say you love me! Because…I *cannot*." Every time I allow myself to care for someone by means of endearment or friend-ship, they vanish into oblivion, only to be recalled as a memory whilst the vocabulary changes to past tense. Forthcoming, I shall not permit myself to fall in love someone, because if I lose them, I also render a piece of my heart to be buried with them, metaphorically or even literally. The reality of it is this: Vireo flew away, and I have yet to see him again. Perhaps it was for the best, but I still carry a sorrow inside myself, regretting that I never told Vireo what kind of hold he had on me or fondness I had for him. It is possible that his ignorance—in the sense of never knowing—was for the best; otherwise, he might have remained the rest of his life in the same place, tied down to me and never fulfilling his potential or seeing what the world has to offer.

The silence is foreboding and humiliating to both parties who choose to endure it. "If that is what you desire, then I will go." Searching for some sign or rebuttal to my previous claim, he does not move a muscle. The only sign is my stunned expression staring open-mouthed at the sudden defeat. What more is there to say? Have we not gone over everything a thousand times?

Pursing his lips, he closes his eyes and takes a quick inhale. When he opens his eyelids, he stares past me, sauntering off in that direction before getting the last word: "Just know that the only reason I am agreeing to this is because I hope you will come back to me. I truly believe that you—Azalea Stanton—are my one true love, whether or not you choose to accept it. I just want you realize that I am wholeheartedly in love with you, in every way possible. I will never stop loving you. My heart shall only ever beat for you—it has been in your possession since the beginning."

With that, Francis makes his way down the rest of the lane, stealing one last glance at me as I stand before Aspenmoore. He certainly knows how to make a heartfelt declaration and an exit. I could barely get a word in edgewise! Not that I could think of any response to quash or unburden the hope that Francis holds to for us to someday be together.

If this is for the best, why does it feel like everything has been reduced to shambles?

Chapter 21

HIRAETH

FEAR IS THE PRISON of the mind; this is a lesson I have come to learn and accept. In the entirety of Earth's population, I cannot be the only person to regret a decision made whilst overcome by emotion.

"Just know that the only reason I am agreeing to this is because I hope you will come back to me. I truly believe that you—Azalea Stanton—are my one true love, whether or not you choose to accept it. I just want you realize that I am wholeheartedly in love with you, in every way possible. I will never stop loving you. My heart shall only ever beat for you—it has been in your possession since the beginning."

No matter how many times I shake the words from my head, they return, pulsing with elevated levels of intensity each time. From *Pride and Prejudice* to *Wuthering Heights*, Mr. Darcy and Elizabeth Bennet to Heathcliff and Catherine, I have devoured the words said between two souls destined to be with each other, and with a childish fantasy I wondered if the day might come when a young man may utter something as romantically poetic as that. What my imagination failed to include was the realistic factor of unrequited or impossible love and how excruciating it is to refuse such a declaration! Oh, well…a thought for another time; for now, I shall tuck it into the back of my mind and call it forth at some later date.

The sunlight of daybreak begins to peek through the window, only to find my bed vacant and untouched. With a perplexed face and a sudden onset of worry, the sun travels through the dining room windows, locating me in all my lonesomeness.

The fork falls from my grasp and clangs feebly on the table, making a small indent. I am tired in more ways than one. The exhaustion of the events that have transpired, operating without a wink of sleep, fletcherizing my breakfast in the hope that the lump lodged in my throat will disappear before I swallow, and everything that lies ahead have all taken their toll on me! Besides Pa, Mother, Mrs. Southerland, Francis, and myself, the rest of Winfield have yet to hear of the news. How can I go to school, take an exam, and withhold vital information while everyone questions why Elspeth is not there? How can I sit there and lie?

The empty chairs in the dining room hold bewildered looks, as this is the first occasion the Stanton clan is not together. As soon as the pancakes were done cooking, Mother wrapped a shawl around herself and took off towards the Augustines' house. With the return of warmer days, Pa has returned to work in town. Seems like food is the last thing on everyone's mind, or maybe the haunting feeling of death that this house now holds has driven them away—I too would madly dash away if there was any hope of escaping it or if I did not dread the school day ahead. I try to push away the flutter in my stomach with a deep inhale; nevertheless, it remains permanently fixated on inflicting anxiety.

The journey to the white building, where the river turns to a brook and where children rush to six months out of the year, feels fictitious, as if it is someone else's feet that carry me. Upon entering, the general mood is vivacious; noise fills the room from the countless misconducts that Hasting is not here to witness. The teacher's desk is inhabited by one of the younger boys, who waves a ruler around, pointing at the chalkboard behind him as if he is the schoolmaster. Nannie prances up to me, her eyes lively and hair swaying as she skips.

"Can you believe it is the last day of the school term? Let us take our seats. I suspect Mr. Hasting shall be here any moment!" I give a half-hearted smile and follow her to our bench, where Ophelia is scratching her name in a book.

"There!" Leaning back to admire the signature that took twice the time it should have, she nearly jumps out of her skin when she realizes we have sat down next to her. "You nearly scared me half to death! Here, Azalea. You have yet to sign your name in the autograph book. It is a tradition we do every year. Look, there is mine from fifth grade! I wrote a poem that year, something concerning a seagull and the ocean…" She stares at the booklet intensely as she hands it to me as if trying to locate her piece from three years ago.

Every inch of the page is filled with scribbles of signatures—varying degrees of flourish or blotchy writing—short poems that were either thought of in the moment or plagiarized from others, and small drawings. A pen materializes in my hand, and I sign away with a hint of joy brimming at my lips. Regardless of the challenges this term has brought, I have fulfilled my childhood desire of attending school and having friends!

As the other girls over our shoulders converse loudly, Nannie leans in to whisper, "Are you quite alright? You seem tired." My muscles tense as if readying myself for a fight. I shake the feeling away and finish dotting my John Hancock with an air of resolution.

Clearing my throat and sliding the opened booklet back to its owner, I respond without making eye contact. "Yes, dear. The umm…studying kept me up most of the night." Whilst scanning the room, for no reason other than avoiding my friend's peculiar and all-knowing leer, my green eyes locate Francis. How can he laugh and talk up a storm as if a life-altering thing did not take place within the last twenty-four hours? Maybe the declaration he made was not genuine after all; if it were, then why does he appear so jubilant?

Whether or not it was believable, my explanation to Nannie suffices, and the schoolmaster enters the room shortly after, bringing a lethal hush amongst the children.

Once the papers are passed around and the time chalked up on the board, the infinite sound of ink bottles clicking with the tapping of quills and illimitable scratching of the point on paper are the only din that dare to subsist in the room. I nearly faint dead away when Hasting surveys the room to find Elspeth missing and calls out the question of her whereabouts, to which there is no answer.

When I find a moment of respite during the insufferable exam, my attention wavers to Francis, who I can just barely see over Nannie's and Ophelia's shoulders. Not once does he so much as peek at me! Does his impertinent manner translate to something else? Perhaps I was right, we cannot maintain a friendship.

When the exam sheets are collected, the bell rings to announce the end of the term. An uproar comes as everyone gathers their things and spills onto the front lawn.

"It was a piece of cake! I don't know why you were so worried," Phoebe exclaims with an air of confidence to Matilda as they pass by.

"Goodbye, dear! I will see you at church on Sunday!" Nannie yells, waving a goodbye to Ophelia, then exchanging hugs with some of the other girls.

I pick at the skin around my nails, standing on my tiptoes and trying to locate Francis but failing miserably. In my distracted state, I did not notice Daphne coming up behind me. Jumping out of my skin when she taps me on the shoulder, I clasp a palm to the base of my throat and say with a laugh, "Daphne, you gave me a fright!" I daresay she looks more startled than I do!

Twitching the corner of her lips, she scans the crowd, then returns her attention to me. "Have you seen Elspeth lately?" The query sends my blood running cold.

Swatting at a lock of hair that tickles the tip of my nose, I stammer, "No, I…well…why do you ask?" *What are you really asking?* She narrows her eyes as if that will cause me to relent and pour over with information. Maybe that works on getting the other girls to fess up, but I shall do my very best to uphold the secret Elspeth tried to keep in solitary! Daphne's stare bores into my skin, not in a rude or menacing way, but as if she is aware that some vital factoid is being withheld.

Correcting her posture like a well-rehearsed young lady, she equips a cordial grin. "It is funny you should say that! You see, my house is on the corner of Lem Turner Road, the very route you take to walk to and from school." *Oh, no.* "Imagine my shock yesterday afternoon when, a while after I arrive home, out of the front window I see Azalea Stanton, Francis Southerland, and Elspeth Augustine all trudging up the lane toward Aspenmoore!" *How did I not see this coming?* A hasty peer over my shoulder confirms that Nannie is occupied. She would be heartbroken to know that I lied to her.

"I can explain…Elspeth, she…" Daphne purses her lips and raises her brows like a mother awaiting to hear a child's excuse for wrongdoing. I gesture wildly and squint whilst trying to think of a falsehood that could sound candid. Why can I not think of something? Elspeth was sick and we were helping her? What could exonerate us of any suspicion without revealing that Elspeth was in labor? Several moments pass and nothing resembling a complete sentence has come from my mouth.

Like a knight in shining armor, Francis interrupts the discussion, jumping in as if part of it from the beginning. His charming approach and mature etiquette are no match for Daphne. "How did your exam go, Daphne? That equation on page two of the arithmetic portion was rather difficult, was it not?"

Blinking several times, utterly confused at the sudden diversion of the chat, she replies, "I suppose so."

"If you will excuse us, Azalea and I must bid farewell to some of the upperclassmen. See you around!" He ushers me along with a benign pull at my arm. We traipse past her, and after circling to the other side of the thinning horde, we are lost from view.

Massaging the pulsing headache at my temples, I brush the stress off and convey my gratitude. "Thank you, Francis! She just caught me off guard and I—"

Holding up a hand and turning his face away, the words are put off. Sensing the silence, he meets my hurt stare head-on. "That is the last time I will ever save you, Azalea. I cannot keep doing *this*." Waving his wrist to emphasize the word, he bites the corner of his lip as if trying to articulate something that he has been contemplating. "I meant what I said. Therefore, we can no longer be around one another. Goodbye." Abruptly taking my hand in his, he places a kiss on my skin, quickly releasing his gentle grip.

Seeing him walk away causes a throb from within, bringing about the question of if I want to run after him. *No, I made a decision to protect myself; there is no going back!*

With nobody else to bid farewell or make promises to see, I clutch my books to my chest and plod back home, avoiding the trail in the grove.

⌒

A balmy breeze sweeps by, extending an invitation to the flowers to be carried along with it. This is a season distinguished by flowery beginnings, the enchanting sight of ducklings following their parents into the river, squirrels scratching at the dirt whilst chittering to each other, and the brilliance of the ethereal light touching the mountaintops. An appreciation for nature is the sustenance for imagination, for creation and all that it entails.

Storm nuzzles his nose into the crook of my neck as I titter and stroke his crown. Hanging on to the fence with my arms crossed and the heels of my shoes balancing on a board, I settle my chin on my wrist and watch my companion as he goes back to grazing the verdant pasture. This part of the fence is located on an idyllic corner of the forest, off the beaten path where I can be isolated from mankind with my perceptive mind as a form of entertainment.

The grass truly is greener on the other side, isn't it? A year ago, I was standing in the kitchen of our home in Lorretta, pruning flowers, observing their docile nature as they gazed at me with imploring eyes when Mother came down the stairs announcing our trip to Brockschmidt. *I often think of how many days, hours, and minutes have passed and how I have spent each one thinking about you.* A ladder-to-heaven stretches to the soil as an oblivious cloud shades this spot from the light. Is it not mind boggling to think that whilst day shines here, on the other side of the globe, the moon is its parallel? Maybe it is a reminder: where there is a world of darkness, the sun shall always come again.

Some people may prognosticate to try to find some detail that may come to their aid or be utilized to work to their advantage. I, however, have always thought human nature—whether it be mistakes or triumphs— repeats itself. Thus, looking back on history may unveil crucial advice.

"After all this time, I still do not know how to live without her! Every moment that went by while she was alive was wasted as if it never mattered. How do I…how can I keep living without her?"

"Don't dwell too much on the past because you might miss the future. Azalea, you cannot be angry at the world for what has happened to you! You must move on, forgive what has happened but don't forget her. And try not to feel guilty for living." Colleen's euphonic voice comes to my ear as if spoken next to me.

"I thought I made peace with the world! When will life move on from her death? I shall never be truly happy until it does…"

"I still search for you; when someone laughs, when a moment aches of your presence, in the sunrise and wide-open fields. It's been forever since your

name has been spoken aloud." That was the first entry I ever wrote in the journal; it is like the words are drawn up in the sky before my eyes…

"*You have to let me go.*" Florence. A mournful grin comes to me at the sound of such a memory.

"*What if I can't? I know you are at peace. I just wish I was too.*"

Almost a year since she passed. Similar events have recently transpired, but I find myself changed. After all, I am not the same person I was last May. Somewhere in between then and now, I healed. After a while, the pain and grief changes; it is no longer a form of guilt that gnaws at my heart and makes me feel selfish for criticizing God's plan. It is now a lesson learned and a dull heartache that arrives in moments when I need Florence's presence. She was the light of my life, and when that disappeared, I was left in darkness with only thoughts to keep me company in that lonely place. Since then, I have found happiness in people, in warm hugs and welcoming smiles, in God's love and creation, and most importantly, within myself. Florence has taught me a great many things, even in death. Francis was right. Time doesn't heal wounds; your willingness does. Only you can heal yourself. Maybe that wasn't the only thing he was right about…but that is something for a later date. For the longest time, I thought God was punishing me when in actuality he was telling me to look for the lessons in each tribulation.

"There is a secret that I must unburden upon you, for not a soul on Earth knows it." Storm flicks his tail curiously. I do not care what others may think of me for talking to the sky, for when I look up, all I can see is my sister's affable face. Some things you can bottle up inside yourself for a lifetime, but with every question that a stranger asks, with every memory that is recalled in the past tense, and with every vision of her, a crack is inflicted upon the glass. At some point, it grows beyond repair and one day shatters, letting out every article that was retained. I am aware of the fact that I have said this before, but it has never applied more than now.

This is the breaking point, the climax and the conclusion, the verge of collapse and restoration. The exigency to speak my truth aloud has brought me here. Therefore, I shall release every thought that I have wanted to express since the day Florence departed this world…

"Every day since you died, I have held on to this affliction in more ways than one." My soft fingertips systematically pull the small patch of black cloth out of my dress pocket. "I cut this cloth from the dress I wore when we bid our final farewell to you in Lorretta." I twirl the article between my fingers. The end is not truly final so long as it lives on in someone else's mind and heart. "It is customary to wear black after someone has passed. Then suddenly, as if one day the veil of sorrow has been lifted by holy hands, the black evanesces. It is a sign of moving on and resuming life. Whilst everyone else paraded around in their colors and shades of contentment, I remained, stuck on the final page of your book, petrified of abandoning the darkness and walking into the light because I assumed it translated into abandoning you.

"I have moved on from your death. The heartache, however, has not abandoned me, even after it was forced to the surface. So, I could not go without the black cloth that I hold in the palm of my hand because, Florence, I feel as though the longing for your presence, your smile and laugh, and everything else that you entail shall forevermore dwell in me and this cloth. Part of me wants to hang on to this grief because I have grown so accustomed to it that I'm not sure who I am without it dwelling within the confines of my soul. I have a great many things that remind me of you and have felt your touch, but this cloth serves as a reminder of the day that a part of me died as well. For whatever reason, by keeping it in my possession I feel like I still have the old carefree and rebellious Azalea here with me. It has taken some time, but Elspeth's death made me realize that I am not the same person I was last year and that I cannot keep holding on to the false hope that I am. Though I have learned, laughed, and lived since then, for me, everything stopped when you left because even when the world progressed, I did not. I remained fixated on the past—wishing I could change it—and the emotions tied to it."

There are no tears, sobs, or screams begging to go back in time and reverse it all. I have…I *am* accepting it as God's will because it is now that I have come to fully acknowledge that her life was not cut short, nor was her impact on the world unfulfilled. "My dear sister, I wish you could have witnessed the impact you have imposed and all that you have contributed to my existence!"

"A part of my heart has grown fond of this emotion, for it reminds me of my only sister and the life we shared. And if it goes, I fear the world and everybody residing in it will take it to mean I am forgetting you!" Nothing dares to breathe, chirp, or tweet; utter and complete silence engulfs me. "I could only stop missing you if I relinquished the entirety of myself! I know that I may always see you merely by closing my eyes."

The wind picks up and, with my permission, carries the piece of the black cloth along with it. I hold on to the knowledge that as long as that scrap of fabric is still on Earth, a part of it shall lay claim to the memory of Florence Mae Stanton.

"I cannot keep living in the past—this, I know. The present is a gift that I must enjoy while it lasts. My heart longs for you now, and conceivably it will for the rest of my life. But this is the point of no return. I can no longer be dependent on that pain to serve as a reminder of you. Instead of carrying the grief, I will carry the recollections and think of them fondly as happy days that may continue instead of somber memories that taunt me with how life used to be. You were right…you *are* right: happiness is here." I point at my chest as if able to reach in, clasp the emotion in my grasp, and pull it out for all to see. "I just have to let myself revel in it."

"Azalea, may I ask something of you?" Nannie says. Orange light from the sun's rays bathe the meadow we walk through. A flower crown, crafted whilst we strolled and stepped through the grasses, sits on my head, tied by my white hair ribbon. Following a noiseless and unobtrusive nod, she twiddles her thumbs and says gently after hesitating, "Do you ever miss Wyoming?"

A grin brims on my lips as a laugh is brought about, confusing my faithful friend further. If I were asked this same thing a few months ago, my answer would have been impulsive and injudicious; no doubt it would have been sincere at the time, but it the same cannot be said as of now.

"Before today, I could never truly allow myself to revel in every aspect of Winfield for fear of it disappearing just as everything I have ever obtained has done. Even now, I sometimes wonder if this is all some elaborate fantasy that I am responsible for creating. At any moment, it may fade away: Aspenmoore, gallivanting through the grove whilst the woodnote plays, attending school… And when it does—fade away that is—I shall be back on the roof espying the dawn breaking through the specks of snow on the apex of the mountains. It is not an eerie feeling, as one would speculate, almost like a peaceful dream from which you have yet to awaken."

⌒

"The worst pain isn't constant; it creeps into your soul as night falls, it leaves a dull ache in a seemingly joyful moment, it's the kind that remains through it all."

LANGUAGE OF FLOWERS

Persimmon............................ Bury me amid nature's beauty

Vetch .... I cling to thee

Forget me not .... Forget me not

Zinnia................................... I mourn your absence

Freesia.................................. Lasting friendship

Thornless rose .... Love at first sight

Clover (white) .... Think of me

Cinquefoil............................. Beloved daughter

Azalea .... Take care of yourself for me

Geranium .... True friendship

Carnation (red)....................... My heart breaks for you

Yarrow .... Cure for a broken heart

Hazel (Corylus)....................... Reconciliation

Gerber Daisy........................... Cheerfulness

Dogwood................................ Love undiminished by adversity

Carnation (Striped) .... I cannot be with you

Celandine .... Joys to come

Cosmos.................................. Joy in love and life

Cranberry .... Cure for the heartache

Primrose................................ I cannot live without you

Michaelmas Daisy.................... Farewell my beloved

ABOUT THE AUTHOR

HANNAH BREE CAMPBELL is the critically acclaimed teen author of The Eunoia Series. Since its release, Campbell has watched Eunoia compete in prestigious book awards, travel the world, and meet readers from various walks of life. With her richly researched historical settings and compelling characters, Campbell's books transport readers to another time, making stories come alive on the page. Whether she is hiking a mountain in Alaska or delving into a new writing project, Hannah always brings her trademark enthusiasm and dedication to everything she does. "I have given the world Eunoia, and now I want to give Eunoia the world."